EVERYMAN, I will go with thee,

and be thy guide,

In thy most need to go by thy side

Thirteen Famous Ghost Stories

Edited and Selected by

Peter Underwood

DENT: LONDON, MELBOURNE AND TORONTO
EVERYMAN'S LIBRARY
DUTTON: NEW YORK

Printed in Great Britain by C. Nicholls & Company Ltd,
The Philips Park Press, Manchester

for
J.M. DENT & SONS LTD
Aldine House · Albemarle Street · London

This book is set in Times New Roman 327, 9 on 10 pt.

No. 749 Hardback ISBN 0 460 00749 1
No. 1749 Paperback ISBN 0 460 01749 7

British Library Cataloguing in Publication Data
Thirteen famous ghost stories
ISBN 0-460-00749-1
ISBN 0-460-01749-7 Pbk
1. Underwood, Peter
823'.01 PZ1
Ghost stories, English
Short stories, English

Published in the U.S.A. by arrangement
with J.M. Dent & Sons Ltd

Contents

Acknowledgments

The editor and publishers acknowledge permission to include the following copyright stories in this collection:

Adam and Charles Black Ltd for 'The Dream' by A.J. Alan; A.P. Watt and Son and the Estate of the late E.F. Benson for 'Caterpillars', originally published in *The Room in the Tower* by E.F. Benson; Michael D. Balfour, The Garnstone Press and the Estate of the late Algernon Blackwood for 'Secret Worship', originally published in *John Silence* by Algernon Blackwood; The Society of Authors as the literary representative of the Estate of the late W.W. Jacobs for 'The Monkey's Paw' by W.W. Jacobs; Edward Arnold Limited and the Estate of the late M.R. James for *Martin's Close* by M.R. James; A.P. Watt and Son, the Executors of the Estate of Mrs Elsie Bambridge and The Macmillan Company of London and Basingstoke for 'They' originally published in *Traffics and Discoveries* by Rudyard Kipling; and A.M. Heath & Co. Ltd and the Estate of the late Arthur Machen for 'Change' originally published in *The Children of the Pool* by Arthur Machen.

Despite exercising the utmost care and diligence the publishers have been unsuccessful in their efforts to ascertain the owner of the rights of 'When I Was Dead' by Vincent O'Sullivan.

Introduction

These thirteen stories – an ominous number perhaps for the readers' peace of mind – represent different types of classic ghost stories, from gentle excursions into the darker side of nature to terrifying tales of terror; such stories are as old as man himself and indeed it is likely that the first story ever invented by man was a ghost story; since then there have been few people in any civilization who have not enjoyed the rare and special pleasure of a really frightening story, well told by a master of the macabre.

Someone once said that if love stories are available day-dreams, ghost stories are available nightmares. Nightmares are perhaps the most horrible ordeals that the human mind has to undergo, since it has no barrier against them; self-conjured terrors that can terrify the mind that brought them into being. Yet, sometimes we enjoy nightmares for there *is* a secret pleasure in being frightened, and the unknown world really does lie just beyond the material world. We are not as ordinary as we think and the day comes when we realize, as we surely must, that no man is totally secure and that the edge of the world beyond this world is just a step beyond the familiar and comfortable world we live in. Occasionally we enter an empty room and something tells us that it is not empty, that someone or something lies in hiding, watching—but the feeling is dismissed as imagination. I wonder. Could it be that at such times we are close to something that is not of this world? That a primitive sixth sense warns us of a primeval danger, a danger that has not materialized . . . yet.

As president of the century-old Ghost Club I suppose I know a little about the subject of ghosts from several different points of view and it may be that I have heard as many stories of ghosts and hauntings—first-hand—as any man alive, but true hauntings and true ghost stories are *usually* much less frightening than the ghosts of fiction.

I remember Walter de la Mare telling me of the time that he almost saw a ghost. He was staying in a haunted house and in 'the grey hours just before daybreak' (as he put it) he found himself awake with the certain knowledge that there was a ghost in the room. He knew that e was fully conscious and awake, although he had not opened his eyes, and he lay there and reasoned with himself: if he turned his head and opened his eyes, he would see a ghost; then, whatever happened next, he would not get to sleep again for hours; better not to look. He kept his eyes closed and soon went back to sleep. Yet he told me he always regretted 'so abject a welcome' to one who probably meant him no harm and who would, in all probability, never visit him again. So Walter de la Mare created for himself a ghost: a ghost of memory and what might have been.

The ghosts of fact and those of fiction are usually separated by several factors but they are linked by the essential ingredient of any successful ghost story: an element of fear—fear of the unknown and perhaps the unknowable, and the gnawing possibility that it just might be true. That is what makes a good ghost story and occasionally a classic one for fear is a feature that can be used in many different ways.

I have special reasons for including every story in this collection. Ambrose Bierce's 'The Damned Thing' is here because something of that strange man's powerful work had to be included and because this particular story was a favourite of Boris Karloff, a man whose trade was the personification of fear on stage and screen; a gentle man whose like we shall not see again. The life and death of Ambrose Bierce (1842–1914?) was almost as strange as the grim stories that flowed from his pen, although his only education came from reading his father's books. Perhaps the loneliest of all ghost-story writers, his first published story was called 'The Haunted Valley' and, embittered by bereavements, he joined General 'Pancho' Villa's revolutionary forces and disappeared in Mexico in 1914, leaving behind a wealth of weird tales of the supernatural of which 'The Damned Thing' (originally published in a volume called *In the Midst of Life*, 1871) is a typical and disturbing example.

A.J. Alan (1883–1940) was a very different type of man. The name was the pseudonym of Leslie Lambert, a Civil Servant at the Foreign Office, who in 1924 broadcast one of his short stories in that languid, shy, genteel voice that so exactly suited the material, and from then until his death in a Norwich nursing home (he lived at Potter Heigham) his rare broadcasts, no more than three a year, were eagerly awaited by connoisseurs of the short story. In common with much of Somerset Maugham's work, A.J. Alan's stories were supposed to be personal experiences; in fact the strange and peculiar adventures he related had mostly occurred to his acquaintances, who were frequently startled to hear half-forgotten episodes of their lives twisted into a story; episodes that they had related in an unguarded moment to the slightly built, middle-aged, monocled and natty Leslie Lambert. His broadcasts were rehearsed again and again with Leslie sitting in a dinner-jacket on a high stool, his story pasted onto cardboard to ensure that no rustle of paper disturbed the atmosphere and, during the week preceding each broadcast, to ensure that his voice was in good shape, he neither smoked nor drank alcohol.

The two original collections of A.J. Alan's spoken tales have now become collectors' items. His stories are quite delightful; there is always humour and often outright laughter but the shadow of the supernatural is never far away; a spellbinder extraordinary, he usually apologizes with polite insincerity for having curdled your blood. His story 'The Dream' opens this collection and it is probably the best of A.J. Alan's contributions to the *genre*.

'Caterpillars' is a lightly-written but progressively horror-laden story that touches a raw spot and produces a shudder of 'frozen terror'. Its author, E.F. Benson (1867–1940), was the son of an Archbishop of Canterbury, an archaeologist, a novelist and a Mayor of the Cinque Port of Rye. He also wrote biographies of Charlotte Brontë and King Edward VII. He used to say that his spooky stories were 'written in the hope of giving some pleasant qualms . . . and perhaps cause an occasional glance to be cast into corners and dark places . . . to make sure that nothing unusual lurked in the shadows. . . .' E.F. Benson is one of the few ghost-story writers whose stories never disappoint and they frequently have the very effect he speaks of.

One of the memorable pleasures of The Ghost Club some years ago was the likelihood of an encounter with Algernon Blackwood (1869–1951), a charming raconteur with a commanding presence, an unforgettable face and an enormous knowledge of the occult. A son of Sir Arthur Blackwood and Sidney, Duchess of Manchester, he went to Canada when he was twenty where a wide variety of jobs in different locales provided him with background information for his many weird stories. He made his reputation with a volume of five stories centred on the personality of Dr John Silence, psychic investigator, and 'Secret Worship' is one of those stories. Blackwood always maintained that his stories possessed more than a grain of truth and that they were really dramatized emotions that he had experienced in various places. 'Secret Worship', he told me, owed its birth to a Moravian school at Koenigsfeld in the Black Forest where he had spent an unhappy eighteen months learning German and where talking in any other language was punished by half-rations at

9

meal-times. Revisiting the place many years later he experienced again the sense of disgust at the over-strict, semi-military discipline, yet the settlement had an almost saintly atmosphere and some mysterious law of compensation operated in Blackwood and he set the story in medieval Satan Worship . . .

Charles Dickens (1812–70) was also a member of The Ghost Club but he was before my time! The hardship of his early years, the people he met and the places he visited are vividly and uniquely reflected in his many books; indeed, apart from Shakespeare, no author has produced such a number and variety of immortal characters. It has been said that Dickens invented the Christmas ghost; be that as it may, he certainly popularized the Christmas ghost story with his *Christmas Carol* (1843) and this often verbose writer is strangely economical with words in 'The Signalman', a straight-forward ghost story that has the ring of truth and almost certainly had its roots in a factual experience.

'When I Was Dead' is a gem of a ghost story: short, succulent and thought-provoking. I am indebted to Montague Summers for intro-ducing me to this story that was first published in 1896, the year before Bram Stoker's *Dracula*, but unlike that powerful story Vincent O'Sullivan's work is completely undated and might have been written yesterday. There is a light but sure touch about his stories that cause them to return again and again to the mind of the reader.

W.W. Jacobs' 'The Monkey's Paw' is here because it has been one of my favourite stories for almost as long as I can remember and because I like to think the story told about a stage production of the classic story is true. It is said that a member of the audience com-plained, after seeing the play, that the awful thing revealed when the door is flung open at the end was offensive and in bad taste and the producer should have left it to the imagination of the audience – which is what he had done . . . W.W. Jacobs (1863–1943) was born in the London Docks area where his father was overseer of a wharf and many of Jacobs' stories are of the sea and seamen. He wrote many humorous stories, some plays and one or two very effective tales of horror, of which 'The Monkey's Paw' is undoubtedly the best.

M.R. James (1862–1936) was Provost of Eton and a celebrated scholar, an antiquary and author of some delightfully gruesome tales, originally written to entertain his favourite friends at Christmas time. Dr Montague James had definite ideas as to how a ghost story ought to be laid out to be really effective and among his rules were:

the setting should be fairly familiar, the majority of the characters and their talk should be such as the reader might meet or hear any day and the ghost should be malevolent or odious. His success in producing original ghost stories is beyond argument and 'Martin's Close' is characteristic of his work in this field.

It is not always realized that Rudyard Kipling (1865–1936) wrote a number of grisly and powerful stories; in contrast 'They' is, to quote Somerset Maugham, 'a fine and deeply moving effort of the imagination'. In 1899 Kipling's eldest daughter died from pneumonia while the family was on a visit to New York and there is little doubt that this exquisite story was born out of his enduring grief at her loss. This contribution by an acknowledged master of the short story has a haunting quality that is only found in the very best ghost stories.

'The Haunted and the Haunters' is a grim story that well illustrates the profound interest in strange and occult happenings of Edward Bulwer, first Baron Lytton of Knebworth (1803–73), for years the most popular author in England. This story is supposed to have been founded on the occurrences reported to have taken place at London's famous Victorian haunted house, 50 Berkeley Square. At all events Lytton steeped himself in the byways of mysterious lore and Dickens, visiting him in 1861, found him 'a little weird occasionally regarding magic and spirits'; originating from the pen of a man who 'saturated his mind with the love of magic', 'The Haunted and the Haunters' has been described as 'the most terrifying ghost story ever written'.

Arthur Machen (1863–1947) was the son of a clergyman; he was a strange, introspective, solitary man and his stories, works of imagination that deal with elemental forces of evil, with spells and with malign and ancient powers, obviously originated in the dark depths of his unconscious. His famous short story 'The Bowmen', published in 1915, brought him fame. It told of St George bringing the ancient archers of Agincourt to the rescue of the British army during the retreat from Mons, and it was so vivid that thousands of people insisted on believing that it was true; I have talked with more than one old soldier who has told me that he was there and saw the spectral bowmen. 'Change', the piece I have chosen for this anthology, is a powerful story of primitive forces and the reversion of the established order of things.

Edith Nesbit (1858–1924) was a novelist and writer of childrens' books that included *The Story of the Treasure Seekers* and *The Railway Children* but she also wrote stories about the return of the dead that are themselves masterpieces. Such a one is 'Mansize in

Marble' and also the short and simple but oddly believable and disturbing story of 'John Charrington's Wedding', which is included in this selection. Edith Nesbit was educated at a French convent, in Germany and at Brighton, and all these places and the people she met and the circumstances she became involved in have contributed to her writings; her success came, however, when she was the first author to portray young people as real human beings and one wonders whether her ghost stories, with their indefinable 'real' quality, gentle atmosphere and waft of the disturbingly uncanny, may not stand the test of time even longer than her delightful books for children.

Mrs Edith Wharton (1862–1937) was born in New York where she married Edward Wharton in 1885. After travelling far and wide they settled in Paris in 1906 but Edward became insane and they were divorced in 1912. Mrs Wharton excelled in the medium of the short story; almost all of her published stories are excellent and special and different. In 'Afterward' we encounter that vague but convincing air of reality and normality that is suddenly disturbed by an increasing dread of the unknown, of things not being as they appear or as they should be; a sickening slip of perception or perhaps a heightened awareness; followed by a frightening realization of what has really happened.

Not long ago I was invited to read a classic ghost story of my choice at a literary evening held by our local Heritage Society and I chose 'The Monkey's Paw' by W.W. Jacobs. Afterwards a member of the audience came up to me and said, kindly but seriously, that she could never forgive me for reading that particular story. It was one she had read as a girl and she had never forgotten it; hearing it again had reminded her of its strange attraction and worrying possibility; it was a story that had given her many sleepless nights. Such is the power of a good ghost story.

And as the shadows lengthen and the sounds of daylight fade, as the forces of darkness take control and the whisper of the wind among the branches becomes full of a strange meaning and purpose, draw your chair closer to the fire and read about adventures that echo strangely in the mind afterwards. And as you ask yourself whether such things can really be, remember that truth truly is stranger than fiction. In the course of this selection I think I can promise readers a few uncomfortable moments . . . and I wouldn't answer that tap at the door if I were you . . .

The Ghost Club, 1977   Peter Underwood

A.J. Alan

The Dream

They've asked me to tell you about another of my experiences, and I think it wouldn't be a bad idea to try and describe to you a dream I often have.

Before describing the dream itself it may be as well to explain a few things about it.

First of all, I've had it some fifteen or twenty years altogether at quite irregular intervals. Sometimes it gives me a miss for two years, at others it will happen twice in six months. There's no knowing.

It began—to visit me—when I was eight or nine years old, and I used to think then that it was just the same dream each time, but it wasn't, and it isn't. The general setting, or *locale*, is the same, but there's a gradual moving forward of events which makes it somewhat interesting—to me, at any rate—and just a bit creepy.

It always begins in exactly the same way. I am walking up a broad flight of stairs in a very large house. The carpet is dark-blue and very thick, so thick that you sink right in.

The walls are all white.

The time, as a rule, is between eleven and twelve at night. It's evidently a party I'm coming to, and I'm rather late for it. My left forefinger is poking a piece of paper down into my waistcoat pocket, and I'm aware in some occult way that it's the ticket for my hat and coat.

The whole place seems deserted except for me, not even anyone to take my name and announce me. In fact, I'm not *rather* late, I'm *very* late.

At the top of the stairs there's a broad sort of landing-place, and, immediately facing me, a very massive mahogany door with a large cut-glass knob. Through this door I go.

In my very young days I used to have quite a job to push it open, but now it's merely heavy and solid.

There's a screen inside the door which cuts me off from the rest of the room, and it just gives me the opportunity to pull down my waistcoat. I walk, with a certain amount of diffidence, round the screen. It's a great big room—very high and brilliantly lighted. The walls are white and the carpet blue—like the stairs—and the furniture is very dark oak.

The scene is rather peculiar. There must be at least forty or fifty men in the room, and they are all sitting on chairs in front of a little platform against the far wall. They aren't sitting in rows, but just anyhow. It looks as though they've drawn up their chairs as near the platform as they can get. I expect that's what happens, really, but I've never got there early enough to see.

They are all much of the same class, as far as general appearance goes; but their ages are widely different. They range from twenty or less right up to seventy and more.

I used to wonder, many years ago, what it was all about, but now I realize that all these people are watching, with very great interest, a conversation which is taking place between a man and a woman. Incidentally, she is the only woman in the room.

These two are sitting on chairs on the dais or platform. It's quite a low platform really—not more than a foot high.

I say they're watching the conversation because I'm sure that unless one happens to be in the very front row it isn't possible to catch more than a word here and there.

The *man* on the platform doesn't call for any particular remark— at least, I don't know—it *is* rather funny about him.

He is evidently just one of the audience who has been invited up, as it were, and I've usually seen him a few times before in the body of the room. But the thing is that once a man has spent the evening on the platform he never appears again.

Now we come to the lady. She is very beautiful—almost too beautiful to be respectable. In fact, if one didn't actually know——. However, when I say respectable, I don't mean that she would faint clean away if anyone said damn; but one would hesitate before digging her in the ribs on short acquaintance.

As far as I can tell, she's on the tall side, and very graceful. I've never seen her standing up. She looks as though she could dance well. By dance I mean waltz, of course. She has lovely copper-coloured hair, and she's had the sense not to cut it off. She apparently believes in looking like a woman and not like an ungainly boy. Most unfashionable—but then you must remember that this is a dream.

She's usually dressed in a simple black evening-frock and a hat. The hat is rather of the—I think it's called the turban type. It's a little difficult to describe. It's got a sort of asprey—no, osprey—thing that points backwards and downwards, rather like the tail of the comet does. I think Miss Lily Elsie wore something like that in *The Merry Widow* (if she doesn't mind my dragging her in).

When I say she's wearing a *simple* black frock, I mean one of those simple little frocks which you can pick up anywhere for fifty or sixty guineas.

And it's never the same dress twice.

While she's sitting down she isn't having a perpetual struggle to make her skirt cover her knees. Not that I've any quarrel with knees —*qua* knees—but those rows of bony excrescences which stick out at you in the Tube, well, surely some of them might be left to the imagination. In fact, if things go on as they are doing now, one won't want an imagination at all, and then what?

To go back to the lady's hat for a moment, I must confess that it rather beats me—why she's wearing one at all, that is—because she must be in her own house.

You can tell that from the way she behaves—I mean, that she's obviously acting as hostess, and her manner is a treat to watch.

She sits quietly in her chair without looking as if she'd been spilt into it, and she doesn't fidget. She hasn't any of those irritating little affectations which one often sees. She doesn't drag out a repair outfit every two minutes and plaster a lot of stuff on her face. Perhaps she doesn't have to. I don't believe she'd even powder her nose in public. Oh, I know that on this subject I'm only a locust crying in the wilderness, but it *is* refreshing to see anyone who isn't ashamed of her complexion.

I've mentioned before that the conversation, or whatever it is, between the good lady and the man on the platform is so quiet that I've never been able to hear her voice, but there's no doubt in my mind that it's the kind that anyone vulgar, who wished to be extra offensive, would describe as a 'refained voice'; but he wouldn't be there, so it doesn't matter.

I've racked my brains trying to imagine what on earth they can be talking about for such a long time. In the early part *she* seems to be asking questions and getting very deferential answers. Perhaps she's applying some sort of test. Later on it's more as though she is giving information or instructions, and he just puts in a word here and there.

At about half-past twelve she usually lights a cigarette. Between you and me, I think it's a signal as much as anything to tell all the rest of us that we can smoke if we like. Some of us do.

Now, it's rather a funny thing about the time. More often than not the place where I'm standing gives me a view of a clock there is on the mantelpiece. It's one of those clocks which pretend they haven't got any works, like the women of the present day. You know them —er—the clocks. All you can see is a sheet of plate-glass with the figures and hands on it, and the hands go round in some mysterious way. This clock goes and it's right. *How* do I know it's right—let's see—how *do* I know it's right? Oh, yes, because it always indicates the time of about one hour after I've gone to sleep, and that may vary quite a lot.

As regards the age of the lady—well, it's a little hard to say. In my extreme youth she was about as old as an aunt. When I grew up she seemed more like a sister, and now I'm blowed if I know how old she is. Early thirties probably. It's rather unusual to grow *past* anyone.

I think I said at the beginning that there aren't quite enough chairs for everyone, and those who come late—like me—have to stand up at the back. All the same, it becomes apparent every now and then during the evening that there *is* a vacant chair a little way in. It's always a mystery to me *how* this happens, because no one would ever seem to go out (only a blind man would), but when it *does* happen one of the men at the back sort of tiptoes in and takes it.

We just settle amongst ourselves who—like you do in the Tube— 'That's all right, I'm getting out at the next station'—you know. A man who has once sat down always has a chair after that, so you see there's a process going on all through the years whereby everyone gradually works forward to the front and eventually finishes up on the platform. It has often, undoubtedly, been my turn to take a vacant chair, but some instinct has always warned me not to. Even our hostess has noticed it, and she's occasionally looked at me as though to say: 'Aren't you going to sit down?' but I've always half-shaken my head and let someone else have it—the chair, that is. Then she has given a slight, very slight, shrug of the shoulders, and I've felt rather ungracious and left it at that. I know *now* why I don't sit down, and I'll tell you about that presently.

It's extremely difficult to give you the facts about this dream in their proper order, because there isn't a proper order, and it differs in so many ways from ordinary dreams. There are none of the mad things in it that you ordinarily get. . . . The one I'm telling you about is so abnormally normal.

The one constantly variable factor is the man on the platform, and it's rotten bad luck that I've always been too late to see how he comes to be chosen out of all the others. He was once just sitting down, but that's the nearest I've ever got.

It used to strike me what a rag it would be if only I could recognize anyone there. After all, it stands to reason that all these other people must be dreaming, too—and then we could compare notes next day.

Well, one night the man on the platform was a man, a rather famous man, whom I knew very well. When I say I knew him very well, I really mean that I knew his secretary very well, which is infinitely better, believe me. So next morning I rang her up—the secretary—and said, 'I say, I wish you'd fix me up an appointment with the old man some time during the day, because I want to see him very particularly'. And she said, 'I'm afraid you can't because he was found dead in bed this morning'.

Wasn't it just my luck? Fearful hard lines on him, too, of course, but it absolutely dished my chance of finding out what the dream meant.

However, the Fates were kind. Three or four years later I again saw a man on the platform whom I knew perfectly well. His name was Ribblechick, but he couldn't help that, poor chap. He recognized me, too, and we grinned at each other, and I thought now it's all right—he'll have heard her speak, and will be able to tell me what she is—if not who.

So next morning I trotted round—they lived quite near us—and will you believe it, the whole house was upside down. He, poor old Ribblechick, had been found dead in bed, too. Heart-failure they said it was.

Please don't think that I'm suggesting for a moment that it was anything but the purest coincidence that these two unfortunate people happened to die in the same way. But all the same, each time I dream my dream nowadays, and a chair does fall vacant, I still let someone else have it, and the good lady still shrugs her shoulders.

E.F. Benson

Caterpillars

I saw a month or two ago in an Italian paper that the Villa Cascana, in which I once stayed, had been pulled down, and that a manufactory of some sort was in process of erection on its site. There is therefore no longer any reason for refraining from writing of those things which I myself saw (or imagined I saw) in a certain room and on a certain landing of the villa in question, nor from mentioning the circumstances which followed, which may or may not (according to the opinion of the reader) throw some light on, or be somehow connected with this experience.

The Villa Cascana was in all ways but one a perfectly delightful house, yet, if it were standing now, nothing in the world—I use the phrase in its literal sense—would induce me to set foot in it again, for I believe it to have been haunted in a very terrible and practical manner. Most ghosts, when all is said and done, do not do much harm; they may perhaps terrify, but the person whom they visit usually gets over their visitation. They may on the other hand be entirely friendly and beneficent. But the appearances in the Villa Cascana were not beneficent, and had they made their 'visit' in a very slightly different manner, I do not suppose I should have got over it more than Arthur Inglis did.

The house stood on an ilex-clad hill not far from Sestri di Levante on the Italian Riviera, looking out over the iridescent blues of that enchanted sea, while behind it rose the pale green chestnut woods that climb up the hillsides till they give place to the pines that, black in contrast with them, crown the slopes. All round it the garden in the luxuriance of mid-spring bloomed and was fragrant, and the scent of magnolia and rose, borne on the salt freshness of the winds from the sea, flowed like a stream through the cool, vaulted rooms.

On the ground floor a broad pillared *loggia* ran round three sides of the house, the top of which formed a balcony for certain rooms on the first floor. The main staircase, broad and of grey marble steps, led up from the hall to the landing outside these rooms, which were three in number, namely, two big sitting-rooms and a bedroom arranged *en suite*. The latter was unoccupied, the sitting-rooms were in use. From here the main staircase continued up to the second floor, where were situated certain bedrooms, one of which I occupied, while on the other side of the first-floor landing some half-dozen steps led to another suite of rooms, where, at the time I am speaking of, Arthur Inglis, the artist, had his bedroom and studio. Thus the landing outside my bedroom, at the top of the house, commanded both the landing of the first floor, and also the steps that led to Inglis' rooms. Jim Stanley and his wife, finally (whose guest I was), occupied rooms in another wing of the house, where also were the servants' quarters.

I arrived just in time for lunch on a brilliant noon of mid-May. The garden was shouting with colour and fragrance, and not less delightful after my broiling walk up from the *marina*, should have been the coming from the reverberating heat and blaze of the day into the marble coolness of the villa. Only (the reader has my bare word for this, and nothing more), the moment I set foot in the house I felt that something was wrong. This feeling, I may say, was quite vague, though very strong, and I remember that when I saw letters waiting for me on the table in the hall I felt certain that the explanation was here: I was convinced that there was bad news of some sort for me. Yet when I opened them I found no such explanation of my premonition: my correspondents all reeked of prosperity. Yet this clear miscarriage of a presentiment did not dissipate my uneasiness. In that cool fragrant house there was something wrong.

I am at pains to mention this because it may explain why it was that, though I am as a rule so excellent a sleeper that the extinction of a light on getting into bed is apparently contemporaneous with being called on the following morning, I slept very badly on my first night in the Villa Cascana. It may also explain that fact that when I did sleep (if it was indeed in sleep that I saw what I thought I saw) I dreamed in a very vivid and original manner, original, that is to say, in the sense that something which, as far as I knew, had never previously entered into my consciousness, usurped it then. But since, in addition to this evil premonition, certain words and events occurring during the rest of the day, might have suggested something of what I thought happened that night, it will be well to relate them.

After lunch, then, I went round the house with Mrs Stanley, and during our tour she referred, it is true, to the unoccupied bedroom on the first floor, which opened out of the room where we had lunched.

'We left that unoccupied,' she said, 'because Jim and I have a charming bedroom and dressing-room, as you saw, in the wing, and if we used it ourselves we should have to turn the dining-room into a dressing-room and have our meals downstairs. As it is, however, we have our little flat there, Arthur Inglis has his little flat in the other passage; and I remembered (aren't I extraordinary?) that you once said that the higher up you were in a house the better you were pleased. So I put you at the top of the house, instead of giving you that room.'

It is true, that a doubt, vaguely as my uneasy premonition, crossed my mind at this. I did not see why Mrs Stanley should have explained all this, if there had not been more to explain. I allow, therefore, that the thought that there was something to explain about the unoccupied bedroom was momentarily present to my mind.

The second thing that may have borne on my dream was this.

At dinner the conversation turned for a moment on ghosts. Inglis, with the certainty of conviction, expressed his belief that anybody who could possibly believe in the existence of supernatural phenomena was unworthy of the name of an ass. The subject instantly dropped. As far as I can recollect, nothing else occurred or was said that could bear on what follows.

We all went to bed rather early, and personally I yawned my way upstairs, feeling hideously sleepy. My room was rather hot, and I threw all the windows wide, and from without poured in the white light of the moon, and the love-song of many nightingales. I undressed quickly, and got into bed, but though I had felt so sleepy before, I now felt extremely wide-awake. But I was quite content to be awake: I did not toss or turn, I felt perfectly happy listening to the song and seeing the light. Then, it is possible, I may have gone to sleep, and what follows may have been a dream. I thought anyhow that after a time the nightingales ceased singing and the moon sank. I thought also that if, for some unexplained reason, I was going to lie awake all night, I might as well read, and I remembered that I had left a book in which I was interested in the dining-room on the first floor. So I got out of bed, lit a candle, and went downstairs. I entered the room, saw on a side-table the book I had come to look for, and then, simultaneously, saw that the door into the unoccupied bedroom was open. A curious grey light, not of dawn nor of moonshine, came out of it, and I looked in. The bed stood just opposite the door, a big four-poster, hung with tapestry at the head. Then I saw that the greyish light of the bedroom came from the bed, or rather from what was on the bed. For it was covered with great caterpillars, a foot or more in length, which crawled over it. They were faintly luminous, and it was the light from them that showed me the room. Instead of the sucker-feet of ordinary caterpillars they had rows of pincers like crabs, and they moved by grasping what they lay on with their pincers, and then sliding their bodies forward. In colour these dreadful insects were yellowish grey, and they were covered with irregular lumps and swellings. There must have been hundreds of them, for they formed a sort of writhing, crawling pyramid on the bed. Occasionally one fell off on to the floor, with a soft fleshy thud, and though the floor was of hard concrete, it yielded to the pincer-feet as if it had been putty, and crawling back, the caterpillar would mount on to the bed again, to rejoin its fearful companions. They appeared to have no faces, so to speak, but at one end of them there was a mouth that opened sideways in respiration.

Then, as I looked, it seemed to me as if they all suddenly became conscious of my presence. All the mouths at any rate were turned in my direction, and next moment they began dropping off the bed with those soft fleshy thuds on to the floor, and wriggling towards me. For one second the paralysis of nightmare was on me, but the next I was running upstairs again to my room, and I remember feeling the cold of the marble steps on my bare feet. I rushed into my bedroom, and slammed the door behind me, and then—I was certainly wide awake now—I found myself standing by my bed with the sweat of terror pouring from me. The noise of the banged doors still rang in my ears. But, as would have been more usual, if this had been mere nightmare, the terror that had been mine when I saw those foul beasts crawling about the bed or dropping softly on to the floor did not cease then. Awake now, if dreaming before, I did not at all recover from the horror of dream: it did not seem to me that I had dreamed. And until dawn, I sat or stood, not daring to lie down, thinking that every rustle or movement that I heard was the approach of the caterpillars. To them and the claws that bit into the cement the wood of the door was child's play: steel would not keep them out.

But with the sweet and noble return of day the horror vanished: the whisper of wind became benignant again: the nameless fear, whatever it was, was smoothed out and terrified me no longer. Dawn broke, hueless at first; then it grew dove-coloured, then the flaming pageant of light spread over the sky.

The admirable rule of the house was that everybody had breakfast

21

where and when he pleased, and in consequence it was not till lunch-time that I met any of the other members of our party, since I had breakfast on my balcony, and wrote letters and other things till lunch. In fact, I got down to that meal rather late, after the other three had begun. Between my knife and fork there was a small pill-box of cardboard, and as I sat down Inglis spoke.

'Do look at that,' he said, 'since you are interested in natural history. I found it crawling on my counterpane last night, and I don't know what it is.'

I think that before I opened the pill-box I expected something of the sort which I found in it. Inside it, anyhow, was a small caterpillar, greyish-yellow in colour, with curious bumps and excrescences on its rings. It was extremely active, and hurried round the box, this way and that. Its feet were unlike the feet of any caterpillar I ever saw: they were like the pincers of a crab. I looked, and shut the lid down again.

'No, I don't know it,' I said, 'but it looks rather unwholesome. What are you going to do with it?'

'Oh, I shall keep it,' said Inglis. 'It has begun to spin: I want to see what sort of a moth it turns into.'

I opened the box again, and saw that these hurrying movements were indeed the beginning of the spinning of the web of its cocoon. Then Inglis spoke again.

'It has got funny feet, too,' he said. 'They are like crabs' pincers. What's the Latin for crab? Oh, yes, Cancer. So in case it is unique, let's christen it: "Cancer Inglisensis".'

Then something happened in my brain, some momentary piecing together of all that I had seen or dreamed. Something in his words seemed to me to throw light on it all, and my own intense horror at the experience of the night before linked itself on to what he had just said. In effect, I took the box and threw it, caterpillar and all, out of the window. There was a gravel path just outside, and beyond it a fountain playing into a basin. The box fell on to the middle of this.

Inglis laughed.

'So the students of the occult don't like solid facts,' he said. 'My poor caterpillar!'

The talk went off again at once on to other subjects, and I have only given in detail, as they happened, these trivialities in order to be sure myself that I have recorded everything that could have borne on occult subjects or on the subject of caterpillars. But at the moment when I threw the pill-box into the fountain, I lost my head: my only excuse is that, as is probably plain, the tenant of it was, in miniature, exactly what I had seen crowded on to the bed in the unoccupied room. And though this translation of those phantoms into flesh and blood—or whatever it is that caterpillars are made of—ought perhaps to have relieved the horror of the night, as a matter of fact it did nothing of the kind. It only made the crawling pyramid that covered the bed in the unoccupied room more hideously real.

After lunch we spent a lazy hour or two strolling about the garden or sitting in the *loggia*, and it must have been about four o'clock when Stanley and I started off to bathe, down the path that led by the fountain into which I had thrown the pill-box. The water was shallow and clear, and at the bottom of it I saw its white remains. The soaking had disintegrated the cardboard, and it had become no more than a few strips and shreds of sodden paper. The centre of the fountain was a marble Italian Cupid which squirted the water out of a wine-skin held under its arm. And crawling up its leg was the caterpillar. Strange and scarcely credible as it seemed, it must have survived the falling-to-bits of its prison, and made its way to shore, and there it was, out of arm's reach, weaving and waving this way and that as it evolved its cocoon.

Then, as I looked at it, it seemed to me again that, like the cater-pillar I had seen last night, it saw me, and breaking out of the threads that surrounded it, it crawled down the marble leg of the Cupid and began swimming like a snake across the water of the fountain to-wards me. It came with extraordinary speed (the fact of a caterpillar being able to swim was new to me), and in another moment was crawling up the marble lip of the basin. Just then Inglis joined us.

'Why, if it isn't old "Cancer Inglisensis" again,' he said, catching sight of the beast. 'What a tearing hurry it is in.'

We were standing side by side on the path, and when the caterpillar had advanced to within about a yard of us, it stopped, and began waving again, as if in doubt as to the direction in which it should go. Then it appeared to make up its mind, and crawled on to Inglis' shoe.

'It likes me best,' he said, 'but I don't really know that I like it. And as it won't drown I think perhaps——'

He shook it off his shoe on to the gravel path and trod on it.

All the afternoon the air got heavier and heavier with the Sirocco that was without doubt coming up from the south, and that night again I went up to bed feeling very sleepy, but below my drowsiness, so to speak, there was the consciousness, stronger than before, that there was something wrong in the house, that something dangerous was close at hand. But I fell asleep at once, and—how long after I do not know—either woke or dreamed I awoke, feeling that I must get up at once, *or I should be too late*. Then (dreaming or awake) I lay and fought this fear, telling myself that I was but the prey of my own nerves disordered by Sirocco or what not, and at the same time quite clearly knowing in another part of my mind, so to speak, that every moment's delay added to the danger. At last this second feeling became irresistible, and I put on coat and trousers and went out of my room on to the landing. And then I saw that I had already delayed too long, and that I was now too late.

The whole of the landing of the first floor below was invisible under the swarm of caterpillars that crawled there. The folding doors into the sitting-room from which opened the bedroom where I had seen them last night, were shut, but they were squeezing through the cracks of it, and dropping one by one through the keyhole, elongating themselves into mere string as they passed, and growing fat and lumpy again on emerging. Some, as if exploring, were nosing about the steps into the passage at the end of which were Inglis' rooms, others were crawling on the lowest steps of the staircase that led up to where I stood. The landing, however, was completely covered with them: I was cut off. And of the frozen horror that seized me when I saw that, I can give no idea in words.

Then at last a general movement began to take place, and they grew thicker on the steps that led to Inglis' room. Gradually, like some hideous tide of flesh, they advanced along the passage, and I saw the foremost, visible by the pale grey luminousness that came from them, reach his door. Again and again I tried to shout and warn him, in terror all the time that they should turn at the sound of my voice and mount my stair instead, but for all my efforts I felt that no sound came from my throat. They crawled along the hinge-crack of his door, passing through as they had done before, and still I stood there making impotent efforts to shout to him, to bid him escape while there was time.

At last the passage was completely empty: they had all gone, and at that moment I was conscious for the first time of the cold of the marble landing on which I stood barefooted. The dawn was just beginning to break in the Eastern sky.

Six months later I met Mrs Stanley in a country house in England. We talked on many subjects and at last she said:

'I don't think I have seen you since I got that dreadful news about Arthur Inglis a month ago.'

'I haven't heard,' said I.

'No? He has got cancer. They don't even advise an operation, for there is no hope of a cure: he is riddled with it, the doctors say.'

Now during all these six months I do not think a day had passed on which I had not had in my mind the dreams (or whatever you like to call them) which I had seen in the Villa Cascana.

'It is awful, is it not?' she continued, 'and I feel, I can't help feeling, that he may have——'

'Caught it at the villa?' I asked.

She looked at me in blank surprise.

'Why did you say that?' she asked. 'How did you know?'

Then she told me. In the unoccupied bedroom a year before there had been a fatal case of cancer. She had, of course, taken the best advice and had been told that the utmost dictates of prudence would be obeyed so long as she did not put anybody to sleep in the room, which had also been thoroughly disinfected and newly white-washed and painted. But——

Ambrose Bierce

The Damned Thing

By the light of a tallow candle, which had been placed on one end of a rough table, a man was reading something written in a book. It was an old account book, greatly worn; and the writing was not, apparently, very legible, for the man sometimes held the page close to the flame of the candle to get a stronger light upon it. The shadow of a book would then throw into obscurity a half of the room, darkening a number of faces and figures; for besides the reader, eight other men were present. Seven of them sat against the rough log walls, silent and motionless, and, the room being small, not very far from the table. By extending an arm any one of them could have touched the eighth man, who lay on the table, face upward, partly covered by a sheet, his arms at his sides. He was dead.

The man with the book was not reading aloud, and no one spoke; all seemed to be waiting for something to occur; the dead man only was without expectation. From the blank darkness outside came in, through the aperture that served for a window, all the ever unfamiliar noises of night in the wilderness—the long, nameless note of a distant coyote; the stilly pulsing thrill of tireless insects in trees; strange cries of night birds, so different from those of the birds of day; the drone of great blundering beetles, and all that mysterious chorus of small sounds that seem always to have been but half heard when they have suddenly ceased, as if conscious of an indiscretion. But nothing of all this was noted in that company; its members were not overmuch addicted to idle interest in matters of no practical importance; that was obvious in every line of their rugged faces—obvious even in the dim light of the single candle. They were evidently men of the vicinity—farmers and woodmen.

The person reading was a trifle different; one would have said of him that he was of the world, worldly, albeit there was that in his attire which attested a certain fellowship with the organisms of his environment. His coat would hardly have passed muster in San

Francisco; his footgear was not of urban origin, and the hat that lay by him on the floor (he was the only one uncovered) was such that if one had considered it as an article of mere personal adornment he would have missed its meaning. In countenance the man was rather prepossessing, with just a hint of sternness; though that he may have assumed or cultivated as appropriate to one in authority. For he was a coroner. It was by virtue of his office that he had possession of the book in which he was reading; it had been found among the dead man's effects—in his cabin, where the inquest was now taking place.

When the coroner had finished reading he put the book into his breast pocket. At that moment the door was pushed open and a young man entered. He, clearly, was not of mountain birth and breeding; he was clad as those who dwell in cities. His clothing was dusty, however, as from travel. He had, in fact, been riding hard to attend the inquest.

The coroner nodded; no one else greeted him.

'We have waited for you,' said the coroner. 'It is necessary to have done with this business tonight.'

The young man smiled. 'I am sorry to have kept you,' he said. 'I went away, not to evade your summons, but to post to my newspaper an account of what I suppose I am called back to relate.'

The coroner smiled.

'The account that you posted to your newspaper,' he said, 'differs probably from that which you will give here under oath.'

'That,' replied the other, rather hotly and with a visible flush, 'is as you choose. I used manifold paper and have a copy of what I sent. It was not written as news, for it is incredible, but as fiction. It may go as a part of my testimony under oath.'

'But you say it is incredible.'

'That is nothing to you, sir, if I also swear that it is true.'

The coroner was apparently not greatly affected by the young man's manifest resentment. He was silent for some moments, his eyes upon the floor. The men about the sides of the cabin talked in whispers, but seldom withdrew their gaze from the face of the corpse. Presently the coroner lifted his eyes and said: 'We will resume the inquest.'

The men removed their hats. The witness was sworn.

'What is your name?' the coroner asked.

'William Harker.'

'Age?'

'Twenty-seven.'

'You knew the deceased, Hugh Morgan?'

'Yes.'

'You were with him when he died?'

'Near him.'

'How did that happen—your presence, I mean?'

'I was visiting him at this place to shoot and fish. A part of my purpose, however, was to study him, and his odd, solitary way of life. He seemed a good model for a character in fiction. I sometimes write stories.'

'I sometimes read them.'

'Thank you.'

'Stories in general—not yours.'

Some of the jurors laughed. Against a sombre background humour shows high lights. Soldiers in the intervals of battle laugh easily, and a jest in the death chamber conqueres by surprise.

'Relate the circumstances of this man's death,' said the coroner. 'You may use any notes or memoranda that you please.'

The witness understood. Pulling a manuscript from his breast pocket he held it near the candle, and turning the leaves until he found the passage that he wanted, began to read.

2

'"... The sun had hardly risen when we left the house. We were looking for quail, each with a shotgun, but we had only one dog. Morgan said that our best ground was beyond a certain ridge that he pointed out, and we crossed it by a trail through the chaparral. On the other side was comparatively level ground, thickly covered with wild oats. As we emerged from the chaparral, Morgan was but a few yards in advance. Suddenly, we heard, at a little distance to our right, and partly in front, a noise as of some animal thrashing about in the bushes, which we could see were violently agitated.

'" We've started a deer,' I said. 'I wish we had brought a rifle.'

'" Morgan, who had stopped and was intently watching the agitated chaparral, said nothing, but had cocked both barrels of his gun, and was holding it in readiness to aim. I thought him a trifle excited, which surprised me, for he had a reputation for exceptional coolness, even in moments of sudden and imminent peril.

'""Oh, come!' I said. 'You are not going to fill up a deer with quail-shot, are you?'

'"Still he did not reply; but, catching a sight of his face as he turned it slightly toward me, I was struck by the pallor of it. Then I understood that we had serious business on hand, and my first conjecture was that we had 'jumped' a grizzly. I advanced to

Morgan's side, cocking my piece as I moved.

"'The bushes were now quiet, and the sounds had ceased, but Morgan was as attentive to the place as before.

"'What is it? What the devil is it?' I asked.

"'That Damned Thing!' he replied, without turning his head. His voice was husky and unnatural. He trembled visibly.

"'I was about to speak further when I observed the wild oats near the place of the disturbance moving in the most inexplicable way. I can hardly describe it. It seemed as if stirred by a streak of wind, which not only bent it, but pressed it down—crushed it so that it did not rise, and this movement was slowly prolonging itself directly toward us.

"'Nothing that I had ever seen had affected me so strangely as this unfamiliar and unaccountable phenomenon, yet I am unable to recall any sense of fear. I remember—and tell it here because, singularly enough, I recollected it then—that once, in looking care-lessly out of an open window, I momentarily mistook a small tree close at hand for one of a group of larger trees at a little distance away. It looked the same size as the others, but, being more distinctly and sharply defined in mass and detail, seemed out of harmony with them. It was a mere falsification of the law of aërial perspective, but it startled, almost terrified me. We so rely upon the orderly operation of familiar natural laws that any seeming suspension of them is noted as a menace to our safety, a warning of unthinkable calamity. So now the apparently causeless movement of the herbage, and the slow, undeviating approach of the line of disturbance, were distinctly disquieting. My companion appeared actually frightened, and I could hardly credit my senses when I saw him suddenly throw his gun to his shoulder and fire both barrels at the agitated grass! Before the smoke of the discharge had cleared away I heard a loud savage cry—a scream like that of a wild animal—and, flinging his gun upon the ground, Morgan sprang away and ran swiftly from the spot. At the same instant I was thrown violently to the ground by the impact of something unseen in the smoke—some soft, heavy substance that seemed thrown against me with great force.

"'Before I could get upon my feet and recover my gun, which seemed to have been struck from my hands, I heard Morgan crying out as if in mortal agony, and mingling with his cries were such hoarse, savage sounds as one hears from fighting dogs. Inexpressibly terrified, I struggled to my feet and looked in the direction of Morgan's retreat; and may heaven in mercy spare me from another sight like that! At a distance of less than thirty yards was my friend, down upon one knee, his head thrown back at a frightful angle, hatless, his long hair in disorder and his whole body in violent movement from side to side, backward and forward. His right arm was lifted and seemed to lack the hand—at least, I could see none. The other arm was invisible. At times, as my memory now reports this extraordinary scene, I could discern but a part of his body; it was as if he had been partly blotted out—I cannot otherwise express it—then a shifting of his position would bring it all into view again.

'"All this must have occurred within a few seconds, yet in that time Morgan assumed all the posture of a determined wrestler vanquished by superior weight and strength. I saw nothing but him, and him not always distinctly. During the entire incident his shouts and curses were heard, as if through an enveloping uproar of such sounds of rage and fury as I had never heard from the throat of man or brute!

'"For a moment only I stood irresolute, then, throwing down my gun, I ran forward to my friend's assistance. I had a vague belief that he was suffering from a fit or some form of convulsion. Before I could reach his side he was down and quiet. All sounds had ceased, but, with a feeling of such terror as even these awful events had not inspired, I now saw the same mysterious movement of the wild oats prolonging itself from the trampled area about the prostrate man toward the edge of a wood. It was only when it had reached the wood that I was able to withdraw my eyes and look at my companion. He was dead."'

3

The coroner rose from his seat and stood beside the dead man. Lifting an edge of the sheet he pulled it away, exposing the entire body, altogether naked, and showing in the candlelight a clay-like yellow. It had, however, broad maculations of bluish-black, obviously caused by extravasated blood from contusions. The chest and sides looked as if they had been beaten with a bludgeon. There were dreadful lacerations; the skin was torn in strips and shreds.

The coroner moved round to the end of the table and undid a silk handkerchief, which had been passed under the chin and knotted on the top of the head. When the handkerchief was drawn away it exposed what had been the throat. Some of the jurors who had risen to get a better view repented their curiosity and turned away their faces. Witness Harker went to the open window and leaned out across the sill, faint and sick. Dropping the handkerchief upon the dead man's neck, the coroner stepped to an angle of the room, and from a pile of clothing produced one garment after another, each of which he held up a moment for inspection. All were torn, and stiff with blood. The jurors did not make a closer inspection. They seemed rather uninterested. They had, in truth, seen all this before; the only thing that was new to them being Harker's testimony.

'Gentlemen,' the coroner said, 'we have no more evidence, I think. Your duty has been already explained to you; if there is nothing you wish to ask you may go outside and consider your verdict.'

The foreman rose—a tall, bearded man of sixty, coarsely clad.

'I should like to ask one question, Mr Coroner,' he said. 'What asylum did this yer last witness escape from?'

'Mr Harker,' said the coroner, gravely and tranquilly, 'from what asylum did you last escape?'

Harker flushed crimson again, but said nothing, and the seven jurors rose and solemnly filed out of the cabin.

'If you have done insulting me, sir,' said Harker, as soon as he and the officer were left alone with the dead man, ' I suppose I am at liberty to go?'

'Yes.'

Harker started to leave, but paused, with his hand on the door latch. The habit of his profession was strong in him—stronger than his sense of personal dignity. He turned about and said:

'The book that you have there—I recognize it as Morgan's diary. You seemed greatly interested in it; you read in it while I was testifying. May I see it? The public would like——'

'The book will cut no figure in this matter,' replied the official, slipping it into his coat pocket; 'all the entries in it were made before the writer's death.'

As Harker passed out of the house the jury reëntered and stood about the table, on which the now covered corpse showed under the sheet with sharp definition. The foreman seated himself near the candle, produced from his breast pocket a pencil and scrap of paper, and wrote rather laboriously the following verdict, which with various degrees of effort all signed:

'We, the jury, do find that the remains come to their death at the hands of a mountain lion, but some of us thinks, all the same, they had fits.'

4

In the diary of the late Hugh Morgan are certain interesting entries having, possibly, a scientific value as suggestions. At the inquest upon his body the book was not put in evidence; possibly the coroner thought it not worth while to confuse the jury. The date of the first of the entries mentioned cannot be ascertained; the upper part of the leaf is torn away; the part of the entry remaining is as follows:

'. . . would run in a half circle, keeping his head turned always toward the centre and again he would stand still, barking furiously. At last he ran away into the brush as fast as he could go. I thought at first that he had gone mad, but on returning to the house found no other alteration in his manner than what was obviously due to fear of punishment.

'Can a dog see with his nose? Do odours impress some olfactory centre with images of the thing emitting them? . . .

'*September 2*.—Looking at the stars last night as they rose above the crest of the ridge east of the house I observed them successively disappear—from left to right. Each was eclipsed but an instant, and only a few at the same time, but along the entire length of the ridge all that were within a degree or two of the crest were blotted out. It was as if something had passed along between me and them; but I could not see it, and the stars were not thick enough to define its outline. Ugh! I don't like this. . . .'

Several weeks' entries are missing, three leaves being torn from the book.

'*September 27*.—It has been about here again—I find evidences of its presence every day. I watched again all of last night in the same cover, gun in hand, double-charged with buckshot. In the morning the fresh footprints were there, as before. Yet I would have sworn that I did not sleep—indeed, I hardly sleep at all. It is terrible, insupportable! If these amazing experiences are real I shall go mad; if they are fanciful I am mad already.

'*October 3*.—I shall not go—it shall not drive me away. No, this is *my* house, *my* land. God hates a coward. . . .

'*October 5*.—I can stand it no longer; I have invited Harker to pass a few weeks with me—he has a level head. I can judge from his manner if he thinks me mad.

'*October 7*.—I have the solution of the problem; it came to me last night—suddenly, as by revelation. How simple—how terribly simple!

'There are sounds that we cannot hear. At either end of the scale are notes that stir no chord of that imperfected instrument, the human ear. They are too high or too grave. I have observed a flock of blackbirds occupying an entire treetop—the tops of several trees—and all in full song. Suddenly—in a moment—at absolutely the same instant—all spring into the air and fly away. How? They could not all see one another—whole treetops intervened. At no point could a leader have been visible to all. There must have been a signal of warning or command, high and shrill above the din, but by me unheard. I have observed, too, the same simultaneous flight when all were silent, among not only blackbirds, but other birds—quail, for example, widely separated by bushes—even on opposite sides of a hill.

'It is known to seamen that a school of whales basking or sporting on the surface of the ocean, miles apart, with the convexity of the earth between them, will sometimes dive at the same instant—all gone out of sight in a moment. The signal has been sounded—too grave for the ear of the sailor at the masthead and his comrades on the deck—who nevertheless feel its vibrations in the ship as the stones of a cathedral are stirred by the bass of the organ.

'As with sounds, so with colours. At each end of the solar spectrum the chemist can detect the presence of what are known as "actinic" rays. They represent colours—integral colours in the composition of light—which we are unable to discern. The human eye is an imperfect instrument; its range is but a few octaves of the real "chromatic scale". I am not mad; there are colours that we cannot see.

'And, God help me! the Damned Thing is of such a colour!'

Algernon Blackwood

Secret Worship

Harris, the silk merchant, was in South Germany on his way home from a business trip when the idea came to him suddenly that he would take the mountain railway from Strassbourg and run down to revisit his old school after an interval of something more than thirty years. And it was to this chance impulse of the junior partner in Harris Brothers of St Paul's Churchyard that John Silence owed one of the most curious cases of his whole experience, for at that very moment he happened to be tramping these same mountains with a holiday knapsack, and from different points of the compass the two men were actually converging towards the same inn.

Now, deep down in the heart that for thirty years had been concerned chiefly with the profitable buying and selling of silk, this school had left the imprint of its peculiar influence, and, though perhaps unknown to Harris, had strongly coloured the whole of his subsequent existence. It belonged to the deeply religious life of a small Protestant community (which it is unnecessary to specify), and his father had sent him there at the age of fifteen, partly because he would learn the German requisite for the conduct of the silk business, and partly because the discipline was strict, and discipline was what his soul and body needed just then more than anything else.

The life, indeed, had proved exceedingly severe, and young Harris benefited accordingly; for though corporal punishment was unknown, there was a system of mental and spiritual correction which somehow made the soul stand proudly erect to receive it, while it struck at the very root of the fault and taught the boy that his character was being cleaned and strengthened, and that he was not merely being tortured in a kind of personal revenge.

That was over thirty years ago, when he was a dreamy and impressionable youth of fifteen; and now, as the train climbed slowly up the winding mountain gorges, his mind travelled back somewhat lovingly over the intervening period, and forgotten details rose vividly again before him out of the shadows. The life there had been very wonderful, it seemed to him, in that remote mountain village, protected from the tumults of the world by the love and worship of the devout Brotherhood that ministered to the needs of some hundred boys from every country in Europe. Sharply the scenes came back to him. He smelt again the long stone corridors, the hot pine-wood rooms, where the sultry hours of summer study were passed with bees droning through open windows in the sunshine, and German characters struggling in the mind with dreams of English lawns—and then the sudden awful cry of the master in German—

'Harris, stand up! You sleep!'

And he recalled the dreadful standing motionless for an hour, book in hand, while the knees felt like wax and the head grew heavier than a cannon-ball.

The very smell of the cooking came back to him—the daily *Sauerkraut*, the watery chocolate on Sundays, the flavour of the stringy meat served twice a week at *Mittagessen*; and he smiled to think again of the half-rations that was the punishment for speaking English. The very odour of the milk-bowls—the hot sweet aroma that rose from the soaking peasant-bread at the six-o'clock breakfast —came back to him pungently, and he saw the huge *Speisesaal* with the hundred boys in their school uniform, all eating sleepily in silence, gulping down the coarse bread and scalding milk in terror of the bell that would presently cut them short—and, at the far end where the masters sat, he saw the narrow slit windows with the vistas of enticing field and forest beyond.

And this, in turn, made him think of the great barn-like room on the top floor where all slept together in wooden cots, and he heard in memory the clamour of the cruel bell that woke them on winter mornings at five o'clock and summoned them to the stone-flagged *Waschkammer*, where boys and masters alike, after scanty and icy washing, dressed in complete silence.

From this his mind passed swiftly, with vivid picture-thoughts, to other things, and with a passing shiver he remembered how the loneliness of never being alone had eaten into him, and how every-thing—works, meals, sleep, walks, leisure—was done with his 'division' of twenty other boys and under the eyes of at least two masters. The only solitude possible was by asking for half an hour's practice in the cell-like music rooms, and Harris smiled to himself as he recalled the zeal of his violin studies.

Then, as the train puffed laboriously through the great pine forests that cover these mountains with a giant carpet of velvet, he found the pleasanter layers of memory giving up their dead, and he recalled with admiration the kindness of the masters, whom all addressed as Brother, and marvelled afresh at their devotion in burying themselves for years in such a place, only to leave it, in most cases, for the still rougher life of missionaries in the wild places of the world.

He thought once more of the still, religious atmosphere that hung over the little forest community like a veil, barring the distressful world; of the picturesque ceremonies at Easter, Christmas, and New Year; of the numerous feast-days and charming little festivals. The *Beschehr-Fest*, in particular, came back to him—the feast of gifts at Christmas—when the entire community paired off and gave presents, many of which had taken weeks to make or the savings of many days to purchase. And then he saw the midnight ceremony in the church at New Year, with the shining face of the *Prediger* in the pulpit—the village preacher who, on the last night of the old year, saw in the empty gallery beyond the organ loft the faces of all who were to die in the ensuing twelve months, and who at last recognized himself among them, and, in the very middle of his sermon, passed into a state of rapt ecstasy and burst into a torrent of praise.

Thickly the memories crowded upon him. The picture of the small village dreaming its unselfish life on the mountain-tops, clean, wholesome, simple, searching vigorously for its God, and training hundreds of boys in the grand way, rose up in his mind with all the power of an obsession. He felt once more the old mystical enthusiasm, deeper than the sea and more wonderful than the stars; he heard again the winds sighing from leagues of forest over the red roofs in the moonlight; he heard the Brothers' voices talking of the things beyond this life as though they had actually experienced them in the body; and, as he sat in the jolting train, a spirit of unutterable longing passed over his seared and tired soul, stirring in the depths of him a sea of emotions that he thought had long since frozen into immobility.

And the contrast pained him—the idealistic dreamer then, the man of business now—so that a spirit of unworldly peace and beauty known only to the soul in meditation laid its feathered finger upon his heart, moving strangely the surface of the waters.

Harris shivered a little and looked out of the window of his empty carriage. The train had long passed Hornberg, and far below the streams tumbled in white foam down the limestone rocks. In front of him, dome upon dome of wooded mountain stood against the sky. It was October, and the air was cool and sharp, wood-smoke and damp moss exquisitely mingled in it with the subtle odours of the pines. Overhead, between the tips of the highest firs, he saw the first stars peeping, and the sky was a clean, pale amethyst that seemed exactly the colour all these memories clothed themselves with in his mind.

He leaned back in his corner and sighed. He was a heavy man, and he had not known sentiment for years; he was a big man, and it took much to move him, literally and figuratively; he was a man in whom the dreams of God that haunt the soul in youth, though overlaid by the scum that gathers in the fight for money, had not, as with the majority, utterly died the death.

He came back into this little neglected pocket of the years, where so much fine gold had collected and lain undisturbed, with all his semi-spiritual emotions aquiver; and, as he watched the mountain-tops come nearer, and smelt the forgotten odours of his boyhood, something melted on the surface of his soul and left him sensitive to a degree he had not known since, thirty years before, he had lived here with his dreams, his conflicts, and his youthful suffering.

A thrill ran through him as the train stopped with a jolt at a tiny station and he saw the name in large black lettering on the grey stone building, and below it, the number of metres it stood above the level of the sea.

'The highest point on the line!' he exclaimed. 'How well I remember it—Sommerau—Summer Meadow. The very next station is mine!'

And, as the train ran downhill with brakes on and steam shut off, he put his head out of the window and one by one saw the old familiar landmarks in the dusk. They stared at him like dead faces in a dream. Queer, sharp feelings, half poignant, half sweet, stirred in his heart.

'There's the hot, white road we walked along so often with the two Brüder always at our heels,' he thought; 'and there, by Jove, is the turn through the forest to "*Die Galgen*", the stone gallows where they hanged the witches in olden days!'

He smiled a little as the train slid past.

'And there's the copse where the Lilies of the Valley powdered the ground in spring; and, I swear'—he put his head out with a sudden impulse—'if that's not the very clearing where Calame, the French boy, chased the swallow-tail with me, and Bruder Pagel gave us half-rations for leaving the road without permission, and for shouting in our mother tongues!' And he laughed again as the memories came back with a rush, flooding his mind with vivid detail.

The train stopped, and he stood on the grey gravel platform like a

man in a dream. It seemed half a century since he last waited there
with corded wooden boxes, and got into the train for Strassbourg
and home after the two years' exile. Time dropped from him like an
old garment and he felt a boy again. Only, things looked so much
smaller than his memory of them; shrunk and dwindled they looked,
and the distances seemed on a curiously smaller scale.

He made his way across the road to the little Gasthaus, and, as he
went, faces and figures of former schoolfellows—German, Swiss,
Italian, French, Russian—slipped out of the shadowy woods and
silently accompanied him. They flitted by his side, raising their eyes
questioningly, sadly, to his. But their names he had forgotten. Some
of the Brothers, too, came with them, and most of these he remembered by name—Bruder Röst, Bruder Pagel, Bruder Schliemann,
and the bearded face of the old preacher who had seen himself in the
haunted gallery of those about to die—Bruder Gysin. The dark
forest lay all about him like a sea that any moment might rush with
velvet waves upon the scene and sweep all the faces away. The air
was cool and wonderfully fragrant, but with every perfumed breath
came also a pallid memory. . . .

Yet, in spite of the underlying sadness inseparable from such an
experience, it was all very interesting, and held a pleasure peculiarly
its own, so that Harris engaged his room and ordered supper feeling
well pleased with himself, and intending to walk up to the old school
that very evening. It stood in the centre of the community's village,
some four miles distant through the forest, and he now recollected
for the first time that this little Protestant settlement dwelt isolated
in a section of the country that was otherwise Catholic. Crucifixes
and shrines surrounded the clearing like the sentries of a beleaguring
army. Once beyond the square of the village, with its few acres of
field and orchard, the forest crowded up in solid phalanxes, and
beyond the rim of trees began the country that was ruled by the
priests of another faith. He vaguely remembered, too, that the
Catholics had showed sometimes a certain hostility towards the little
Protestant oasis that flourished so quietly and benignly in their
midst. He had quite forgotten this. How trumpery it all seemed now
with his wide experience of life and his knowledge of other countries
and the great outside world. It was like stepping back, not thirty
years, but three hundred.

There were only two others besides himself at supper. One of them,
a bearded, middle-aged man in tweeds, sat by himself at the far end,
and Harris kept out of his way because he was English. He feared he
might be in business, possibly even in the silk business, and that he

would perhaps talk on the subject. The other traveller, however, was a Catholic priest. He was a little man who ate his salad with a knife, yet so gently that it was almost inoffensive, and it was the sight of 'the cloth' that recalled his memory of the old antagonism. Harris mentioned by way of conversation the object of his sentimental journey, and the priest looked up sharply at him with raised eyebrows and an expression of surprise and suspicion that somehow picqued him. He ascribed it to his difference of belief.

'Yes,' went on the silk merchant, pleased to talk of what his mind was so full, 'and it was a curious experience for an English boy to be dropped down into a school of a hundred foreigners. I well remember the loneliness and intolerable Heimweh of it at first.' His German was very fluent.

The priest opposite looked up from his cold veal and potato salad and smiled. It was a nice face. He explained quietly that he did not belong here, but was making a tour of the parishes of Württemberg and Baden.

'It was a strict life,' added Harris. 'We English, I remember, used to call it *Gefängnisleben*—prison life!'

The face of the other, for some unaccountable reason, darkened. After a slight pause, and more by way of politeness than because he wished to continue the subject, he said quietly—

'It was a flourishing school in those days, of course. Afterwards, I have heard——' He shrugged his shoulders slightly, and the odd look—it almost seemed a look of alarm—came back into his eyes. The sentence remained unfinished.

Something in the tone of the man seemed to his listener uncalled for—in a sense reproachful, singular. Harris bridled in spite of himself.

'It has changed?' he asked. 'I can hardly believe——'

'You have not heard, then?' observed the priest gently, making a gesture as though to cross himself, yet not actually completing it. 'You have not heard what happened there before it was abandoned——?'

It was very childish, of course, and perhaps he was overtired and overwrought in some way, but the words and manner of the little priest seemed to him so offensive—so disproportionately offensive—that he hardly noticed the concluding sentence. He recalled the old bitterness and the old antagonism, and for a moment he almost lost his temper.

'Nonsense,' he interrupted with a forced laugh, '*Unsinn!* You must forgive me, sir, for contradicting you. But I was a pupil there myself. I was at school there. There was no place like it. I cannot believe that anything serious could have happened to—to take away its character. The devotion of the Brothers would be difficult to equal anywhere——'

He broke off suddenly, realizing that his voice had been raised unduly and that the man at the far end of the table might understand German; and at the same moment he looked up and saw that this individual's eyes were fixed upon his face intently. They were peculiarly bright. Also they were rather wonderful eyes, and the way they met his own served in some way he could not understand to convey both a reproach and a warning. The whole face of the stranger, indeed, made a vivid impression upon him, for it was a face, he now noticed for the first time, in whose presence one would not willingly have said or done anything unworthy. Harris could not explain to himself how it was he had not become conscious sooner of its presence.

But he could have bitten off his tongue for having so far forgotten himself. The little priest lapsed into silence. Only once he said, looking up and speaking in a low voice that was not intended to be overheard, but that evidently *was* overheard, 'You will find it different.' Presently he rose and left the table with a polite bow that included both the others.

And, after him, from the far end rose also the figure in the tweed suit, leaving Harris by himself.

He sat on for a bit in the darkening room, sipping his coffee and smoking his fifteen-pfennig cigar, till the girl came in to light the oil lamps. He felt vexed with himself for his lapse from good manners, yet hardly able to account for it. Most likely, he reflected, he had been annoyed because the priest had unintentionally changed the pleasant character of his dream by introducing a jarring note. Later he must seek an opportunity to make amends. At present, however, he was too impatient for his walk to the school, and he took his stick and hat and passed out into the open air.

And, as he crossed before the Gasthaus, he noticed that the priest and the man in the tweed suit were already engaged in such deep conversation that they hardly noticed him as he passed and raised his hat.

He started off briskly, well remembering the way, and hoping to reach the village in time to have a word with one of the Brüder. They might even ask him in for a cup of coffee. He felt sure of his welcome, and the old memories were in full possession once more. The hour of return was a matter of no consequence whatever.

It was then just after seven o'clock, and the October evening was drawing in with chill airs from the recesses of the forest. The road plunged straight from the railway clearing into its depths, and in a very few minutes the trees engulfed him and the clack of his boots fell dead and echoless against the seried stems of a million firs. It was very black; one trunk was hardly distinguishable from another. He walked smartly, swinging his holly stick. Once or twice he passed a peasant on his way to bed, and the guttural 'Gruss Got', unheard for so long, emphasized the passage of time, while yet making it seem as nothing. A fresh group of pictures crowded his mind. Again the figures of former schoolfellows flitted out of the forest and kept pace by his side, whispering of the doings of long ago. One reverie stepped hard upon the heels of another. Every turn in the road, every clearing of the forest, he knew, and each in turn brought forgotten associations to life. He enjoyed himself thoroughly.

He marched on and on. There was powdered gold in the sky till the moon rose, and then a wind of faint silver spread silently between the earth and stars. He saw the tips of the fir trees shimmer, and heard them whisper as the breeze turned their needles towards the light. The mountain air was indescribably sweet. The road shone like the foam of a river through the gloom. White moths flitted here and there like silent thoughts across his path, and a hundred smells greeted him from the forest caverns across the years.

Then, when he least expected it, the trees fell away abruptly on both sides, and he stood on the edge of the village clearing.

He walked faster. There lay the familiar outlines of the houses, sheeted with silver; there stood the trees in the little central square with the fountain and small green lawns; there loomed the shape of the church next to the Gasthof der Brüdergemeinde; and just beyond, dimly rising into the sky, he saw with a sudden thrill the mass of the huge school building, blocked castle-like with deep shadows in the moonlight, standing square and formidable to face him after the silences of more than a quarter of a century.

He passed quickly down the deserted village street and stopped close beneath its shadow, staring up at the walls that had once held him prisoner for two years—two unbroken years of discipline and homesickness. Memories and emotions surged through his mind; for the most vivid sensations of his youth had focused about this spot, and it was here he had first begun to live and learn values. Not a single footstep broke the silence, though lights glimmered here and there through cottage windows; but when he looked up at the high walls of the school, draped now in shadow, he easily imagined that

41

well-known faces crowded to the windows to greet him—closed windows that really reflected only moonlight and the gleam of stars.

This, then, was the old school building, standing foursquare to the world, with its shuttered windows, its lofty, tiled roof, and the spiked lightning-conductors pointing like black and taloned fingers from the corners. For a long time he stood and stared. Then, presently, he came to himself again, and realized to his joy that a light still shone in the windows of the *Bruderstube*.

He turned from the road and passed through the iron railings; then climbed the twelve stone steps and stood facing the black wooden door with the heavy bars of iron, a door he had once loathed and dreaded with the hatred and passion of an imprisoned soul, but now looked upon tenderly with a sort of boyish delight.

Almost timorously he pulled the rope and listened with a tremor of excitement to the clanging of the bell deep within the building. And the long-forgotten sound brought the past before him with such a vivid sense of reality that he positively shivered. It was like the magic bell in the fairy-tale that rolls back the curtain of Time and summons the figures from the shadows of the dead. He had never felt so sentimental in his life. It was like being young again. And, at the same time, he began to bulk rather large in his own eyes with a certain spurious importance. He was a big man from the world of strife and action. In this little place of peaceful dreams would he, perhaps, not cut something of a figure?

'I'll try once more,' he thought after a long pause, seizing the iron bell-rope, and was just about to pull it when a step sounded on the stone passage within, and the huge door slowly swung open.

A tall man with a rather severe cast of countenance stood facing him in silence.

'I must apologize—it is somewhat late,' he began a trifle pompously, 'but the fact is I am an old pupil. I have only just arrived and really could not restrain myself.' His German seemed not quite so fluent as usual. 'My interest is so great. I was here in '70.'

The other opened the door wider and at once bowed him in with a smile of genuine welcome.

'I am Bruder Kalkmann,' he said quietly in a deep voice. 'I myself was a master here about that time. It is a great pleasure always to welcome a former pupil.' He looked at him very keenly for a few seconds, and then added, 'I think, too, it is splendid of you to come —very splendid.'

'It is a very great pleasure,' Harris replied, delighted with his reception.

The dimly-lighted corridor with its flooring of grey stone, and the familiar sound of a German voice echoing through it—with the peculiar intonation the Brothers always used in speaking—all combined to lift him bodily, as it were, into the dream-atmosphere of long-forgotten days. He stepped gladly into the building and the door shut with the familiar thunder that completed the reconstruction of the past. He almost felt the old sense of imprisonment, of aching nostalgia, of having lost his liberty.

Harris sighed involuntarily and turned towards his host, who returned his smile faintly and then led the way down the corridor.

'The boys have retired,' he explained, 'and, as you remember, we keep early hours here. But, at least, you will join us for a little while in the *Bruderstube* and enjoy a cup of coffee.' This was precisely what the silk merchant had hoped, and he accepted with an alacrity that he intended to be tempered by graciousness. 'And tomorrow,' continued the Bruder, 'you must come and spend a whole day with us. You may even find acquaintances, for several pupils of your day have come back here as masters.'

For one brief second there passed into the man's eyes a look that made the visitor start. But it vanished as quickly as it came. It was impossible to define. Harris convinced himself it was the effect of a shadow cast by the lamp they had just passed on the wall. He dismissed it from his mind.

'You are very kind, I'm sure,' he said politely. 'It is perhaps a greater pleasure to me than you can imagine to see the place again. Ah'—he stopped short opposite a door with the upper half of glass and peered in—'surely there is one of the music rooms where I used to practise the violin. How it comes back to me after all these years!'

Bruder Kalkmann stopped indulgently, smiling, to allow his guest a moment's inspection.

'You still have the boys' orchestra? I remember I used to play '*zweite Geige*' in it. Bruder Schliemann conducted at the piano. Dear me, I can see him now with his long black hair and—and——' He stopped abruptly. Again the odd, dark look passed over the stern face of his companion. For an instant it seemed curiously familiar.

'We still keep up the pupils' orchestra,' he said, 'but Bruder Schliemann, I am sorry to say——' he hesitated an instant, and then added, 'Bruder Schliemann is dead.'

'Indeed, indeed,' said Harris quickly. 'I am sorry to hear it.' He was conscious of a faint feeling of distress, but whether it arose from the news of his old music teacher's death, or—from something else —he could not quite determine. He gazed down the corridor that

43

lost itself among shadows. In the street and village everything had seemed so much smaller than he remembered, but here, inside the school building, everything seemed so much bigger. The corridor was loftier and longer, more spacious and vast, than the mental picture he had preserved. His thoughts wandered dreamily for an instant.

He glanced up and saw the face of the Bruder watching him with a smile of patient indulgence.

'Your memories possess you,' he observed gently, and the stern look passed into something almost pitying.

'You are right,' returned the man of silk, 'they do. This was the most wonderful period of my whole life in a sense. At the time I hated it——' He hesitated, not wishing to hurt the Brother's feelings.

'According to English ideas it seemed strict, of course,' the other said persuasively, so that he went on.

'——Yes, partly that; and partly the ceaseless nostalgia, and the solitude which came from never being really alone. In English schools the boys enjoy peculiar freedom, you know.'

Bruder Kalkmann, he saw, was listening intently.

'But it produced one result that I have never wholly lost,' he continued self-consciously, 'and am grateful for.'

'*Ach! Wie so, denn?*'

'The constant inner pain threw me headlong into your religious life, so that the whole force of my being seemed to project itself towards the search for a deeper satisfaction—a real resting-place for the soul. During my two years here I yearned for God in my boyish way as perhaps I have never yearned for anything since. Moreover, I have never quite lost that sense of peace and inward joy which accompanied the search. I can never quite forget this school and the deep things it taught me.'

He paused at the end of his long speech, and a brief silence fell between them. He feared he had said too much, or expressed himself clumsily in the foreign language, and when Bruder Kalkmann laid a hand upon his shoulder, he gave a little involuntary start.

'So that my memories perhaps do possess me rather strongly,' he added apologetically; 'and this long corridor, these rooms, that barred and gloomy front door, all touch chords that—that——' His German failed him and he glanced at his companion with an explanatory smile and gesture. But the brother had removed the hand from his shoulder and was standing with his back to him, looking down the passage.

'Naturally, naturally so,' he said hastily without turning round.

'*Es ist doch selbstverständlich.* We shall all understand.'

Then he turned suddenly, and Harris saw that his face had turned most oddly and disagreeably sinister. It may only have been the shadows again playing their tricks with the wretched oil lamps on the wall, for the dark expression passed instantly as they retraced their steps down the corridor, but the Englishman somehow got the impression that he had said something to give offence, something that was not quite to the other's taste. Opposite the door of the *Bruderstube* they stopped. Harris realized that it was late and he had possibly stayed talking too long. He made a tentative effort to leave, but his companion would not hear of it.

'You must have a cup of coffee with us,' he said firmly as though he meant it, 'and my colleagues will be delighted to see you. Some of them will remember you, perhaps.'

The sound of voices came pleasantly through the door, men's voices talking together. Bruder Kalkmann turned the handle and they entered a room ablaze with light and full of people.

'Ah—but your name?' he whispered, bending down to catch the reply; 'you have not told me your name yet.'

'Harris,' said the Englishman quickly as they went in. He felt nervous as he crossed the threshold, but ascribed the momentary trepidation to the fact that he was breaking the strictest rule of the whole establishment, which forbade a boy under severest penalties to come near this holy of holies where the masters took their brief leisure.

'Ah, yes, of course—Harris,' repeated the other as though he remembered it. 'Come in, Herr Harris, come in, please. Your visit will be immensely appreciated. It is really very fine, very wonderful of you to have come in this way.'

The door closed behind them and, in the sudden light which made his sight swim for a moment, the exaggeration of the language escaped his attention. He heard the voice of Bruder Kalkmann introducing him. He spoke very loud, indeed, unnecessarily— absurdly loud, Harris thought.

'Brothers,' he announced, 'it is my pleasure and privilege to introduce to you Herr Harris from England. He has just arrived to make us a little visit, and I have already expressed to him on behalf of us all the satisfaction we feel that he is here. He was, as you re-member, a pupil in the year '70.'

It was a very formal, a very German introduction, but Harris rather liked it. It made him feel important and he appreciated the fact that made it almost seem as though he had been expected.

The black forms rose and bowed; Harris bowed; Kalkmann bowed. Every one was very polite and very courtly. The room swam with moving figures; the light dazzling him after the gloom of the corridor; there was thick cigar smoke in the atmosphere. He took the chair that was offered to him between two of the Brothers, and sat down, feeling vaguely that his perceptions were not quite as keen and accurate as usual. He felt a trifle dazed perhaps, and the spell of the past came strongly over him, confusing the immediate present and making everything dwindle oddly to the dimensions of long ago. He seemed to pass under the mastery of a great mood that was a composite reproduction of all the moods of his forgotten boyhood.

Then he pulled himself together with a sharp effort and entered into the conversation that had begun again to buzz round him. Moreover, he entered into it with keen pleasure, for the Brothers—there were perhaps a dozen of them in the little room—treated him with a charm of manner that speedily made him feel one of themselves. This, again, was a very subtle delight to him. He felt that he had stepped out of the greedy, vulgar, self-seeking world, the world of silk and markets and profit-making—stepped into the cleaner atmosphere where spiritual ideals were paramount and life was simple and devoted. It all charmed him inexpressibly, so that he realized—yes, in a sense—the degradation of his twenty years' absorption in business. This keen atmosphere under the stars where men thought only of their souls, and of the souls of others, was too rarefied for the world he was now associated with. He found himself making comparisons to his own disadvantage—comparisons with the mystical little dreamer that had stepped thirty years before from the stern peace of this devout community, and the man of the world that he had since become—and the contrast made him shiver with a keen regret and something like self-contempt.

He glanced round at the other faces floating towards him through tobacco smoke—this acrid cigar smoke he remembered so well: how keen they were, how strong, placid, touched with the nobility of great aims and unselfish purposes. At one or two he looked particularly. He hardly knew why. They rather fascinated him. There was something so very stern and uncompromising about them, and something, too, oddly, subtly, familiar, that yet just eluded him. But whenever their eyes met his own they held undeniable welcome in them; and some held more—a kind of perplexed admiration, he thought, something that was between esteem and deference. This note of respect in all the faces was very flattering to his vanity.

Coffee was served presently, made by a black-haired Brother who sat in the corner by the piano and bore a marked resemblance to Bruder Schliemann, the musical director of thirty years ago. Harris exchanged bows with him when he took the cup from his white hands, which he noticed were like the hands of a woman. He lit a cigar, offered to him by his neighbour, with whom he was chatting delightfully, and who, in the glare of the lighted match, reminded him sharply for a moment of Bruder Pagel, his former room-master.

'*Es ist wirklich merkwürdig,*' he said, 'how many resemblances I see, or imagine. It is really *very* curious!'

'Yes,' replied the other, peering at him over his coffee cup, 'the spell of the place is wonderfully strong. I can well understand that the old faces rise before your mind's eye—almost to the exclusion of ourselves perhaps.'

They both laughed pleasantly. It was soothing to find his mood understood and appreciated. And they passed on to talk of the mountain village, its isolation, its remoteness from worldly life, its peculiar fitness for meditation and worship, and for spiritual development—of a certain kind.

'And your coming back in this way, Herr Harris, has pleased us all so much,' joined in the Bruder on his left. 'We esteem you for it mostly highly. We honour you for it.'

Harris made a deprecating gesture. 'I fear, for my part, it is only a very selfish pleasure,' he said a trifle unctuously.

'Not all would have had the courage,' added the one who resembled Pagel.

'You mean,' said Harris, a little puzzled, 'the disturbing memories——?'

Bruder Pagel looked at him steadily, with unmistakable admiration and respect. 'I mean that most men hold so strongly to life, and can give up so little for their beliefs,' he said gravely.

The Englishman felt slightly uncomfortable. These worthy men really made too much of his sentimental journey. Besides, the talk was getting a little out of his depth. He hardly followed it.

'The worldly life still has *some* charms for me,' he replied smilingly, as though to indicate that sainthood was not yet quite within his grasp.

'All the more, then, must we honour you for so freely coming,' said the Brother on his left; 'so unconditionally!'

A pause followed, and the silk merchant felt relieved when the conversation took a more general turn, although he noted that it never travelled very far from the subject of his visit and the wonderful situation of the lonely village for men who wished to develop their spiritual powers and practise the rites of a high worship. Others joined in, complimenting him on his knowledge of the language, making him feel utterly at his ease, yet at the same time a little uncomfortable by the excess of their admiration. After all, it was such a very small thing to do, this sentimental journey.

The time passed along quickly; the coffee was excellent, the cigars soft and of the nutty flavour he loved. At length, fearing to outstay his welcome, he rose reluctantly to take his leave. But the others would not hear of it. It was not often a former pupil returned to visit them in this simple, unaffected way. The night was young. If necessary they could even find him a corner in the great *Schlafzimmer* upstairs. He was easily persuaded to stay a little longer. Somehow he had become the centre of the little party. He felt pleased, flattered, honoured.

'And perhaps Bruder Schliemann will play something for us— now.'

It was Kalkmann speaking, and Harris started visibly as he heard the name, and saw the black-haired man by the piano turn with a smile. For Schliemann was the name of his old music director, who was dead. Could this be his son? They were so exactly alike.

'If Bruder Meyer has not put his Amati to bed, I will accompany him,' said the musician suggestively, looking across at a man whom Harris had not yet noticed, and who, he now saw, was the very image of a former master of that name.

Meyer rose and excused himself with a little bow, and the Englishman quickly observed that he had a peculiar gesture as though his neck had a false join on to the body just below the collar and feared it might break. Meyer of old had this trick of movement. He remembered how the boys used to copy it.

He glanced sharply from face to face, feeling as though some silent, unseen process were changing everything about him. All the faces seemed oddly familiar. Pagel, the Brother he had been talking with, was of course the image of Pagel, his former room-master; and Kalkmann, he now realized for the first time, was the very twin of another master whose name he had quite forgotten, but whom he used to dislike intensely in the old days. And, through the smoke, peering at him from the corners of the room, he saw that all the Brothers about him had the faces he had known and lived with long ago—Röst, Fluheim, Meinert, Rigel, Gysin.

He stared hard, suddenly grown more alert, and everywhere saw, or fancied he saw, strange likenesses, ghostly resemblances—more, the identical faces of years ago. There was something queer about it all, something not quite right, something that made him feel uneasy. He shook himself, mentally and actually, blowing the smoke from before his eyes with a long breath, and as he did so he noticed to his dismay that every one was fixedly staring. They were watching him.

This brought him to his senses. As an Englishman, and a foreigner, he did not wish to be rude, or to do anything to make himself foolishly conspicuous and spoil the harmony of the evening. He was a guest, and a privileged guest at that. Besides, the music had already begun. Bruder Schliemann's long white fingers were caressing the keys to some purpose.

He subsided into his chair and smoked with half-closed eyes that yet saw everything.

But the shudder had established itself in his being, and, whether he would or not, it kept repeating itself. As a town, far up some inland river, feels the pressure of the distant sea, so he became aware that mighty forces from somewhere beyond his ken were urging themselves up against his soul in this smoky little room. He began to feel exceedingly ill at ease.

And as the music filled the air his mind began to clear. Like a lifted veil there rose up something that had hitherto obscured his vision. The words of the priest at the railway inn flashed across his brain unbidden: 'You will find it different.' And also, though why he could not tell, he saw mentally the strong, rather wonderful eyes of that other guest at the supper-table, the man who had overheard his conversation, and had later got into earnest talk with the priest. He took out his watch and stole a glance at it. Two hours had slipped by. It was already eleven o'clock.

Schliemann, meanwhile, utterly absorbed in his music, was playing a solemn measure. The piano sang marvellously. The power of a great conviction, the simplicity of great art, the vital spiritual message of a soul that had found itself—all this, and more, were in the chords, and yet somehow the music was what can only be described as impure—atrociously and diabolically impure. And the piece itself, although Harris did not recognize it as anything familiar, was surely the music of a Mass—huge, majestic, sombre? It stalked through the smoky room with slow power, like the passage of something that was mighty, yet profoundly intimate, and as it went there stirred into each and every face about him the signature of the enormous forces of which it was the audible symbol. The countenances round him turned sinister, but not idly, negatively sinister: they grew dark with purpose. He suddenly recalled the face of Bruder Kalkmann in the corridor earlier in the evening. The motives of their secret souls rose to the eyes, and mouths, and foreheads, and hung there for all to see like the black banners of an assembly of ill-starred and fallen creatures. Demons—was the horrible word that flashed through his brain like a sheet of fire.

When this sudden discovery leaped out upon him, for a moment he lost his self-control. Without waiting to think and weigh his extraordinary impression, he did a very foolish but a very natural thing. Feeling himself irresistibly driven by the sudden stress to some kind of action, he sprang to his feet—and screamed! To his own utter amazement he stood up and shrieked aloud!

But no one stirred. No one, apparently, took the slightest notice of his absurdly wild behaviour. It was almost as if no one but himself had heard the scream at all—as though the music had drowned it and swallowed it up—as though after all perhaps he had not really screamed as loudly as he imagined, or had not screamed at all.

Then, as he glanced at the motionless, dark faces before him, something of utter cold passed into his being, touching his very soul. . . . All emotion cooled suddenly, leaving him like a receding tide. He sat down again, ashamed, mortified, angry with himself for behaving like a fool and a boy. And the music, meanwhile, continued to issue from the white and snake-like fingers of Bruder Schliemann, as poisoned wine might issue from the weirdly-fashioned necks of antique phials.

And, with the rest of them, Harris drank it in.

Forcing himself to believe that he had been the victim of some kind of illusory perception, he vigorously restrained his feelings. Then the music presently ceased, and every one applauded and began to talk at once, laughing, changing seats, complimenting the player, and behaving naturally and easily as though nothing out of the way had happened. The faces appeared normal once more. The Brothers crowded round their visitor, and he joined in their talk and even heard himself thanking the gifted musician.

But, at the same time, he found himself edging towards the door, nearer and nearer, changing his chair when possible, and joining the groups that stood closest to the way of escape.

'I must thank you all *tauseadmal* for my little reception and the great pleasure—the very great honour you have done me,' he began in decided tones at length, 'but I fear I have trespassed far too long already in your hospitality. Moreover, I have some distance to walk to my inn.'

A chorus of voices greeted his words. They would not hear of his going—at least not without first partaking of refreshment. They produced pumpernickel from one cupboard, and rye-bread and sausage from another, and all began to talk again and eat. More coffee was made, fresh cigars lighted, and Bruder Meyer took out his violin and began to tune it softly.

'There is always a bed upstairs if Herr Harris will accept it,' said one.

'And it is difficult to find the way out now, for all the doors are locked,' laughed another loudly.

'Let us take our simple pleasures as they come,' cried a third. 'Bruder Harris will understand how we appreciate the honour of this last visit of his.'

They made a dozen excuses. They all laughed, as though the politeness of their words was but formal, and veiled thinly more and more thinly—a very different meaning.

'And the hour of midnight draws near,' added Bruder Kalkmann with a charming smile, but in a voice that sounded to the Englishman like the grating of iron hinges.

Their German seemed to him more and more difficult to understand. He noted that they called him 'Bruder' too, classing him as one of themselves.

And then suddenly he had a flash of keener perception, and realized with a creeping of his flesh that he had all along misinterpreted—grossly misinterpreted all they had been saying. They had talked about the beauty of the place, its isolation and remoteness from the world, its peculiar fitness for certain kinds of spiritual development and worship—yet hardly, he now grasped, in the sense in which he had taken the words. They had meant something different. Their spiritual powers, their desire for loneliness, their passion for worship, were not the powers, the solitude, or the worship that *he* meant and understood. He was playing a part in some horrible masquerade; he was among men who cloaked their lives with religion in order to follow their real purposes unseen of men.

What did it all mean? How had he blundered into so equivocal a situation? Had he blundered into it at all? Had he not rather been led into it, deliberately led? His thoughts grew dreadfully confused, and his confidence in himself began to fade. And why, he suddenly thought again, were they so impressed by the mere fact of his coming to revisit his old school? What was it they so admired and wondered at in his simple act? Why did they set such store upon his having the courage to come, to 'give himself so freely', 'unconditionally' as one of them had expressed it with such a mockery of exaggeration?

Fear stirred in his heart most horribly, and he found no answer to

51

any of his questionings. Only one thing he now understood quite clearly: it was their purpose to keep him here. They did not intend that he should go. And from this moment he realized that they were sinister, formidable and, in some way he had yet to discover, inimical to himself, inimical to his life. And the phrase one of them had used a moment ago—'this *last* visit of his'—rose before his eyes in letters of flame.

Harris was not a man of action, and had never known in all the course of his career what it means to be in a situation of real danger. He was not necessarily a coward, though, perhaps, a man of untried nerve. He realized at last plainly that he was in a very awkward predicament indeed, and that he had to deal with men who were utterly in earnest. What their intentions were he only vaguely guessed. His mind, indeed, was too confused for definite ratiocination, and he was only able to follow blindly the strongest instincts that moved in him. It never occurred to him that the Brothers might all be mad, or that he himself might have temporarily lost his senses and be suffering under some terrible delusion. In fact, nothing occurred to him—he realized nothing—except that he meant to escape—and the quicker the better. A tremendous revulsion of feeling set in and overpowered him.

Accordingly, without further protest for the moment, he ate his pumpernickel and drank his coffee, talking meanwhile as naturally and pleasantly as he could, and when a suitable interval had passed, he rose to his feet and announced once more that he must now take take his leave. He spoke very quietly, but very decidedly. No one hearing him could doubt that he meant what he said. He had got very close to the door by this time.

'I regret,' he said, using his best German, and speaking to a hushed room, 'that our pleasant evening must come to an end, but it is now time for me to wish you all good-night.' And then, as no one said anything, he added, though with a trifle less assurance, 'And I thank you all most sincerely for your hospitality.'

'On the contrary,' replied Kalkman instantly, rising from his chair and ignoring the hand the Englishman had stretched out to him, 'it is we who have to thank you; and we do so most gratefully and sincerely.'

And at the same moment at least half a dozen of the Brothers took up their position between himself and the door.

'You are very good to say so,' Harris replied as firmly as he could manage, noticing this movement out of the corner of his eye, 'but really I had no conception that—my little chance visit could have afforded you so much pleasure.' He moved another step nearer the door, but Bruder Schliemann came across the room quickly and stood in front of him. His attitude was uncompromising. A dark and terrible expression had come into his face.

'But it was *not* by chance that you came, Bruder Harris,' he said so that all the room could hear; 'surely we have not misunderstood your presence here?' He raised his black eyebrows.

'No, no,' the Englishman hastened to reply, 'I was—I am delighted to be here. I told you what pleasure it gave me to find myself among you. Do not misunderstand me, I beg.' His voice faltered a little, and he had difficulty in finding the words. More and more, too, he had difficulty in understanding *their* words.

'Of course,' interposed Bruder Kalkmann in his iron bass, '*we* have not misunderstood. You have come back in the spirit of true and unselfish devotion. You offer yourself freely, and we all appreciate it. It is your willingness and nobility that have so completely won our veneration and respect.' A faint murmur of applause ran round the room. 'What we all delight in—what our great Master will especially delight in—is the value of your spontaneous and voluntary——'

He used a word Harris did not understand. He said '*Opfer*'. The bewildered Englishman searched his brain for the translation, and searched in vain. For the life of him he could not remember what it meant. But the word, for all his inability to translate it, touched his soul with ice. It was worse, far worse, than anything he had imagined. He felt like a lost, helpless creature, and all power to fight sank out of him from that moment.

'It is magnificent to be such a willing——' added Schliemann, sidling up to him with a dreadful leer on his face. He made use of the same word—'*Opfer*'.

'God! What could it all mean? 'Offer himself!' 'True spirit of devotion!' 'Willing,' 'unselfish', 'magnificent!' *Opfer, Opfer, Opfer!* What in the name of heaven did it mean, that strange, mysterious word that struck such terror into his heart?

He made a valiant effort to keep his presence of mind and hold his nerves steady. Turning, he saw that Kalkmann's face was a dead white. Kalkmann! He understood that well enough. *Kalkmann* meant 'Man of Chalk'; he knew that. But what did '*Opfer*' mean? That was the real key to the situation. Words poured through his disordered mind in an endless stream—unusual, rare words he had perhaps heard but once in his life—while '*Opfer*', a word in common use, entirely escaped him. What an extraordinary mockery it all was!

Then Kalkmann, pale as death, but his face hard as iron, spoke a few low words that he did not catch, and the Brothers standing by the walls at once turned the lamps down so that the room became dim. In the half lights he could only just discern their faces and movements.

'It is time,' he heard Kalkmann's remorseless voice continue just behind him. 'The hour of midnight is at hand. Let us prepare. He comes! He comes; Bruder Asmodelius comes!' His voice rose to a chant.

And the sound of that name, for some extraordinary reason, was terrible—utterly terrible; so that Harris shook from head to foot as he heard it. Its utterance filled the air like soft thunder, and a hush came over the whole room. Forces rose all about him, transforming the normal into the horrible, and the spirit of craven fear ran through all his being, bringing him to the verge of collapse.

Asmodelius! Asmodelius! The name was appalling. For he understood at last to whom it referred and the meaning that lay between its great syllables. At the same instant, too, he suddenly understood the meaning of that unremembered word. The import of the word '*Opfer*' flashed upon his soul like a message of death.

He thought of making a wild effort to reach the door, but the weakness of his trembling knees, and the row of black figures that stood between, dissuaded him at once. He would have screamed for help, but remembering the emptiness of the vast building, and the loneliness of the situation, he understood that no help could come that way, and he kept his lips closed. He stood still and did nothing. But he knew now what was coming.

Two of the brothers approached and took him gently by the arm.

'Bruder Asmodelius accepts you,' they whispered; 'are you ready?'

Then he found his tongue and tried to speak. 'But what have I to do with this Bruder Asm—Asmo——?' he stammered, a desperate rush of words crowding vainly behind the halting tongue.

The name refused to pass his lips. He could not pronounce it as they did. He could not pronounce it at all. His sense of helplessness then entered the acute stage, for this inability to speak the name produced a fresh sense of quite horrible confusion in his mind, and he became extraordinarily agitated.

'I came here for a friendly visit,' he tried to say with a great effort, but, to his intense dismay, he heard his voice saying something quite different, and actually making use of that very word they had all used: 'I came here as a willing *Opfer*,' he heard his own voice say, 'and *I am quite ready*.'

He was lost beyond all recall now! Not alone his mind, but the very muscles of his body had passed out of control. He felt that he was hovering on the confines of a phantom or demon-world—a world in which the name they had spoken constituted the Master-name, the word of ultimate power.

What followed he heard and saw as in a nightmare.

'In the half light that veils all truth, let us prepare to worship and adore,' chanted Schliemann, who had preceded him to the end of the room.

'In the mists that protect our faces before the Black Throne, let us make ready the willing victim,' echoed Kalkmann in his great bass.

They raised their faces, listening expectantly, as a roaring sound, like the passing of mighty projectiles, filled the air, far, far away, very wonderful, very forbidding. The walls of the room trembled.

'He comes! He comes! He comes!' chanted the Brothers in chorus.

The sound of roaring died away, and an atmosphere of still and utter cold established itself over all. Then Kalkmann, dark and unutterably stern, turned in the dim light and faced the rest.

'Asmodelius, our *Hauptbruder*, is about us,' he cried in a voice that even while it shook was yet a voice of iron: 'Asmodelius is about us. Make ready.'

There followed a pause in which no one stirred or spoke. A tall Brother approached the Englishman; but Kalkmann held up his hand.

'Let the eyes remain uncovered,' he said, 'in honour of so freely giving himself.' And to his horror Harris then realized for the first time that his hands were already fastened to his sides.

The Brothers retreated again silently, and in the pause that followed all the figures about him dropped to their knees, leaving him standing alone, and as they dropped, in voices hushed with mingled reverence and awe, they cried softly, odiously, appallingly, the name of the Being whom they momentarily expected to appear.

Then, at the end of the room, where the windows seemed to have disappeared so that he saw the stars, there rose into view far up against the night sky, grand and terrible, the outline of a man. A kind of grey glory enveloped it so that it resembled a steel-cased statue, immense, imposing, horrific in its distant splendour; while, at the same time, the face was so spiritually mighty, yet so proudly, so austerely sad, that Harris felt as he stared, that the sight was more than his eyes could meet, and that in another moment the power of vision would fail him altogether, and he must sink into utter nothingness.

So remote and inaccessible hung this figure that it was impossible to gauge anything as to its size, yet at the same time so strangely close, that when the grey radiance from its mightily broken visage, august and mournful, beat down upon his soul, pulsing like some dark star with the powers of spiritual evil, he felt almost as though he were looking into a face no farther removed from him in space than the face of any one of the Brothers who stood by his side.

And then the room filled and trembled with sounds that Harris understood full well were the failing voices of others who had preceded him in a long series down the years. There came first, a plain, sharp cry, as of a man in the last anguish, choking for his breath, and yet, with the very final expiration of it, breathing the name of the Worship—of the dark Being who rejoiced to hear it. The cries of the strangled; the short, running gasp of the suffocated; and the smothered gurgling of the tightened throat, all these, and more, echoed back and forth between the walls, the very walls in which he now stood a prisoner, a sacrificial victim. The cries, too, not alone of the broken bodies, but—far worse—of beaten, broken souls. And as the ghastly chorus rose and fell, there came also the faces of the lost and unhappy creatures to whom they belonged, and, against that curtain of pale grey light, he saw float past him in the air, an array of white and piteous human countenances that seemed to beckon and gibber at him as though he were already one of themselves.

Slowly, too, as the voices rose, and the pallid crew sailed past, that giant form of grey descended from the sky and approached the room that contained the worshippers and their prisoner. Hands rose and sank about him in the darkness, and he felt that he was being draped in other garments than his own; a circlet of ice seemed to run about his head, while round the waist, enclosing the fastened arms, he felt a girdle tightly drawn. At last, about his very throat, there ran a soft and silken touch which, better than if there had been full light, and a mirror held to his face, he understood to be the cord of sacrifice— and of death.

At this moment the Brothers, still prostrate upon the floor, began again their mournful, yet impassioned chanting, and as they did so a strange thing happened. For, apparently without moving or altering its position, the huge Figure seemed, at once and suddenly, to be inside the room, almost beside him, and to fill the space around him to the exclusion of all else.

He was now beyond all ordinary sensations of fear, only a drab feeling as of death—the death of the soul—stirred in his heart. His thoughts no longer even beat vainly for escape. The end was near, and he knew it.

The dreadfully chanting voices rose about him in a wave: 'We worship! We adore! We offer!' The sounds filled his ears and hammered, almost meaningless, upon his brain.

Then the majestic grey face turned slowly downwards upon him, and his very soul passed outwards and seemed to become absorbed in the sea of those anguished eyes. At the same moment a dozen hands forced him to his knees, and in the air before him he saw the arm of Kalkmann upraised, and felt the pressure about his throat grow strong.

It was in this awful moment, when he had given up all hope, and the help of gods or men seemed beyond question, that a strange thing happened. For before his fading and terrified vision there slid, as in a dream of light—yet without apparent rhyme or reason—wholly unbidden and unexplained—the face of that other man at the supper table of the railway inn. And the sight, even mentally, of that strong, wholesome, vigorous English face, inspired him suddenly with a new courage.

It was but a flash of fading vision before he sank into a dark and terrible death, yet, in some inexplicable way, the sight of that face stirred in him unconquerable hope and the certainty of deliverance. It was a face of power, a face, he now realized, of simple goodness such as might have been seen by men of old on the shores of Galilee; a face, by heaven, that could conquer even the devils of outer space.

And, in his despair and abandonments, he called upon it, and called with no uncertain accents. He found his voice in this overwhelming moment to some purpose; though the words he actually used, and whether they were in German or English, he could never remember. Their effect nevertheless, was instantaneous. The Brothers understood, and that grey Figure of evil understood.

For a second the confusion was terrific. There came a great shattering sound. It seemed that the very earth trembled. But all Harris remembered afterwards was that voices rose about him in the clamour of terrified alarm—

'A man of power is among us! A man of God!'

The vast sound was repeated—the rushing through space as of

huge projectiles—and he sank to the floor of the room, unconscious. The entire scene had vanished, vanished like smoke over the roof of a cottage when the wind blows.

And, by his side, sat down a slight, un-German figure—the figure of the stranger at the inn—the man who had the 'rather wonderful eyes'.

When Harris came to himself he felt cold. He was lying under the open sky, and the cool air of field and forest was blowing upon his face. He sat up and looked about him. The memory of the late scene was still horribly in his mind, but no vestige of it remained. No walls or ceiling enclosed him; he was no longer in a room at all. There were no lamps turned low, no cigar smoke, no black forms of sinister worshippers, no tremendous grey Figure hovering beyond the windows.

Open space was about him, and he was lying on a pile of bricks and mortar, his clothes soaked with dew, and the kind stars shining brightly overhead. He was lying, bruised and shaken, among the heaped-up debris of a ruined building.

He stood up and stared about him. There, in the shadowy distance, lay the surrounding forest, and here, close at hand, stood the outline of the village buildings. But, underfoot, beyond question, lay nothing but the broken heaps of stones that betokened a building long since crumbled to dust. Then he saw that the stones were blackened, and that great wooden beams, half burnt, half rotten, made lines through the general debris. He stood, then, among the ruins of a burnt and shattered building, the weeds and nettles proving conclusively that it had lain thus for many years.

The moon had already set behind the encircling forest, but the stars that spangled the heavens threw enough light to enable him to make quite sure of what he saw. Harris, the silk merchant, stood among these broken and burnt stones and shivered.

Then he suddenly became aware that out of the gloom a figure had risen and stood beside him. Peering at him, he thought he recognized the face of the stranger at the railway inn.

'Are *you* real?' he asked in a voice he hardly recognized as his own.

'More than real—I'm friendly,' replied the stranger; 'I followed you up here from the inn.'

Harris stood and stared for several minutes without adding anything. His teeth chattered. The least sound made him start; but the simple words in his own language, and the tone in which they were uttered, comforted him inconceivably.

'You're English too, thank God,' he said inconsequently. 'These German devils——' He broke off and put a hand to his eyes. 'But what's become of them all—and the room—and—and——' The hand travelled down to his throat and moved nervously round his neck. He drew a long, long breath of relief. 'Did I dream everything —everything?' he said distractedly.

He stared wildly about him, and the stranger moved forward and took his arm. 'Come,' he said soothingly, yet with a trace of command in the voice, 'we will move away from here. The high-road, or even the woods will be more to your taste, for we are standing now on one of the most haunted—and most terribly haunted—spots of the whole world.'

He guided his companion's stumbling footsteps over the broken masonry until they reached the path, the nettles stinging their hands, and Harris feeling his way like a man in a dream. Passing through the twisted iron railing they reached the path, and thence made their way to the road, shining white in the night. Once safely out of the ruins, Harris collected himself and turned to look back.

'But, how is it possible?' he exclaimed, his voice still shaking. 'How can it be possible? When I came in here I saw the building in the moonlight. They opened the door. I saw the figures and heard the voices and touched, yes touched their very hands, and saw their damned black faces, saw them far more plainly than I see you now.' He was deeply bewildered. The glamour was still upon his eyes with a degree of reality stronger than the reality even of normal life. 'Was I so utterly deluded?'

Then suddenly the words of the stranger, which he had only half heard or understood, returned to him.

'Haunted?' he asked, looking hard at him; 'haunted, did you say?' He paused in the roadway and stared into the darkness where the building of the old school had first appeared to him. But the stranger hurried him forward.

'We shall talk more safely farther on,' he said. 'I followed you from the inn the moment I realized where you had gone. When I found you it was eleven o'clock——'

'Eleven o'clock,' said Harris, remembering with a shudder.

'——I saw you drop. I watched over you till you recovered consciousness of your own accord, and now—now I am here to guide you safely back to the inn. I have broken the spell—the glamour——'

'I owe you a great deal, sir,' interrupted Harris again, beginning to understand something of the stranger's kindness, 'but I don't understand it all. I feel dazed and shaken.' His teeth still chattered, and spells of violent shivering passed over him from head to foot. He found that he was clinging to the other's arm. In this way they passed beyond the deserted and crumbling village and gained the high-road that led homewards through the forest.

'That school building has long been in ruins,' said the man at his side presently; 'it was burnt down by order of the Elders of the community at least ten years ago. The village has been uninhabited ever since. But the simulacra of certain ghastly events that took place under that roof in past days still continue. And the "shells" of the chief partipants still enact there the dreadful deeds that led to its final destruction, and to the desertion of the whole settlement. They were devil-worshippers!'

Harris listened with beads of perspiration on his forehead that did not come alone from their leisurely pace through the cool night. Although he had seen this man but once before in his life, and had never before exchanged so much as a word with him, he felt a degree of confidence and a subtle sense of safety and well-being in his presence that were the most healing influences he could possibly have wished after the experience he had been through. For all that, he still felt as if he were walking in a dream, and though he heard every word that fell from his companion's lips, it was only the next day that the full import of all he said became fully clear to him. The presence of this quiet stranger, the man with the wonderful eyes which he felt now, rather than saw, applied a soothing anodyne to his shattered spirit that healed him through and through. And this healing influence, distilled from the dark figure at his side, satisfied his first imperative need, so that he almost forgot to realize how strange and opportune it was that the man should be there at all.

It somehow never occurred to him to ask his name, or to feel any undue wonder that one passing tourist should take so much trouble on behalf of another. He just walked by his side, listening to his quiet words, and allowing himself to enjoy the very wonderful experience after his recent ordeal, of being helped, strengthened, blessed. Only once, remembering vaguely something of his reading of years ago, he turned to the man beside him, after some more than usually remarkable words, and heard himself, almost involuntarily it seemed, putting the question: 'Then are you a Rosicrucian, sir, perhaps?' But the stranger had ignored the words, or possibly not heard them, for he continued with his talk as though unconscious of any interruption, and Harris became aware that another somewhat unusual picture had taken possession of his mind, as they walked there side by side through the cool reaches of the forest, and that he had found his imagination suddenly charged with the childhood memory of Jacob wrestling with an angel—wrestling all night with a being of superior quality whose strength eventually became his own.

'It was your abrupt conversation with the priest at supper that first put me upon the track of this remarkable occurrence,' he heard the man's quiet voice beside him in the darkness, 'and it was from him I learned after you left the story of the devil-worship that became secretly established in the heart of this simple and devout little community.'

'Devil-worship! Here——!' Harris stammered, aghast.

'Yes—here—conducted secretly for years by a group of Brothers before unexplained disappearances in the neighbourhood led to its discovery. For where could they have found a safer place in the whole wide world for their ghastly traffic and perverted powers than here, in the very precincts—under cover of the very shadow of saintliness and holy living?'

'Awful, awful!' whispered the silk merchant, 'and when I tell you the words they used to me——'

'I know it all,' the stranger said quietly. 'I saw and heard everything. My plan first was to wait till the end and then to take steps for their destruction, but in the interest of your personal safety'—he spoke with the utmost gravity and conviction—'in the interest of the safety of your soul, I made my presence known when I did, and before the conclusion had been reached——'

'My safety! The danger, then, was real. They were alive and——'
Words failed him. He stopped in the road and turned towards his companion, the shining of whose eyes he could just make out in the gloom.

'It was a concourse of the shells of violent men, spiritually-developed but evil men, seeking after death—the death of the body —to prolong their vile and unnatural existence. And had they accomplished their object you, in turn, at the death of your body, would have passed into their power and helped to swell their dreadful purposes.'

Harris made no reply. He was trying hard to concentrate his mind upon the sweet and common things of life. He even thought of silk and St Paul's Churchyard and the faces of his partners in business.

'For you came all prepared to be caught,' he heard the other's voice like some one talking to him from a distance; 'your deeply introspective mood had already reconstructed the past so vividly, so intensely, that you were *en rapport* at once with any forces of those days that chanced still to be lingering. And they swept you up all unresistingly.'

Harris tightened his hold upon the stranger's arm as he heard. At the moment he had room for one emotion only. It did not seem to him odd that this stranger should have such intimate knowledge of his mind.

'It is, alas, chiefly the evil emotions that are able to leave their photographs upon surrounding scenes and objects,' the other added, 'and who ever heard of a place haunted by a noble deed, or of beautiful and lovely ghosts revisiting the glimpses of the moon? It is unfortunate. But the wicked passions of men's hearts alone seem strong enough to leave pictures that persist; the good are ever too luke-warm.'

The stranger sighed as he spoke. But Harris, exhausted and shaken as he was to the very core, paced by his side, only half listening. He moved as in a dream still. It was very wonderful to him, this walk home under the stars in the early hours of the October morning, the peaceful forest all about them, mist rising here and there over the small clearings, and the sound of water from a hundred little invisible streams filling in the pauses of the talk. In after life he always looked back to it as something magical and impossible, something that had seemed too beautiful, too curiously beautiful, to have been quite true. And, though at the time he heard and understood but a quarter of what the stranger said, it came back to him afterwards, staying with him till the end of his days, and always with a curious, haunting sense of unreality, as though he had enjoyed a wonderful dream of which he could recall only faint and exquisite portions.

But the horror of the earlier experience was effectually dispelled; and when they reached the railway inn, somewhere about three o'clock in the morning, Harris shook the stranger's hand gratefully, effusively, meeting the look of those rather wonderful eyes with a full heart, and went up to his room, thinking in a hazy, dream-like way of the words with which the stranger had brought their conversation to an end as they left the confines of the forest—

'And if thought and emotion can persist in this way so long after the brain that sent them forth has crumbled into dust, how vitally important it must be to control their very birth in the heart, and guard them with the keenest possible restraint.'

But Harris, the silk merchant, slept better than might have been expected, and with a soundness that carried him half-way through the day. And when he came downstairs and learned that the stranger had already taken his departure, he realized with keen regret that he had never once thought of asking his name.

'Yes, he signed in the visitors' book,' said the girl in reply to his question.

And he turned over the blotted pages and found there, the last entry, in a very delicate and individual handwriting—

'*John Silence*, London.'

Charles Dickens

The Signalman

'Halloa! Below there!'

When he heard a voice thus calling to him, he was standing at the door of his box, with a flag in his hand, furled round its short pole. One would have thought, considering the nature of the ground, that he could not have doubted from what quarter the voice came; but instead of looking up to where I stood on the top of the steep cutting nearly over his head, he turned himself about and looked down the Line. There was something remarkable in his manner of doing so, though I could not have said for my life what. But I know it was remarkable enough to attract my notice, even though his figure was foreshortened and shadowed, down in the deep trench, and mine was high above him, so steeped in the glow of an angry sunset, that I had shaded my eyes with my hand before I saw him at all.

'Halloa! Below!'

From looking down the Line, he turned himself about again, and, raising his eyes, saw my figure high above him.

'Is there any path by which I can come down and speak to you?'

He looked up at me without replying, and I looked down at him without pressing him too soon with a repetition of my idle question. Just then there came a vague vibration in the earth and air, quickly changing into a violent pulsation, and an oncoming rush that caused me to start back, as though it had force to draw me down. When such vapour as rose to my height from this rapid train had passed me, and was skimming away over the landscape, I looked down again, and saw him refurling the flag he had shown while the train went by.

I repeated my inquiry. After a pause, during which he seemed to regard me with fixed attention, he motioned with his rolled-up flag towards a point on my level, some two or three hundred yards distant. I called down to him: 'All right!' and made for that point. There, by dint of looking closely about me, I found a rough zigzag descending path notched out, which I followed.'

The cutting was extremely deep, and unusually precipitous. It was made through a clammy stone, that became oozier and wetter as I went down. For these reasons, I found the way long enough to give me time to recall a singular air of reluctance or compulsion with which he had pointed out the path.

When I came down low enough upon the zigzag descent to see him again, I saw that he was standing between the rails on the way by which the train had lately passed, in an attitude as if he were waiting for me to appear. He had his left hand at his chin, and his left elbow rested on his right hand, crossed over his breast. His attitude was one of such expectation and watchfulness that I stopped a moment, wondering at it.

I resumed my downward way, and stepping out upon the level of the railroad, and drawing nearer to him, saw that he was a dark sallow man, with a dark beard and rather heavy eyebrows. His post was in as solitary and dismal a place as ever I saw. On either side, a dripping-wet wall of jagged stone, excluding all view but a strip of sky; the perspective one way only a crooked prolongation of this great dungeon; the shorter perspective in the other direction terminating in a gloomy red light, and the gloomier entrance to a black tunnel, in whose massive architecture there was a barbarous, depressing, and forbidding air. So little sunlight ever found its way to this spot, that it had an earthy, deadly smell; and so much cold wind rushed through it, that it struck chill to me, as if I had left the natural world.

Before he stirred, I was near enough to him to have touched him. Not even then removing his eyes from mine, he stepped back one step, and lifted his hand.

This was a lonesome post to occupy (I said), and it had riveted my attention when I looked down from up yonder. A visitor was a rarity, I should suppose; not an unwelcome rarity, I hoped? In me, he merely saw a man who had been shut up within narrow limits all his life, and who, being at last set free, had a newly-awakened interest in these great works. To such purpose I spoke to him; but I am far from sure of the terms I used; for, besides that I am not happy in opening any conversation, there was something in the man that daunted me.

He directed a most curious look towards the red light near the tunnel's mouth, and looked all about it, as if something were missing from it, and then looked at me.

That light was part of his charge? Was it not?

He answered in a low voice: 'Don't you know it is?'

The monstrous thought came into my mind, as I perused the fixed eyes and the saturnine face, that this was a spirit, not a man. I have speculated since, whether there may have been infection in his mind.

In my turn, I stepped back. But in making the action, I detected in his eyes some latent fear of me. This put the monstrous thought to flight.

'You look at me,' I said, forcing a smile, 'as if you had a dread of me.'

'I was doubtful,' he returned, 'whether I had seen you before.'

'Where?'

He pointed to the red light he had looked at.

'There?' I said.

Intently watchful of me, he replied (but without sound), 'Yes.'

'My good fellow, what should I do there? However, be that as it may, I never was there, you may swear.'

'I think I may,' he rejoined. 'Yes; I am sure I may.'

His manner cleared, like my own. He replied to my remarks with readiness, and in well-chosen words. Had he much to do there? Yes; that was to say, he had enough responsibility to bear; but exactness and watchfulness were what was required of him, and of actual work—manual labour—he had next to none. To change that signal, to trim those lights, and to turn this iron handle now and then, was all he had to do under that head. Regarding those many long and lonely hours of which I seemed to make so much, he could only say that the routine of his life had shaped itself into that form, and he had grown used to it. He had taught himself a language down here—if only to know it by sight, and to have formed his own crude ideas of its pronunciation, could be called learning it. He had also worked at fractions and decimals, and tried a little algebra; but he was, and had been as a boy, a poor hand at figures. Was it necessary for him when on duty always to remain in that channel of damp air, and could he never rise into the sunshine from between those high stone walls? Why, that depended upon times and circumstances. Under some conditions there would be less upon the Line than under others, and the same held good as to certain hours of the day and night. In bright weather, he did choose occasions for getting a little above these lower shadows; but, being at all times liable to be called by his electric bell, and at such times listening for it with redoubled anxiety, the relief was less than I would suppose.

He took me into his box, where there was a fire, a desk for an official book in which he had to make certain entries, a telegraphic instrument with its dial, face, and needles, and the little bell of which he had spoken. On my trusting that he would excuse the remark that he had been well educated, and (I hoped I might say without offence), perhaps educated above that station, he observed that instances of slight incongruity in such wise would rarely be found wanting among large bodies of men; that he had heard it was so in workhouses, in the police force; even in that last desperate resource, the army; and that he knew it was so, more or less, in any great railway staff. He had been, when young (if I could believe it, sitting in that hut—he scarcely could), a student of natural philosophy, and had attended lectures; but he had run wild, misused his opportunities, gone down, and never risen again. He had no complaint to offer about that. He had made his bed, and he lay upon it. It was far too late to make another.

All that I have here condensed he said in a quiet manner, with his grave dark regards divided between me and the fire. He threw in the word, 'Sir', from time to time, and especially when he referred to his youth—as though to request me to understand that he claimed to be nothing but what I found him. He was several times interrupted by the little bell, and had to read off messages, and send replies. Once he had to stand without the door, and display a flag as a train passed, and make some verbal communication to the driver. In the discharge of his duties, I observed him to be remarkably exact and vigilant, breaking off his discourse at a syllable, and remaining silent until what he had to do was done.

In a word, I should have set this man down as one of the safest of men to be employed in that capacity, but for the circumstance that while he was speaking to me he twice broke off with a fallen colour, turned his face towards the little bell when it did NOT ring, opened the door of the hut (which was kept shut to exclude the unhealthy damp), and looked out towards the red light near the mouth of the tunnel. On both of these occasions, he came back to the fire with the inexplicable air upon him which I had remarked, without being able to define, when we were so far asunder.

Said I, when I rose to leave him, 'You almost make me think that I have met with a contented man.'

(I am afraid I must acknowledge that I said it to lead him on.)

'I believe I used to be so,' he rejoined, in the low voice in which he had first spoken; 'but I am troubled, Sir, I am troubled.'

He would have recalled the words if he could. He had said them, however, and I took them up quickly.

'With what? What is your trouble?'

'It is very difficult to impart, Sir. It is very, very difficult to speak of. If ever you make me another visit, I will try to tell you.'

'But I expressly intend to make you another visit. Say, when shall it be?'

'I go off early in the morning, and I shall be on again at ten o'clock tomorrow night, Sir.'

'I will come at eleven.'

He thanked me, and went out at the door with me. 'I'll show my white light, Sir,' he said, in his peculiar low voice, 'till you have found the way up. When you have found it, don't call out! And when you are at the top, don't call out!'

His manner seemed to make the place strike colder to me, but I said no more than, 'Very well.'

'And when you come down tomorrow night, don't call out! Let me ask you a parting question. What made you cry, "Halloa! Below there!" tonight?'

'Heaven knows,' said I. 'I cried something to that effect——'

'Not to that effect, Sir. Those were the very words. I know them well.'

'Admit those were the very words. I said them, no doubt, because I saw you below.'

'For no other reason?'

'What other reason could I possibly have?'

'You had no feeling that they were conveyed to you in any supernatural way?'

'No.'

He wished me good night, and held up his light. I walked by the side of the down Line of rails (with a very disagreeable sensation of a train coming behind me) until I found the path. It was easier to mount than to descend, and I got back to my inn without any adventure.

Punctual to my appointment, I placed my foot on the first notch of the zigzag next night, as the distant clocks were striking eleven. He was waiting for me at the bottom, with his white light on. 'I have not called out,' I said, when we came close together; 'may I speak now?' 'By all means, Sir.' 'Good night, then, and here's my hand.' 'Good night, Sir, and here's mine.' With that we walked side by side to his box, entered it, closed the door, and sat down by the fire.

'I have made up my mind, Sir,' he began, bending forward as soon as we were seated, and speaking in a tone but a little above a whisper, 'that you shall not have to ask me twice what troubles me. I took you for someone else yesterday evening. That troubles me.'

'That mistake?'

'No. That someone else.'

'Who is it?'

'I don't know.'

'Like me?'

'I don't know. I never saw the face. The left arm is across the face, and the right arm is waved—violently waved. This way.'

I followed his action with my eyes, and it was the action of an arm gesticulating, with the utmost passion and vehemence, 'For God's sake, clear the way!'

'One moonlight night,' said the man, 'I was sitting here, when I heard a voice cry, "Halloa! Below there!" I started up, looked from that door, and saw this Someone else standing by the red light near the tunnel, waving as I just now showed you. The voice seemed hoarse with shouting, and it cried: "Look out! Look out!" And then again: "Halloa! Below there! Look out!" I caught up my lamp, turned it on red, and ran towards the figure, calling, "What's wrong? What has happened? Where?" It stood just outside the blackness of the tunnel. I advanced so close upon it that I wondered at its keeping the sleeve across its eyes. I ran right up at it, and had my hand stretched out to pull the sleeve away, when it was gone.'

'Into the tunnel?' said I.

'No. I ran on into the tunnel, five hundred yards. I stopped, and held my lamp above my head, and saw the figures of the measured distance, and saw the wet stains stealing down the walls and trickling through the arch. I ran out again faster than I had run in (for I had a mortal abhorrence of the place upon me), and I looked all round the red light with my own red light, and I went up the iron ladder to the gallery atop of it, and I came down again, and ran back here. I telegraphed both ways. "An alarm has been given. Is anything wrong?" The answer came back, both ways, "All well".'

Resisting the slow touch of a frozen finger tracing out my spine, I showed him how that this figure must be a deception of his sense of sight; and how that figures, originating in disease of the delicate nerves that minister to the functions of the eye, were known to have often troubled patients, some of whom had become conscious of the nature of their affliction, and had even proved it by experiments upon themselves. 'As to an imaginary cry,' said I, 'do but listen for a moment to the wind in this unnatural valley while we speak so low, and to the wild harp it makes of the telegraph wires.'

That was all very well, he returned, after we had sat listening for a while, and he ought to know something of the wind and the wires— he who so often passed long winter nights there, alone and watching.

But he would beg to remark that he had not finished.

I asked his pardon, and he slowly added these words, touching my arm:

'Within six hours after the Appearance, the memorable accident on this Line happened, and within ten hours the dead and wounded were brought along through the tunnel over the spot where the figure had stood.'

A disagreeable shudder crept over me, but I did my best against it. It was not to be denied, I rejoined, that this was a remarkable coincidence, calculated deeply to impress his mind. But it was unquestionable that remarkable coincidences did continually occur, and they must be taken into account in dealing with such a subject. Though to be sure I must admit, I added (for I thought I saw that he was going to bring the objection to bear upon me), men of common sense did not allow much for coincidences in making the ordinary calculations of life.

He again begged to remark that he had not finished.

I again begged his pardon for being betrayed into interruptions.

'This,' he said, again laying his hand upon my arm, and glancing over his shoulder with hollow eyes, 'was just a year ago. Six or seven months passed, and I had recovered from the surprise and shock, when one morning, as the day was breaking, I, standing at the door, looked towards the red light, and saw the spectre again.' He stopped, with a fixed look at me.

'Did it cry out?'

'No. It was silent.'

'Did it wave its arm?'

'No. It leaned against the shaft of the light, with both hands before the face. Like this.'

Once more I followed his action with my eyes. It was an action of mourning. I have seen such an attitude in stone figures on tombs.

'Did you go up to it?'

'I came in and sat down, partly to collect my thoughts, partly because it had turned me faint. When I went to the door again, daylight was above me, and the ghost was gone.'

'But nothing followed? Nothing came of this?'

He touched me on the arm with his forefinger twice or thrice, giving a ghastly nod each time:

'That very day, as a train came out of the tunnel, I noticed, at a carriage window on my side, what looked like a confusion of hands and heads, and something waved. I saw it just in time to signal the driver, Stop! He shut off, and put his brake on, but the train drifted past here a hundred and fifty yards or more. I ran after it, and, as I went along, heard terrible screams and cries. A beautiful young lady had died instantaneously in one of the compartments, and was brought in here, and laid down on this floor between us.'

Involuntarily I pushed my chair back, as I looked from the boards at which he pointed to himself.

'True, Sir. True. Precisely as it happened, so I tell it you.'

I could think of nothing to say, to any purpose, and my mouth was very dry. The wind and the wires took up the story with a long lamenting wail.

He resumed. 'Now, Sir, mark this, and judge how my mind is troubled. The spectre came back a week ago. Ever since, it has been there, now and again, by fits and starts.'

'At the light?'

'At the Danger-light.'

'What does it seem to do?'

He repeated, if possible with increased passion and vehemence, that former gesticulation of 'For God's sake, clear the way!'

Then he went on. 'I have no peace or rest for it. It calls to me, for many minutes together, in an agonized manner, "Below there! Look out! Look out!" It stands waving to me. It rings my little bell——'

I caught at that. 'Did it ring your bell yesterday evening when I was here, and you went to the door?'

'Twice.'

'Why, see,' said I, 'how your imagination misleads you. My eyes were on the bell, and my ears were open to the bell, and if I am a living man, it did NOT ring at those times. No, nor at any other time, except when it was rung in the natural course of physical things by the station communicating with you.'

He shook his head. 'I have never made a mistake as to that yet, Sir. I have never confused the spectre's ring with the man's. The ghost's ring is a strange vibration in the bell that it derives from nothing else, and I have not asserted that the bell stirs to the eye. I don't wonder that you failed to hear it. But *I* heard it.'

'And did the spectre seem to be there, when you looked out?'

'It WAS there.'

'Both times?'

He repeated firmly: 'Both times.'

'Will you come to the door with me, and look for it now?'

He bit his under lip as though he were somewhat unwilling, but arose. I opened the door, and stood on the step, while he stood in the doorway. There was the Danger-light. There was the dismal

71

mouth of the tunnel. There were the high, wet stone walls of the cutting. There were the stars above them.

'Do you see it?' I asked him, taking particular note of his face. His eyes were prominent and strained, but not very much more so, perhaps, than my own had been when I had directed them earnestly towards the same spot.

'No,' he answered. 'It is not there.'

'Agreed,' said I.

We went in again, shut the door, and resumed our seats. I was thinking how best to improve this advantage, if it might be called one, when he took up the conversation in such a matter-of-course way, so assuming that there could be no serious question of fact between us, that I felt myself placed in the weakest of positions.

'By this time you will fully understand, Sir,' he said, 'that what troubles me so dreadfully is the question: What does the spectre mean?'

I was not sure, I told him, that I did fully understand.

'What is its warning against?' he said, ruminating, with his eyes on the fire, and only by times turning them on me. 'What is the danger? Where is the danger? There is danger overhanging somewhere on the Line. Some dreadful calamity will happen. It is not to be doubted this third time, after what has gone before. But surely this is a cruel haunting of *me*. What can *I* do?'

He pulled out his handkerchief, and wiped the drops from his heated forehead.

'If I telegraph Danger, on either side of me, or on both, I can give no reason for it,' he went on, wiping the palms of his hands. 'I should get into trouble, and do no good. They would think I was mad. This is the way it would work: Message: "Danger! Take care!" Answer: "What Danger? Where?" Message: "Don't know. But, for God's sake, take care!" They would displace me. What else could they do?'

His pain of mind was most pitiable to see. It was the mental torture of a conscientious man, oppressed beyond endurance by an unintelligible responsibility involving life.

'When it first stood under the Danger-light,' he went on, putting his dark hair back from his head, and drawing his hands outward across and across his temples in an extremity of feverish distress, 'why not tell me where that accident was to happen—if it must happen? Why not tell me how it could be averted—if it could have been averted? When on its second coming it hid its face, why not tell me, instead, "She is going to die. Let them keep her at home"? If it came, on those two occasions, only to show me that its warnings were true, and so to prepare me for the third, why not warn me plainly now? And I, Lord help me! A mere poor signalman on this solitary station! Why not go to somebody with credit to be believed and power to act?'

When I saw him in this state, I saw that for the poor man's sake, as well as for the public safety, what I had to do for the time was to compose his mind. Therefore, setting aside all question of reality or unreality between us, I represented to him that whoever thoroughly discharged his duty must do well, and that at least it was his comfort that he understood his duty, though he did not understand these confounding Appearances. In this effort I succeeded far better than in the attempt to reason him out of his conviction. He became calm; the occupations incidental to his post as the night advanced began to make larger demands on his attention: and I left him at two in the morning. I had offered to stay through the night, but he would not hear of it.

That I more than once looked back at the red light as I ascended the pathway, that I did not like the red light, and that I should have slept but poorly if my bed had been under it, I see no reason to conceal. Nor did I like the two sequences of the accident and the dead girl. I see no reason to conceal that either.

But what ran most in my thoughts was the consideration how ought I to act, having become the recipient of this disclosure? I had proved the man to be intelligent, vigilant, painstaking, and exact; but how long might he remain so, in his state of mind? Though in a subordinate position, still he held a most important trust, and would I (for instance) like to stake my own life on the chances of his continuing to execute it with precision?

Unable to overcome a feeling that there would be something treacherous in my communicating what he had told me to his superiors in the Company, without first being plain with himself and proposing a middle course to him, I ultimately resolved to offer to accompany him (otherwise keeping his secret for the present) to the wisest medical practitioner we could hear of in those parts, and to take his opinion. A change in his time of duty would come round next night, he had apprised me, and he would be off an hour or two after sunrise, and on again soon after sunset. I had appointed to return accordingly.

Next evening was a lovely evening, and I walked out early to enjoy it. The sun was not yet quite down when I traversed the field-path near the top of the deep cutting. I would extend my walk for an hour, I said to myself, half an hour on and half an hour back, and it would then be time to go to my signalman's box.

Before pursuing my stroll, I stepped to the brink, and mechanically looked down, from the point from which I had first seen him. I cannot describe the thrill that seized upon me, when, close at the mouth of the tunnel, I saw the appearance of a man, with his left sleeve across his eyes, passionately waving his right arm.

—The nameless horror that oppressed me passed in a moment, for in a moment I saw that this appearance of a man was a man indeed, and that there was a little group of other men standing at a short distance, to whom he seemed to be rehearsing the gesture he made. The Danger-light was not yet lighted. Against its shaft, a little low hut, entirely new to me, had been made of some wooden supports and tarpaulin. It looked no bigger than a bed.

—With an irresistible sense that something was wrong—with a flashing self-reproachful fear that fatal mischief had come of my leaving the man there, and causing no one to be sent to overlook or correct what he did—I descended the notched path with all the speed I could make.

'What is the matter?' I asked the men.

'Signalman killed this morning, Sir.'

'Not the man belonging to that box?'

'Yes, sir.'

'Not the man I know?'

'You will recognize him, Sir, if you knew him,' said the man who spoke for the others, solemnly uncovering his own head, and raising an end of the tarpaulin, 'for his face is quite composed.'

'Oh, how did this happen, how did this happen?' I asked, turning from one to another as the hut closed in again.

'He was cut down by an engine, Sir. No man in England knew his work better. But somehow he was not clear of the outer rail. It was just at broad day. He had struck the light, and had the lamp in his hand. As the engine came out of the tunnel, his back was towards her, and she cut him down. That man drove her, and was showing how it happened. Show the gentleman, Tom.'

The man, who wore a rough dark dress, stepped back to his former place at the mouth of the tunnel.

'Coming round the curve in the tunnel, Sir,' he said, 'I saw him at the end, like as if I saw him down a perspective glass. There was no time to check speed, and I knew him to be very careful. As he didn't seem to take heed of the whistle, I shut it off when we were running down upon him, and called to him as loud as I could call.'

'What did you say?'

'I said, "Below there! Look out! Look out! For God's sake, clear the way!"'

I started.

'Ah! it was a dreadful time, Sir. I never left off calling to him. I put this arm before my eyes not to see, and I waved this arm to the last; but it was no use.'

Without prolonging the narrative to dwell on any one of its curious circumstances more than on any other, I may, in closing it, point out the coincidence that the warning of the Engine-Driver included, not only the words which the unfortunate Signalman had repeated to me as haunting him, but also the words which I myself—not he—had attached, and that only in my own mind, to the gesticulation he had imitated.

W.W. Jacobs

The Monkey's Paw

1

Without, the night was cold and wet, but in the small parlour of Laburnam Villa the blinds were drawn and the fire burned brightly. Father and son were at chess, the former, who possessed ideas about the game involving radical changes, putting his king into such sharp and unnecessary perils that it even provoked comment from the white-haired old lady knitting placidly by the fire.

'Hark at the wind,' said Mr White, who, having seen a fatal mistake after it was too late, was amiably desirous of preventing his son from seeing it.

'I'm listening,' said the latter, grimly surveying the board as he stretched out his hand. 'Check.'

'I should hardly think that he'd come tonight,' said his father, with his hand poised over the board.

'Mate,' replied the son.

'That's the worst of living so far out,' bawled Mr White, with sudden and unlooked-for violence; 'of all the beastly, slushy, out-of-the-way places to live in, this is the worst. Pathway's a bog, and the road's a torrent. I don't know what people are thinking about. I suppose because only two houses in the road are let, they think it doesn't matter.'

'Never mind, dear,' said his wife, soothingly; 'perhaps you'll win the next one.'

Mr White looked up sharply, just in time to intercept a knowing glance between mother and son. The words died away on his lips, and he hid a guilty grin in his thin grey beard.

'There he is,' said Herbert White, as the gate banged to loudly and heavy footsteps came toward the door.

The old man rose with hospitable haste, and opening the door, was heard condoling with the new arrival. The new arrival also condoled with himself, so that Mrs White said, 'Tut, tut!' and coughed gently as her husband entered the room, followed by a tall, burly man, beady of eye and rubicund of visage.

'Sergeant-Major Morris,' he said, introducing him.

The sergeant-major shook hands, and taking the proffered seat by the fire, watched contentedly while his host got out whisky and tumblers and stood a small copper kettle on the fire.

At the third glass his eyes got brighter, and he began to talk, the little family circle regarding with eager interest this visitor from distant parts, as he squared his broad shoulders in the chair and spoke of wild scenes and doughty deeds; of wars and plagues and strange peoples.

'Twenty-one years of it,' said Mr White, nodding at his wife and son. 'When he went away he was a slip of a youth in the warehouse. Now look at him.'

'He don't look to have taken much harm,' said Mrs White, politely.

'I'd like to go to India myself,' said the old man, 'just to look round a bit, you know.'

'Better where you are,' said the sergeant-major, shaking his head. He put down the empty glass, and sighing softly, shook it again.

'I should like to see those old temples and fakirs and jugglers,' said the old man. 'What was that you started telling me the other day about a monkey's paw or something, Morris?'

'Nothing,' said the soldier hastily. 'Leastways nothing worth hearing.'

'Monkey's paw?' said Mrs White, curiously.

'Well, it's just a bit of what you might call magic, perhaps,' said the sergeant-major off-handedly.

His three listeners leaned forward eagerly. The visitor absent-mindedly put his empty glass to his lips and then set it down again. His host filled it for him.

'To look at,' said the sergeant-major, fumbling in his pocket, 'it's just an ordinary little paw, dried to a mummy.'

He took something out of his pocket and proffered it. Mrs White drew back with a grimace, but her son, taking it, examined it curiously.

'And what is there special about it?' inquired Mr White as he took it from his son, and having examined it, placed it upon the table.

'It had a spell put on it by an old fakir,' said the sergeant-major, 'a very holy man. He wanted to show that fate ruled people's lives,

77

and that those who interfered with it did so to their sorrow. He put a spell on it so that three separate men could each have three wishes from it.'

His manner was so impressive that his hearers were conscious that their light laughter jarred somewhat.

'Well, why don't you have three, sir?' said Herbert White cleverly.

The soldier regarded him in the way that middle age is wont to regard presumptuous youth. 'I have,' he said quietly, and his blotchy face whitened.

'And did you really have the three wishes granted?' asked Mrs White.

'I did,' said the sergeant-major, and his glass tapped against his strong teeth.

'And has anybody else wished?' persisted the old lady.

'The first man had his three wishes. Yes,' was the reply; 'I don't know what the first two were, but the third was for death. That's how I got the paw.'

His tones were so grave that a hush fell upon the group.

'If you've had your three wishes, it's no good to you now, then, Morris,' said the old man at last. 'What do you keep it for?'

The soldier shook his head. 'Fancy, I suppose,' he said slowly. 'I did have some idea of selling it, but I don't think I will. It has caused enough mischief already. Besides, people won't buy. They think it's a fairy tale; some of them, and those who do think anything of it want to try it first and pay me afterward.'

'If you could have another three wishes,' said the old man, eyeing him keenly, 'would you have them?'

'I don't know,' said the other. 'I don't know.'

He took the paw, and dangling it between his forefinger and thumb, suddenly threw it upon the fire. White, with a slight cry, stooped down and snatched it off.

'Better let it burn,' said the soldier solemnly.

'If you don't want it, Morris,' said the other, 'give it to me.'

'I won't,' said his friend doggedly. 'I threw it on the fire. If you keep it, don't blame me for what happens. Pitch it on the fire again like a sensible man.'

The other shook his head and examined his new possession closely. 'How do you do it?' he inquired.

'Hold it up in your right hand and wish aloud,' said the sergeant-major, 'but I warn you of the consequences.'

'Sounds like the *Arabian Nights*,' said Mrs White, as she rose and began to set the supper. 'Don't you think you might wish for four pairs of hands for me?'

Her husband drew the talisman from his pocket, and then all three burst into laughter as the sergeant-major, with a look of alarm on his face, caught him by the arm.

'If you must wish,' he said gruffly, 'wish for something sensible.'

Mr White dropped it back into his pocket, and placing chairs, motioned his friend to the table. In the business of supper the talisman was partly forgotten, and afterwards the three sat listening in an enthralled fashion to a second instalment of the soldier's adventures in India.

'If the tale about the monkey's paw is not more truthful than those he has been telling us,' said Herbert, as the door closed behind their guest, just in time for him to catch the last train, 'we shan't make much out of it.'

'Did you give him anything for it, father?' inquired Mrs White, regarding her husband closely.

'A trifle,' said he, colouring slightly. 'He didn't want it, but I made him take it. And he pressed me again to throw it away.'

'Likely,' said Herbert, with pretended horror. 'Why, we're going to be rich, and famous and happy. Wish to be an emperor, father, to begin with; then you can't be hen-pecked.'

He darted round the table, pursued by the maligned Mrs White armed with an antimacassar.

Mr White took the paw from his pocket and eyed it dubiously. 'I don't know what to wish for, and that's a fact,' he said slowly. 'It seems to me I've got all I want.'

'If you only cleared the house, you'd be quite happy wouldn't you?' said Herbert, with his hand on his shoulder. 'Well, wish for two hundred pounds, then; that'll just do it.'

His father, smiling shamefacedly at his own credulity, held up the talisman, as his son, with a solemn face, somewhat marred by a wink at his mother, sat down at the piano and struck a few impressive chords.

'I wish for two hundred pounds,' said the old man distinctly.

A fine crash from the piano greeted the words, interrupted by a shuddering cry from the old man. His wife and son ran toward him.

'It moved,' he cried, with a glance of disgust at the object as it lay on the floor. 'As I wished, it twisted in my hand like a snake.'

'Well, I don't see the money,' said his son as he picked it up and placed it on the table, 'and I bet I never shall.'

'It must have been your fancy, father,' said his wife, regarding him anxiously.

He shook his head. 'Never mind, though; there's no harm done, but it gave me a shock all the same.'

They sat down by the fire again while the two men finished their pipes. Outside, the wind was higher than ever, and the old man started nervously at the sound of a door banging upstairs. A silence unusual and depressing settled upon all three, which lasted until the old couple rose to retire for the night.

'I expect you'll find the cash tied up in a big bag in the middle of your bed,' said Herbert, as he bade them good night, 'and something horrible squatting up on top of the wardrobe watching you as you pocket your ill-gotten gains.'

He sat alone in the darkness, gazing at the dying fire, and seeing faces in it. The last face was so horrible and so simian that he gazed at it in amazement. It got so vivid that, with a little uneasy laugh, he felt on the table for a glass containing a little water to throw over it. His hand grasped the monkey's paw, and with a little shiver he wiped his hands on his coat and went up to bed.

2

In the brightness of the wintry sun next morning as it streamed over the breakfast table he laughed at his fears. There was an air of prosaic wholesomeness about the room which it had lacked on the previous night, and the dirty, shrivelled little paw was pitched on the sideboard with a carelessness which betokened no great belief in its virtues.

'I suppose all old soldiers are the same,' said Mrs White. 'The idea of our listening to such nonsense! How could wishes be granted in these days? And if they could, how could two hundred pounds hurt you, father?'

'Might drop on his head from the sky,' said the frivolous Herbert.

'Morris said the things happened so naturally,' said his father, 'that you might if you so wished attribute it to coincidence.'

'Well, don't break into the money before I come back,' said Herbert as he rose from the table. 'I'm afraid it'll turn you into a mean, avaricious man, and we shall have to disown you.'

His mother laughed, and following him to the door, watched him down the road; and returning to the breakfast table, was very happy at the expense of her husband's credulity. All of which did not prevent her from scurrying to the door at the postman's knock, nor prevent her from referring somewhat shortly to retired sergeant-majors of bibulous habits when she found that the post brought a tailor's bill.

'Herbert will have some more of his funny remarks, I expect, when he comes home,' she said, as they sat at dinner.

'I dare say,' said Mr White, pouring himself out some beer; 'but for all that, the thing moved in my hand; that I'll swear to.'

'You thought it did,' said the old lady soothingly.

'I say it did,' replied the other. 'There was no thought about it; I had just—— What's the matter?'

His wife made no reply. She was watching the mysterious movements of a man outside, who, peering in an undecided fashion at the house, appeared to be trying to make up his mind to enter. In mental connection with the two hundred pounds, she noticed that the stranger was well dressed, and wore a silk hat of glossy newness. Three times he paused at the gate, and then walked on again. The fourth time he stood with his hand upon it, and then with sudden resolution flung it open and walked up the path. Mrs White at the same moment placed her hands behind her, and hurriedly unfastening the strings of her apron, put that useful article of apparel beneath the cushion of her chair.

She brought the stranger, who seemed ill at ease, into the room. He gazed at her furtively, and listened in a preoccupied fashion as the old lady apologized for the appearance of the room, and her husband's coat, a garment which he usually reserved for the garden. She then waited as patiently as her sex would permit, for him to broach his business, but he was at first strangely silent.

'I—was asked to call,' he said at last, and stooped and picked a piece of cotton from his trousers. 'I come from "Maw and Meggins".'

The old lady started. 'Is anything the matter?' she asked breathlessly. 'Has anything happened to Herbert? What is it? What is it?'

Her husband interposed. 'There, there, mother,' he said hastily. 'Sit down, and don't jump to conclusions. You've not brought bad news, I'm sure, sir;' and he eyed the other wistfully.

'I'm sorry——' began the visitor.

'Is he hurt?' demanded the mother wildly.

The visitor bowed in assent. 'Badly hurt,' he said quietly, 'but he is not in any pain.'

'Oh, thank God!' said the old woman, clasping her hands. 'Thank God for that! Thank——'

She broke off suddenly as the sinister meaning of the assurance dawned upon her and she saw the awful confirmation of her fears in the other's averted face. She caught her breath, and turning to her slower-witted husband, laid her trembling old hand upon his. There was a long silence.

'He was caught in the machinery,' said the visitor at length in a low voice.

'Caught in the machinery,' repeated Mr White, in a dazed fashion, 'yes.'

He sat staring blankly out at the window, and taking his wife's hand between his own, pressed it as he had been wont to do in their old courting-days nearly forty years before.

'He was the only one left to us,' he said, turning gently to the visitor. 'It is hard.'

The other coughed, and rising, walked slowly to the window. 'The firm wished me to convey their sincere sympathy with you in your great loss,' he said, without looking round. 'I beg that you will understand I am only their servant and merely obeying orders.'

There was no reply; the old woman's face was white, her eyes staring, and her breath inaudible; on the husband's face was a look such as his friend the sergeant-major might have carried into his first action.

'I was to say that Maw and Meggins disclaim all responsibility,' continued the other. 'They admit no liability at all, but in consideration of your son's services, they wish to present you with a certain sum as compensation.'

Mr White dropped his wife's hand, and rising to his feet, gazed with a look of horror at his visitor. His dry lips shaped the words, 'How much?'

'Two hundred pounds,' was the answer.

Unconscious of his wife's shriek, the old man smiled faintly, put out his hands like a sightless man, and dropped, a senseless heap, to the floor.

3

In the huge new cemetery, some two miles distant, the old people buried their dead, and came back to a house steeped in shadow and silence. It was all over so quickly that at first they could hardly realize it, and remained in a state of expectation as though of something else to happen—something else which was to lighten this load, too heavy for old hearts to bear.

But the days passed, and expectation gave place to resignation— the hopeless resignation of the old, sometimes miscalled, apathy. Sometimes they hardly exchanged a word, for now they had nothing to talk about, and their days were long to weariness.

It was about a week after that the old man, waking suddenly in the night, stretched out his hand and found himself alone. The room was in darkness, and the sound of subdued weeping came from the window. He raised himself in bed and listened.

'Come back,' he said tenderly. 'You will be cold.'

'It is colder for my son,' said the old woman, and wept afresh.

The sound of her sobs died away on his ears. The bed was warm, and his eyes heavy with sleep. He dozed fitfully, and then slept until a sudden wild cry from his wife awoke him with a start.

'The paw!' she cried wildly. 'The monkey's paw!'

He started up in alarm. 'Where? Where is it? What's the matter?'

She came stumbling across the room towards him. 'I want it,' she said quietly. 'You've not destroyed it?'

'It's in the parlour, on the bracket,' he replied, marvelling. 'Why?'

She cried and laughed together, and bending over, kissed his cheek.

'I only just thought of it,' she said hysterically. 'Why didn't I think of it before? Why didn't *you* think of it?'

'Think of what?' he questioned.

'The other two wishes,' she replied rapidly. 'We've only had one.'

'Was not that enough?' he demanded fiercely.

'No,' she cried triumphantly; 'we'll have one more. Go down and get it quickly, and wish our boy alive again.'

The man sat up in bed and flung the bedclothes from his quaking limbs. 'Good God, you are mad!' he cried, aghast.

'Get it,' she panted; 'get it quickly, and wish—— Oh, my boy, my boy!'

Her husband struck a match and lit the candle. 'Get back to bed,' he said unsteadily. 'You don't know what you are saying.'

'We had the first wish granted,' said the old woman feverishly; 'why not the second?'

'A coincidence,' stammered the old man.

'Go and get it and wish,' cried his wife, quivering with excitement.

The old man turned and regarded her, and his voice shook. 'He has been dead ten days, and besides he—I would not tell you else, but—I could only recognize him by his clothing. If he was too terrible for you to see then, how now?'

'Bring him back,' cried the old woman, and dragged him toward the door. 'Do you think I fear the child I have nursed?'

He went down in the darkness, and felt his way to the parlour, and then to the mantelpiece. The talisman was in its place, and a horrible fear that the unspoken wish might bring his mutilated son before him ere he could escape from the room seized upon him, and he caught his breath as he found that he had lost the direction of the door. His brow cold with sweat, he felt his way round the table, and groped along the wall until he found himself in the small passage with the unwholesome thing in his hand.

Even his wife's face seemed changed as he entered the room. It was white and expectant, and to his fears seemed to have an unnatural look upon it. He was afraid of her.

'*Wish!*' she cried, in a strong voice.

'It is foolish and wicked,' he faltered.

'*Wish!*' repeated his wife.

He raised his hand. 'I wish my son alive again.'

The talisman fell to the floor, and he regarded it fearfully. Then he sank trembling into a chair as the old woman, with burning eyes, walked to the window and raised the blind.

He sat until he was chilled with the cold, glancing occasionally at the figure of the old woman peering through the window. The candle-end, which had turned below the rim of the china candlestick, was throwing pulsating shadows on the ceiling and walls, until, with a flicker larger than the rest, it expired. The old man, with an unspeakable sense of relief at the failure of the talisman, crept back to his bed, and a minute or two afterwards the old woman came silently and apathetically beside him.

Neither spoke, but lay silently listening to the ticking of the clock. A stair creaked, and a squeaky mouse scurried noisily through the wall. The darkness was oppressive, and after lying for some time screwing up his courage, he took the box of matches, and striking one, went downstairs for a candle.

At the foot of the stairs the match went out, and he paused to strike another; and at the same moment a knock, so quiet and stealthy as to be scarcely audible, sounded on the front door.

The matches fell from his hand and spilled in the passage. He stood motionless, his breath suspended until the knock was repeated. Then he turned and fled swiftly back to his room, and closed the door behind him. A third knock sounded through the house.

'*What's that?*' cried the old woman, starting up.

'A rat', said the old man in shaking tones—'a rat. It's passed me on the stairs.'

His wife sat up in bed listening. A loud knock resounded through the house.

'It's Herbert!' she screamed. 'It's Herbert!'

She ran to the door, but her husband was before her, and catching her by the arm, held her tightly.

'What are you going to do?' he whispered hoarsely.

'It's my boy; it's Herbert!' she cried, struggling mechanically. 'I forgot it was two miles away. What are you holding me for? Let go. I must open the door.'

'For God's sake don't let it in,' cried the old man, trembling.

'You're afraid of your own son,' she cried, struggling. 'Let me go. I'm coming, Herbert; I'm coming.'

There was another knock, and another. The old woman with a sudden wrench broke free and ran from the room. Her husband followed to the landing, and called after her appealingly as she hurried downstairs. He heard the chain rattle back and the bottom bolt drawn slowly and stiffly from the socket. Then the old woman's voice, strained and panting.

'The bolt,' she cried loudly. 'Come down. I can't reach it.'

But her husband was on his hands and knees groping wildly on the floor in search of the paw. If he could only find it before the thing outside got in. A perfect fussilade of knocks reverberated through the house, and he heard the scraping of a chair as his wife put it down in the passage against the door. He heard the creaking of the bolt as it came slowly back, and at the same moment he found the monkey's paw, and frantically breathed his third and last wish.

The knocking ceased suddenly, although the echoes of it were still in the house. He heard the chair drawn back, and the door opened. A cold wind rushed up the staircase, and a long loud wail of disappointment and misery from his wife gave him courage to run down to her side, and then to the gate beyond. The street lamp flickering opposite shone on a quiet and deserted road.

M.R. James

Martin's Close

Some few years back I was staying with the rector of a parish in the West, where the society to which I belong owns property. I was to go over some of this land; and, on the first morning of my visit, soon after breakfast, the estate carpenter and general handyman, John Hill, was announced as in readiness to accompany us. The rector asked which part of the parish we were to visit that morning. The estate map was produced, and when we had showed him our round, he put his finger on a particular spot. 'Don't forget,' he said, 'to ask John Hill about Martin's Close when you get there. I should like to hear what he tells you.' 'What ought he to tell us?' I said. 'I haven't the slightest idea,' said the rector, 'or, if that is not exactly true, it will do till lunch-time.' And here he was called away.

We set out. John Hill is not a man to withhold such information as he possesses on any point, and you may gather from him much that is of interest about the people of the place and their talk. An unfamiliar word, or one that he thinks ought to be unfamiliar to you, he will usually spell—as c-o-b cob, and the like. It is not, however, relevant to my purpose to record his conversation before the moment when we reached Martin's Close. The bit of land is notice-able, for it is one of the smallest enclosures you are likely to see—a very few square yards, hedged in with quickset on all sides, and without any gate or gap leading into it. You might take it for a small cottage garden long deserted, but that it lies away from the village and bears no trace of cultivation. It is at no great distance from the road, and is part of what is there called a moor, in other words, a rough upland pasture cut up into largish fields.

'Why is this little bit hedged off so?' I asked, and John Hill (whose answer I cannot represent as perfectly as I should like) was not at fault. 'That's what we call Martin's Close, sir; 'tes a curious thing 'bout that bit of land, sir; goes by the name of Martin's Close, sir. M-a-r-t-i-n Martin. Beg pardon, sir, did Rector tell you to make enquiry of me 'bout that, sir?' 'Yes he did.' 'Ah, I thought so much, sir. I was tell'n Rector 'bout that last week, and he was very much interested. It 'pears there's a murderer buried there, sir, by the name of Martin. Old Mr Samuel Saunders, that formerly lived yurr at what we call Southtown, sir, he had a long tale 'bout that, sir; terrible murder done 'pon a young woman, sir. Cut her throat and cast her in the water down yurr.' 'Was he hung for it?' 'Yes, sir, he was hung just up yurr on the roadway, by what I've 'eard, on the Holy Innocents' Day, many 'undred years ago, by the man that went by the name of the bloody judge; terrible red and bloody, I've 'eard.' 'Was his name Jefferies, do you think?' 'Might be possible 'twas—Jefferies—J-e-f—Jefferies. I reckon 'twas, and the tale I've 'eard many times from Mr Saunders, how this young man Martin—George Martin—was troubled before his cruel action come to light by the young woman's sperit.' 'How was that, do you know?' 'No, sir, I don't exactly know how 'twas with it; but by what I've 'eard he was fairly tormented; and rightly tu. Old Mr Saunders, he told a history regarding a cupboard down yurr in the New Inn. According to what he related, this young woman's sperit come out of this cupboard; but I don't recollact the matter.'

This was the sum of John Hill's information. We passed on, and in due time I reported what I had heard to the Rector. He was able to show me from the parish account-books that a gibbet had been paid for in 1684, and a grave dug in the following year, both for the benefit of George Martin; but he was unable to suggest any one in the parish, Saunders being now gone, who was likely to throw any further light on the story.

Naturally, upon my return to the neighbourhood of libraries, I made search in the more obvious places. The trial seemed to be nowhere reported. A newspaper of the time, and one or more news-letters, however, had some short notices, from which I learnt that, on the ground of local prejudice against the prisoner (he was described as a young gentleman of a good estate) the venue had been moved from Exeter to London; that Jefferies had been the judge, and death the sentence, and that there had been some 'singular passages' in the evidence. Nothing further transpired till September of this year. A friend who knew me to be interested in Jefferies then sent me a leaf torn out of a secondhand bookseller's catalogue with the entry: JEFFERIES, JUDGE: *Interesting old MS. trial for murder*, and so forth, from which I gathered, to my delight, that I could become possessed, for a very few shillings, of what seemed to be a verbatim report, in shorthand, of the Martin trial. I telegraphed for the manuscript and got it. It was a thin bound volume, provided with a title written in longhand by some one in the eighteenth century, who had also added this note: 'My father, who took these notes in court, told me that the prisoner's friends had made interest with Judge Jefferies that no report should be put out: he had intended doing this himself when times were better, and had shew'd it to the Revd Mr Glanvil, who incourag'd his design very warmly, but death surpriz'd them both before it could be brought to an accomplishment.'

The initials W. G. are appended; I am advised that the original reporter may have been T. Gurney, who appears in that capacity in more than one State trial.

This was all that I could read for myself. After no long delay I heard of some one who was capable of deciphering the shorthand of the seventeenth century, and a little time ago the type-written copy of the whole manuscript was laid before me. The portions which I shall communicate here help to fill in the very imperfect outline which subsists in the memories of John Hill and, I suppose, one or two others who live on the scene of the events.

The report begins with a species of preface, the general effect of which is that the copy is not that actually taken in court, though it is a true copy in regard of the notes of what was said; but that the writer has added to it some 'remarkable passages' that took place during the trial, and has made this present fair copy of the whole, intending at some favourable time to publish it; but has not put it into longhand, lest it should fall into the possession of unauthorised persons, and he or his family deprived of the profit.

The report then begins:

This case came on to be tried on Wednesday, the 19th of November, between our sovereign lord the King, and George Martin Esquire, of (I take leave to omit some of the place-names), at a sessions of oyer and terminer and gaol delivery, at the Old Bailey, and the prisoner, being in Newgate, was brought to the bar.

Clerk of the Crown: George Martin, hold up thy hand (which he did).

Then the indictment was read, which set forth that the prisoner 'not having the fear of God before his eyes, but being moved and seduced by the instigation of the devil, upon the 15th day of May, in the 36th year of our sovereign lord King Charles the Second, with force and arms in the parish aforesaid, in and upon Ann Clark, spinster, of the same place, in the peace of God and of our said sovereign lord the King then and there being, feloniously, wilfully, and of your malice aforethought, did make an assault and with a certain knife value a penny, the throat of the said Ann Clark then and there did cut, of the which wound the said Ann Clark then and there did die, and the body of the said Ann Clark did cast into a certain pond of water situate in the same parish (with more that is not material to our purpose) against the peace of our sovereign lord the King, his crown and dignity.'

Then the prisoner prayed a copy of the indictment.

L.C.J. (Sir George Jefferies): What is this? Sure you know that is never allowed. Besides, here is a plain indictment as ever I heard; you have nothing to do but to plead to it.

Pris.: My lord, I apprehend there may be matter of law arising out of the indictment, and I would humbly beg the court to assign me counsel to consider of it. Besides, my lord, I believe it was done in another case: copy of the indictment was allowed.

L.C.J.: What case was that?

Pris.: Truly, my lord, I have been kept close prisoner ever since I came up from Exeter Castle, and no one allowed to come at me and no one to advise with.

L.C.J.: But I say, what was that case you allege?

Pris.: My lord, I cannot tell your lordship precisely the name of the case, but it is in my mind that there was such an one, and I would humbly desire——

L.C.J.: All this is nothing. Name your case, and we will tell you whether there be any matter for you in it. God forbid but you should have anything that may be allowed you by law; but this is against law, and we must keep the course of the court.

Att. Gen. (Sir Robert Sawyer): My lord, we pray for the King that he may be asked to plead.

Cl. of Ct.: Are you guilty of the murder whereof you stand indicted, or not guilty?

Pris.: My lord, I would humbly offer this to the court. If I plead now, shall I have an opportunity after to except against the indictment?

L.C.J.: Yes, yes, that comes after verdict; that will be saved to you, and counsel assigned if there be matter of law; but that which you have now to do is to plead.

Then after some little parleying with the court (which seemed strange upon such a plain indictment) the prisoner pleaded, *Not Guilty*.

Cl. of Ct.: Culprit. How wilt thou be tried?

Pris.: By God and my country.

Cl. of Ct.: God send thee a good deliverance.

L.C.J.: Why, how is this? Here has been a great to-do that you should not be tried at Exeter by your country, but be brought here to London, and now you ask to be tried by your country. Must we send you to Exeter again?

Pris.: My lord, I understood it was the form.

L.C.J.: So it is, man: we spoke only on the way of pleasantness. Well, go on and swear the jury.

So they were sworn. I omit the names. There was no challenging on the prisoner's part, for, as he said, he did not know any of the persons called. Thereupon the prisoner asked for the use of pen, ink, and paper, to which the L.C.J. replied: 'Ay, ay, in God's name let him have it.' Then the usual charge was delivered to the jury, and the case opened by the junior counsel for the King, Mr Dolben.

The Atorrney-General followed:

May it please your lordship, and you gentlemen of the jury, I am of counsel for the King against the prisoner at the bar. You have heard that he stands indicted for a murder done upon the person of a young girl. Such crimes as this you may perhaps reckon not to be uncommon, and, indeed, in these times, I am sorry to say it, there is scarce any fact so barbarous and unnatural but what we may hear almost daily instances of it. But I must confess that in this murder that is charged upon the prisoner, there are some particular features that mark it out to be such as I hope has but seldom if ever been perpetrated upon English ground. For as we shall make it appear, the person murdered was a poor country girl (whereas the prisoner is a gentleman of a proper estate) and, besides that, was one to whom Providence had not given the full use of her intellects, but was what is termed among us commonly an innocent or natural: such an one, therefore, as one would have supposed a gentleman of the prisoner's quality more likely to overlook, or, if he did notice her, to be moved to compassion for her unhappy condition, than to lift up his hand against her in the very horrid and barbarous manner which we shall show you he used.

Now to begin at the beginning and open the matter to you orderly: About Christmas of last year, that is the year 1683, this gentleman, Mr Martin, having newly come back into his own country from the University of Cambridge, some of his neighbours, to show him what civility they could (for his family is one that stands in very good repute all over that country) entertained him here and there at their Christmas merrymakings, so that he was constantly riding to and

fro, from one house to another, and sometimes, when the place of
his destination was distant, or for other reasons, as the unsafeness
of the roads, he would be constrained to lie the night at an inn. In
this way it happened that he came, a day or two after the Christmas,
to the place where this young girl lived with her parents, and put up
at the inn there, called the New Inn, which is, as I am informed, a
house of good repute. Here was some dancing going on among the
people of the place, and Ann Clark had been brought in, it seems, by
her elder sister to look on; but being, as I have said, of weak understanding, and, besides that, very uncomely in her appearance, it was
not likely that she should take much part in the merriment; and
accordingly was but standing by in a corner of the room. The
prisoner at the bar, seeing her, one must suppose by way of a jest,
asked her would she dance with him. And in spite of what her sister
and others could say to prevent it and to dissuade her——

L.C.J.: Come, Mr Attorney, we are not set here to listen to tales
of Christmas parties in taverns. I would not interrupt you, but sure
you have more weighty matters than this. You will be telling us next
what tune they danced to.

Att.: My lord, I would not take up the time of the court with
what is not material: but we reckon it to be material to show how
this unlikely acquaintance begun: and as for the tune, I believe,
indeed, our evidence will show that even that hath a bearing on the
matter in hand.

L.C.J.: Go on, go on, in God's name: but give us nothing that is
impertinent.

Att.: Indeed, my lord, I will keep to my matter. But, gentlemen,
having now shown you, as I think, enough of this first meeting
between the murdered person and the prisoner, I will shorten my
tale so far as to say that from then on there were frequent meetings
of the two: for the young woman was greatly tickled with having got
hold (as she conceived it) of so likely a sweetheart, and he being once
a week at least in the habit of passing through the street where she
lived, she would be always on the watch for him; and it seems they
had a signal arranged: he should whistle the tune that was played at
the tavern: it is a tune, as I am informed, well known in that country,
and has a burden, *'Madam, will you walk, will you talk with me?'*

L.C.J.: Ay, I remember it in my own country, in Shropshire. It
runs somehow thus, doth it not? (Here his lordship whistled a part
of a tune, which was very observable, and seemed below the dignity
of the court. And it appears he felt it so himself, for he said): But this
is by the mark, and I doubt it is the first time we have had dance-

tunes in this court. The most part of the dancing we give occasion for is done at Tyburn. (Looking at the prisoner, who appeared very much disordered.) You said the tune was material to your case, Mr Attorney, and upon my life I think Mr Martin agrees with you. What ails you, man? staring like a player that sees a ghost!

Pris.: My lord, I was amazed at hearing such trivial, foolish things as they bring against me.

L.C.J.: Well, well, it lies upon Mr Attorney to show whether they be trivial or not: but I must say, if he has nothing worse than this he has said, you have no great cause to be in amaze. Doth it not lie something deeper? But go on, Mr Attorney.

Att.: My lord and gentlemen—all that I have said so far you may indeed very reasonably reckon as having an appearance of triviality. And, to be sure, had the matter gone no further than the humouring of a poor silly girl by a young gentleman of quality, it had been very well. But to proceed. We shall make it appear that after three or four weeks the prisoner became contracted to a young gentlewoman of that country, one suitable every way to his own condition, and such an arrangement was on foot that seemed to promise him a happy and a reputable living. But within no very long time it seems that this young gentlewoman, hearing of the jest that was going about that countryside with regard to the prisoner and Ann Clark, conceived that it was not only an unworthy carriage on the part of her lover, but a derogation to herself that he should suffer his name to be sport for tavern company: and so without more ado she, with the consent of her parents, signified to the prisoner that the match between them was at an end. We shall show you that upon the receipt of this intelligence the prisoner was greatly enraged against Ann Clark as being the cause of his misfortune, (though indeed there was nobody answerable for it but himself,) and that he made use of many outrageous expressions and threatenings against her, and subsequently upon meeting with her both abused her and struck at her with his whip: but she, being but a poor innocent, could not be persuaded to desist from her attachment to him, but would often run after him testifying with gestures and broken words the affection she had to him: until she was become, as he said, the very plague of his life. Yet, being that affairs in which he was now engaged necessarily took him by the house in which she lived, he could not (as I am willing to believe he would otherwise have done) avoid meeting with her from time to time. We shall further show you that this was the posture of things up to the 15th day of May in this present year. Upon that day the prisoner comes riding through the village, as of custom, and met with the young woman: but in place of passing her by, as he had lately done, he stopped, and said some words to her with which she appeared wonderfully pleased, and so left her; and, after that day she was nowhere to be found, notwithstanding a strict search was made for her. The next time of the prisoner's passing through the place, her relations inquired of him whether he should know anything of her whereabouts; which he totally denied. They expressed to him their fears lest her weak intellects should have been upset by the attention he had showed her, and so she might have committed some rash act against her own life, calling him to witness the same time how often they had beseeched him to desist from taking notice of her, as fearing trouble might come of it: but this, too, he easily laughed away. But in spite of this light behaviour, it was noticeable in him that about this time his carriage and demeanour changed, and it was said of him that he seemed a troubled man. And here I come to a passage to which I should not dare to ask your attention, but that it appears to me to be founded in truth, and is supported by testimony deserving of credit. And, gentlemen, to my judgment it doth afford a great instance of God's revenge against murder, and that He will require the blood of the innocent.

—;Here Mr Attorney made a pause, and shifted with his papers: and it was thought remarkable by me and others, because he was a man not easily dashed.)

L.C.J.: Well, Mr Attorney, what is your instance?

Att.: My lord, it is a strange one, and the truth is that, of all the cases I have been concerned in, I cannot call to mind the like of it. But to be short, gentlemen, we shall bring you testimony that Ann Clark was seen after this 15th of May, and that, at such time as she was so seen, it was impossible she could have been a living person.

(Here the people made a hum, and a good deal of laughter, and the Court called for silence, and when it was made):

L.C.J.: Why, Mr Attorney, you might save up this tale for a week; it will be Christmas by that time, and you can frighten your cook-maids with it (at which the people laughed again, and the prisoner also, as it seemed). God, man, what are you prating of—ghosts and Christmas jigs and tavern company—and here is a man's life at stake! (To the prisoner): And you, sir, I would have you know there is not so much occasion for you to make merry neither. You were not brought here for that, and if I know Mr Attorney, he has more in his brief that he has shown yet. Go on, Mr Attorney. I need not, mayhap, have spoken so sharply, but you must confess your course is something unusual.

Att.: Nobody knows it better than I my lord: but I shall bring it to an end with a round turn. I shall show you, gentlemen, that Ann Clark's body was found in the month of June, in a pond of water, with the throat cut: that a knife belonging to the prisoner was found in the same water: that he made efforts to recover the said knife from the water: that the coroner's quest brought in a verdict against the prisoner at the bar, and that therefore he should by course have been tried at Exeter: but that, suit being made on his behalf, on account that an impartial jury could not be found to try him in his own country, he hath had that singular favour shown him that he should be tried here in London. And so we will proceed to call our evidence.

Then the facts of the acquaintance between the prisoner and Ann Clark were proved, and also the coroner's inquest. I pass over this portion of the trial, for it offers nothing of special interest.

Sarah Arscott was next called and sworn.

Att.: What is your occupation?
S.: I keep the New Inn at——
Att.: Do you know the prisoner at the bar?
S.: Yes; he was often at our house since he come first at Christmas of last year.
Att.: Did you know Ann Clark?
S.: Yes, very well.
Att.: Pray, what manner of person was she in her appearance?
S.: She was a very short thick-made woman: I do not know what else you would have me say.
Att.: Was she comely?
S.: No, not by no manner of means: she was very uncomely, poor child! She had a great face and hanging chops and a very bad colour like a puddock.
L.C.J.: What is that, mistress? What say you she was like?
S.: My lord, I ask pardon; I heard Esquire Martin say she looked like a puddock in the face; and so she did.
L.C.J.: Did you that? Can you interpret her, Mr Attorney?
Att.: My lord, I apprehend it is the country word for a toad?
L.C.J.: Oh, a hop-toad! Ay, go on.

Att.: Will you give an account to the jury of what passed between you and the prisoner at the bar in May last?

S.: Sir, it was this. It was about nine o'clock the evening after that Ann did not come home, and I was about my work in the house; there was no company there only Thomas Snell, and it was foul weather. Esquire Martin came in and called for some drink, and I, by way of pleasantry, I said to him, ''Squire, have you been looking after your sweetheart?' and he flew out at me in a passion and desired I would not use such expressions. I was amazed at that, because we were accustomed to joke with him about her.

L.C.J.: Who, her?

S.: Ann Clark, my lord. And we had not heard the news of his being contracted to a young gentlewoman elsewhere, or I am sure I should have used better manners. So I said nothing, but being I was a little put out, I begun singing, to myself as it were, the song they danced to the first time they met, for I thought it would prick him. It was the same that he was used to sing when he come down the street; I have heard it very often: *'Madam, will you walk, will you talk with me?'* And it fell out that I needed something that was in the kitchen. So I went out to get it, and all the time I went on singing, something louder and more bold-like. And as I was there all of a sudden I thought I heard some one answering outside the house, but I could not be sure because of the wind blowing so high. So when I stopped singing, and now I heard it plain, saying, *'Yes, sir, I will walk, I will talk with you,'* and I knew the voice for Ann Clark's voice.

Att.: How did you know it to be her voice?

S.: It was impossible I could be mistaken. She had a dreadful voice, a kind of a squalling voice, in particular if she tried to sing. And there was nobody in the village that could counterfeit it, for they often tried. So, hearing that, I was glad, because we were all in an anxiety to know what was gone with her: for though she was a natural, she had a good disposition and was very tractable: and says I to myself, 'What, child! are you returned, then?' and I ran from the front room, and said to Squire Martin as I passed by, 'Squire, here is your sweetheart back again: shall I call her in?' and with that I went to open the door; but Squire Martin he caught hold of me, and it seemed to me he was out of his wits, or near upon. 'Hold, woman,' says he, 'in God's name!' and I know not what else: he was all of a shake. Then I was angry, and said I, 'What! are you not glad that poor child is found?' and I called to Thomas Snell and said, 'If the Squire will not let me, do you open the door and call her in.' So

Thomas Snell went and opened the door, and the wind setting that way blew in and overset the two candles that was all we had lighted: and Esquire Martin fell away from holding me; I think he fell down on the floor, but we were wholly in the dark, and it was a minute or two before I got a light again: and while I was feeling for the fire-box, I am not certain but I heard some one step 'cross the floor, and I am sure I heard the door of the great cupboard that stands in the room open and shut to. Then, when I had a light again, I see Esquire Martin on the settle, all white and sweaty as if he had swounded away, and his arms hanging down; and I was going to help him; but just then it caught my eye that there was something like a bit of a dress shut into the cupboard door, and it came to my mind I had heard that door shut. So I thought it might be some person had run in when the light was quenched, and was hiding in the cupboard. So I went up closer and looked: and there was a bit of a black stuff cloak, and just below it an edge of a brown stuff dress, both sticking out of the shut of the door: and both of them was low down, as if the person that had them on might be crouched down inside.

Att.: What did you take it to be?

S.: I took it to be a woman's dress.

Att.: Could you make any guess whom it belonged to? Did you know anyone who wore such a dress?

S.: It was common stuff, by what I could see. I have seen many women wearing such a stuff in our parish.

Att.: Was it like Ann Clark's dress?

S.: She used to wear just such a dress: but I could not say on my oath it was hers.

Att.: Did you observe anything else about it?

S.: I did notice that it looked very wet: but it was foul weather outside.

L.C.J.: Did you feel of it, mistress?

S.: No, my lord, I did not like to touch it.

L.C.J.: Not like? Why that? Are you so nice that you scruple to feel of a wet dress?

S.: Indeed, my lord, I cannot very well tell why: only it had a nasty ugly look about it.

L.C.J.: Well, go on.

S.: Then I called again to Thomas Snell, and bid him come to me and catch any one that come out when I should open the cupboard door, 'for,' says I, 'there is some one hiding within, and I would know what she wants.' And with that Squire Martin gave a sort of a cry or a shout and ran out of the house into the dark, and I felt the cupboard door pushed out against me while I held it, and Thomas Snell helped me: but for all we pressed to keep it shut as hard as we could, it was forced out against us, and we had to fall back.

L.C.J.: And pray what came out—a mouse?

S.: No, my lord, it was greater than a mouse, but I could not see what it was: it fleeted very swift over the floor and out at the door.

L.C.J.: But come; what did it look like? Was it a person?

S.: My lord, I cannot tell what it was, but it ran very low, and it was of a dark colour. We were both daunted by it, Thomas Snell and I, but we made all the haste we could after it to the door that stood open. And we looked out, but it was dark and we could see nothing.

L.C.J.: Was there no tracks of it on the floor? What floor have you there?

S.: It is a flagged floor and sanded, my lord, and there was an appearance of a wet track on the floor, but we could make nothing of it, neither Thomas Snell nor me, and besides, as I said, it was a foul night.

L.C.J.: Well, for my part, I see not—though to be sure it is an odd tale she tells—what you would do with this evidence.

Att.: My lord, we bring it to show the suspicious carriage of the prisoner immediately after the disappearance of the murdered person: and we ask the jury's consideration of that; and also to the matter of the voice heard without the house.

Then the prisoner asked some questions not very material, and Thomas Snell was next called, who gave evidence to the same effect as Mrs Arscott, and added the following:

Att.: Did anything pass between you and the prisoner during the time Mrs Arscott was out of the room?

Th.: I had a piece of twist in my pocket.

Att.: Twist of what?

Th.: Twist of tobacco, sir, and I felt a disposition to take a pipe of tobacco. So I found a pipe on the chimney-piece, and being it was twist, and in regard of me having by an oversight left my knife at my house, and me not having over many teeth to pluck at it, as your lordship or any one else may have a view by their ow eyesight——

L.C.J.: What is the man talking about? Come to the matter, fellow! Do you think we sit here to look at your teeth?

Th.: No, my lord, nor I would not you should do, God forbid! I know your honours have better employment, and better teeth, I would not wonder.

L.C.J.: Good God, what a man is this! Yes, I *have* better teeth, and that you shall find if you keep not to the purpose.

Th.: I humbly ask pardon, my lord, but so it was. And I took upon me, thinking no harm, to ask Squire Martin to lend me his knife to cut my tobacco. And he felt first of one pocket and then of another and it was not there at all. And says I, 'What! have you lost your knife, Squire?' And up he gets and feels again and he sat down, and such a groan as he gave, 'Good God?' he says, 'I must have left it there.' 'But,' says I, 'Squire, by all appearance it is *not* there. Did you set a value on it,' says I, 'you might have it cried.' But he sat there and put his head between his hands and seemed to take no notice to what I said. And then it was Mistress Arscott come tracking back out of the kitchen place.

Asked if he heard the voice singing outside the house, he said, 'No,' but the door into the kitchen was shut, and there was a high wind: but says that no one could mistake Ann Clark's voice.

Then a boy, William Reddaway, about thirteen years of age, was called, and by the usual questions, put by the Lord Chief Justice, it was ascertained that he knew the nature of an oath. And so he was sworn. His evidence referred to a time about a week later.

Att.: Now, child, don't be frighted: there is no one here will hurt you if you speak the truth.

L.C.J.: Ay, if he speak the truth. But remember, child, thou art in the presence of the great God in heaven and earth, that hath the keys of hell, and of us that are the king's officers, and have the keys of Newgate; and remember, too, there is a man's life in question; and if thou tellest a lie, and by that means he comes to an ill end, thou art no better than his murderer; and so speak the truth.

Att.: Tell the jury what you know, and speak out. Where were you on the evening of the 23rd of May last?

L.C.J.: Why, what does such a boy as this know of days. Can you mark the day, boy?

W.: Yes, my lord, it was the day before our feast, and I was to spend sixpence there, and that falls a month before Midsummer Day.

One of the Jury: My lord, we cannot hear what he says.

L.C.J.: He says he remembers the day because it was the day before the feast they had there, and he had sixpence to lay out. Set him up on the table there. Well, child, and where wast thou then?

W.: Keeping cows on the moor, my lord.

But, the boy using the country speech, my lord could not well

apprehend him, and so asked if there was any one that could interpret him, and it was answered the parson of the parish was there,
and he was accordingly sworn and so the evidence given. The boy
said——

'I was on the moor about six o'clock and sitting behind a bush of
furze near a pond of water: and the prisoner came very cautiously
and looking about him, having something like a long pole in his
hand, and stopped a good while as if he would be listening, and then
began to feel in the water with the pole: and I being very near the
water—not about five yards—heard as if the pole struck up against
something that made a wallowing sound, and the prisoner dropped
the pole and threw himself on the ground, and rolled himself about
very strangely with his hands to his ears, and so after a while got up
and went creeping away.'

Asked if he had had any communication with the prisoner, 'Yes,
a day or two before, the prisoner, hearing I was used to be on the
moor, he asked me if I had seen a knife laying about, and said he
would give sixpence to find it. And I said I had not seen any such
thing, but I would ask about. Then he said he would give me sixpence
to say nothing, and so he did.

L.C.J.: And was that the sixpence you were to lay out at the feast?
W.: Yes, if you please, my lord.

Asked if he had observed anything particular as to the pond of
water, he said, 'No, except that it begun to have a very ill smell and
the cows would not drink of it for some days before.'

Asked if he had ever seen the prisoner and Ann Clark in company
together, he began to cry very much, and it was a long time before
they could get him to speak intelligibly. At last the parson of the
parish, Mr Matthews, got him to be quiet, and the question being
put to him again, he said he had seen Ann Clark waiting on the moor
for the prisoner at some way off, several times since last Christmas.

Att.: Did you see her close, so as to be sure it was she?
W.: Yes, quite sure.
L.C.J.: How quite sure, child?
W.: Because she would stand and jump up and down and clap her
arms like a goose (which he called by some country name; but the
parson explained it to be a goose). And then she was of such a shape
that it could not be no one else.

Att.: What was the last time that you so saw her?

Then the witness began to cry again and clung very much to Mr

Matthews, who bid him not to be frightened. And so at last he told this story: that on the day before their feast (being the same evening that he had before spoken of) after the prisoner had gone away, it being then twilight, and he very desirous to get home, but afraid for the present to stir from where he was lest the prisoner should see him, remained some few minutes behind the bush, looking on the pond, and saw something dark come up out of the water at the edge of the pond furthest away from him, and so up the bank. And when it got to the top where he could see it plain against the sky, it stood up and flapped the arms up and down, and then run off very swiftly in the same direction the prisoner had taken: and being asked very strictly who he took it to be, he said upon his oath that it could be nobody but Ann Clark.

Thereafter his master was called, and gave evidence that the boy had come home very late that evening and been chided for it, and that he seemed very much amazed, but could give no account of the reason.

Att.: My lord, we have done with our evidence for the King.

Then the Lord Chief Justice called upon the prisoner to make his defence; which he did, though at no great length, and in a very halting way, saying that he hoped the jury would not go about to take his life on the evidence of a parcel of country people and children that would believe any idle tale; and that he had been very much prejudiced in his trial; at which the L.C.J. interrupted him, saying that he had had singular favour shown to him in having his trial removed from Exeter, which the prisoner acknowledging, said that he meant rather that since he was brought to London there had not been care taken to keep him secured from interruption and disturbance. Upon which the L.C.J. ordered the Marshal to be called, and questioned him about the safe keeping of the prisoner, but could find nothing: except the Marshal said that he had been informed by the underkeeper that they had seen a person outside his door or going up the stairs to it: but there was no possibility the person should have got in. And it being inquired further what sort of person this might be, the Marshal could not speak to it save by hearsay, which was not allowed. And the prisoner, being asked if this was what he meant, said so, he knew nothing of that, but it was very hard that a man should not be suffered to be at quiet when his life stood on it. But it was observed he was very hasty in his denial. And so he said no more, and called no witnesses. Whereupon the Attorney-General spoke to the jury. (A full report of what he said is given, and, if time allowed, I would extract that portion in which he dwells on the alleged appearance of the murdered person: he quotes some authorities of ancient date, as St Augustine *de cura pro mortuis gerenda*—a favourite book of reference with the old writers on the supernatural—and also cites some cases which may be seen in Glanvil's, but more conveniently in Mr Lang's books. He does not, however, tell us more of those cases than is to be found in print.)

The Lord Chief Justice then summed up the evidence for the jury. His speech, again, contains nothing that I find worth copying out: but he was naturally impressed with the singular character of the evidence, saying that he had never heard such given in his experience; but that there was nothing in law to set it aside, and that the jury must consider whether they believed these witnesses or not.

And the jury, after a very short consultation, brought the prisoner in Guilty.

So he was asked whether he had anything to say in arrest of judgment, and pleaded that his name was spelt wrong in the indictment, being Martin with an I, whereas it should be with a Y. But this was overruled as not material, Mr Attorney saying, moreover, that he could bring evidence to show that the prisoner by times wrote it as it was laid in the indictment. And the prisoner, having nothing further to offer, sentence of death was passed upon him, and that he should be hanged in chains upon a gibbet near the place where the fact was committed, and that execution should take place upon the 28th December next ensuing, being Innocents' Day.

Thereafter the prisoner, being to all appearance in a state of desperation, made shift to ask the L.C.J. that his relations might be allowed to come to him during the short time he had to live.

L.C.J.: Ay, with all my heart, so it be in the presence of the keeper; and Ann Clark may come to you as well, for what I care.

At which the prisoner broke out and cried to his lordship not to use such words to him, and his lordship very angrily told him he deserved no tenderness at any man's hands for a cowardly butcherly murderer that had not the stomach to take the reward of his deeds: 'and I hope to God,' said he, 'that she will be with you by day and by night till an end is made of you.' Then the prisoner was removed, and, so far as I saw, he was in a swound, and the court broke up.

I cannot refrain from observing that the prisoner during all the time of the trial seemed to be more uneasy than is commonly the case even in capital causes: that, for example, he was looking narrowly among the people and often turning round very sharply, as if some person might be at his ear. It was also very noticeable at this trial what a silence the people kept, and further (though this might not be otherwise than natural in that season of the year) what a darkness and obscurity there was in the court room, lights being brought in not long after two o'clock in the day, and yet no fog in the town.

It was not without interest that I heard lately from some young men who had been giving a concert in the village I speak of, that a very cold reception was accorded to the song which has been mentioned in this narrative: *'Madam, will you walk?'* It came out in some talk they had next morning with some of the local people, that that song was regarded with an invincible repugnance—it was not so, they believed, at North Tawton—but here it was reckoned to be unlucky. However, why that view was taken no one had the shadow of an idea.

Rudyard Kipling

'They'

One view called me to another; one hill-top to its fellow, half across the county, and since I could answer at no more trouble than the snapping forward of a lever, I let the county flow under my wheels. The orchid-studded flats of the East gave way to the thyme, ilex, and grey grass of the Downs; these again to the rich cornland and fig-trees of the lower coast, where you carry the beat of the tide on your left hand for fifteen level miles; and when at last I turned inland through a huddle of rounded hills and woods I had run myself clean out of my known marks. Beyond that precise hamlet which stands godmother to the capital of the United States, I found hidden villages where bees, the only things awake, boomed in eighty-foot lindens that overhung grey Norman churches; miraculous brooks diving under stone bridges built for heavier traffic than would ever vex them again; tithe-barns larger than their churches, and an old smithy that cried out aloud how it had once been a hall of the Knights of the Temple. Gipsies I found on a common where the gorse, bracken, and heath fought it out together up a mile of Roman road; and a little farther on I disturbed a red fox rolling dog-fashion in the naked sunlight.

As the wooded hills closed about me I stood up in the car to take the bearings of that great Down whose ringed head is a landmark for fifty miles across the low countries. I judged that the lie of the country would bring me across some westward-running road that went to his feet, but I did not allow for the confusing veils of the woods. A quick turn plunged me first into a green cutting brim-full of liquid sunshine, next into a gloomy tunnel where last year's dead leaves whispered and scuffled about my tyres. The strong hazel stuff meeting overhead had not been cut for a couple of generations at least, nor had any axe helped the moss-cankered oak and beech to spring above them. Here the road changed frankly into a carpeted ride on whose brown velvet spent primrose-clumps showed like jade, and a few sickly, white-stalked bluebells nodded together. As the slope favoured I shut off the power and slid over the whirled leaves, expecting every moment to meet a keeper; but I only heard a jay, far off, arguing against the silence under the twilight of the trees.

Still the track descended. I was on the point of reversing and working my way back on the second speed ere I ended in some swamp, when I saw sunshine through the tangle ahead and lifted the brake.

It was down again at once. As the light beat across my face my fore-wheels took the turf of a great lawn from which sprang horsemen ten feet high with levelled lances, monstrous peacocks, and sleek round-headed maids of honour—blue, black, and glistening—all of clipped yew. Across the lawn—the marshalled woods besieged it on three sides—stood an ancient house of lichened and weatherworn stone, with mullioned windows and roofs of rose-red tile. It was flanked by semi-circular walls, also rose-red, that closed the lawn on the fourth side, and at their feet a box hedge grew man-high. There were doves on the roof about the slim brick chimneys, and I caught a glimpse of an octagonal dove-house behind the screening wall.

Here, then, I stayed; a horseman's green spear laid at my breast; held by the exceeding beauty of that jewel in that setting.

'If I am not packed off for a trespasser, or if this knight does not ride a wallop at me,' thought I, 'Shakespeare and Queen Elizabeth at least must come out of that half-open garden door and ask me to tea.'

A child appeared at an upper window, and I thought the little thing waved a friendly hand. But it was to call a companion, for presently another bright head showed. Then I heard a laugh among the yew-peacocks, and turning to make sure (till then I had been watching the house only) I saw the silver of a fountain behind a hedge thrown up against the sun. The doves on the roof cooed to the cooing water; but between the two notes I caught the utterly happy chuckle of a child absorbed in some light mischief.

The garden door—heavy oak sunk deep in the thickness of the wall—opened further: a woman in a big garden hat set her foot slowly on the time-hollowed stone step and as slowly walked across the turf. I was forming some apology when she lifted up her head and I saw that she was blind.

'I heard you,' she said. 'Isn't that a motor car?'

'I'm afraid I've made a mistake in my road. I should have turned off up above—I never dreamed——' I began.

'But I'm very glad. Fancy a motor car coming into the garden!

It will be such a treat——' She turned and made as though looking about her. 'You—you haven't seen any one, have you—perhaps?'

'No one to speak to, but the children seemed interested at a distance.'

'Which?'

'I saw a couple up at the window just now, and I think I heard a little chap in the grounds.'

'Oh, lucky you!' she cried, and her face brightened. 'I hear them, of course, but that's all. You've seen them and heard them?'

'Yes,' I answered. 'And if I know anything of children, one of them's having a beautiful time by the fountain yonder. Escaped, I should imagine.'

'You're fond of children?'

I gave her one or two reasons why I did not altogether hate them.

'Of course, of course,' she said. 'Then you understand. Then you won't think it foolish if I ask you to take your car through the gardens, once or twice—quite slowly. I'm sure they'd like to see it. They see so little, poor things. One tries to make their life pleasant, but——' she threw out her hands towards the woods. 'We're so out of the world here.'

'That will be splendid,' I said. 'But I can't cut up your grass.'

She faced to the right. 'Wait a minute,' she said. 'We're at the South gate, aren't we? Behind those peacocks there's a flagged path. We call it the Peacocks' Walk. You can't see it from here, they tell me, but if you squeeze along by the edge of the wood you can turn at the first peacock and get on to the flags.'

It was sacrilege to wake that dreaming house-front with the clatter of machinery, but I swung the car to clear the turf, brushed along the edge of the wood and turned in on the broad stone path where the fountain-basin lay like one star-sapphire.

'May I come too?' she cried. 'No, please don't help me. They'll like it better if they see me.'

She felt her way lightly to the front of the car, and with one foot on the step she called: 'Children, oh, children! Look and see what's going to happen!'

The voice would have drawn lost souls from the Pit, for the yearning that underlay its sweetness, and I was not surprised to hear an answering shout behind the yews. It must have been the child by the fountain, but he fled at our approach, leaving a little toy boat in the water. I saw the glint of his blue blouse among the still horsemen.

Very disposedly we paraded the length of the walk and at her request backed again. This time the child had got the better of his panic, but stood far off and doubting.

'The little fellow's watching us,' I said. 'I wonder if he'd like a ride.'

'They're very shy still. Very shy. But, oh, lucky you to be able to see them! Let's listen.'

I stopped the machine at once, and the humid stillness, heavy with the scent of box, cloaked us deep. Shears I could hear where some gardener was clipping; a mumble of bees and broken voices that might have been the doves.

'Oh, unkind!' she said weariedly.

'Perhaps they're only shy of the motor. The little maid at the window looks tremendously interested.'

'Yes?' She raised her head. 'It was wrong of me to say that. They are really fond of me. It's the only thing that makes life worth living —when they're fond of you, isn't it? I daren't think what the place would be without them. By the way, is it beautiful?'

'I think it is the most beautiful place I have ever seen.'

'So they all tell me. I can feel it, of course, but that isn't quite the same thing.'

'Then have you never——?' I began, but stopped abashed.

'Not since I can remember. It happened when I was only a few months old, they tell me. And yet I must remember something, else how could I dream about colours? I see light in my dreams, and colours, but I never see *them*. I only hear them just as I do when I'm awake.'

'It's difficult to see faces in dreams. Some people can, but most of us haven't the gift,' I went on, looking up at the window where the child stood all but hidden.

'I've heard that too,' she said. 'And they tell me that one never sees a dead person's face in a dream. Is that true?'

'I believe it is—now I come to think of it.'

'But how is it with yourself—yourself?' The blind eyes turned towards me.

'I have never seen the faces of my dead in any dream,' I answered.

'Then it must be as bad as being blind.'

The sun had dipped behind the woods and the long shades were possessing the insolent horsemen one by one. I saw the light die from off the top of a glossy-leafed lance and all the brave hard green turn to soft black. The house, accepting another day at end, as it had accepted an hundred thousand gone, seemed to settle deeper into its rest among the shadows.

'Have you ever wanted to?' she said after the silence.

'Very much sometimes,' I replied. The child had left the window as the shadows closed upon it.

'Ah! So've I, but I don't suppose it's allowed. . . . Where d'you live?'

'Quite the other side of the county—sixty miles and more, and I must be going back. I've come without my big lamps.'

'But it's not dark yet. I can feel it.'

'I'm afraid it will be by the time I get home. Could you lend me someone to set me on my road at first? I've utterly lost myself.'

'I'll send Madden with you to the cross-roads. We are so out of the world, I don't wonder you were lost! I'll guide you round to the front of the house; but you will go slowly, won't you, till you're out of the grounds? It isn't foolish, do you think?'

'I promise you I'll go like this,' I said, and let the car start herself down the flagged path.

We skirted the left wing of the house, whose elaborately cast lead guttering alone was worth a day's journey; passed under a great rose-grown gate in the red wall, and so round to the high front of the house, which in beauty and stateliness as much excelled the back as that all others I had seen.

'Is it so very beautiful?' she said wistfully when she heard my raptures. 'And you like the lead figures too? There's the old azalea garden behind. They say that this place must have been made for children. Will you help me out, please? I should like to come with you as far as the cross-roads, but I mustn't leave them. Is that you, Madden? I want you to show this gentleman the way to the cross-roads. He has lost his way, but—he has seen them.'

A butler appeared noiselessly at the miracle of old oak that must be called the front door, and slipped aside to put on his hat. She stood looking at me with open blue eyes in which no sight lay, and I saw for the first time that she was beautiful.

'Remember,' she said quietly, 'if you are fond of them you will come again,' and disappeared within the house.

The butler in the car said nothing till we were nearly at the lodge gates, where catching a glimpse of a blue blouse in a shrubbery I swerved amply lest the devil that leads little boys to play should drag me into child-murder.

'Excuse me,' he asked of a sudden, 'but why did you do that, sir?'

'The child yonder.'

'Our young gentleman in blue?'

'Of course.'

'He runs about a good deal. Did you see him by the fountain, sir?'

'Oh, yes, several times. Do we turn here?'

'Yes, sir. And did you 'appen to see them upstairs too?'

'At the upper window? Yes.'

'Was that before the mistress come out to speak to you, sir?'

'A little before that. Why d'you want to know?'

He paused a little. 'Only to make sure that—that they had seen the car, sir, because with children running about, though I'm sure you're driving particularly careful, there might be an accident. That was all, sir. Here are the cross-roads. You can't miss your way from now on. Thank you, sir, but that isn't *our* custom, not with——'

'I beg your pardon,' I said, and thrust away the British silver.

'Oh, it's quite right with the rest of 'em as a rule. Good-bye, sir.'

He retired into the armour-plated conning-tower of his caste and walked away. Evidently a butler solicitous for the honour of his house, and interested, probably through a maid, in the nursery.

Once beyond the signposts at the cross-roads I looked back, but the crumpled hills interlaced so jealously that I could not see where the house had lain. When I asked its name at a cottage along the road, the fat woman who sold sweetmeats there gave me to understand that people with motors cars had small right to live—much less to 'go about talking like carriage folk'. They were not a pleasant-mannered community.

When I retraced my route on the map that evening I was little wiser. Hawkin's Old Farm appeared to be the Survey title of the place, and the old County Gazetteer, generally so ample, did not allude to it. The big house of those parts was Hodnington Hall, Georgian with early Victorian embellishments, as an atrocious steel engraving attested. I carried my difficulty to a neighbour—a deep-rooted tree of that soil—and he gave me a name of a family which conveyed no meaning.

A month or so later—I went again, or it may have been that my car took the road of her own volition. She over-ran the fruitless Downs, threaded every turn of the maze of lanes below the hills, drew through the high-walled woods, impenetrable in their full leaf, came out at the cross-roads where the butler had left me, and a little farther on developed an internal trouble which forced me to turn her in on a grass way-waste that cut into a summer-silent hazel wood. So far as I could make sure by the sun and a six-inch Ordnance map, this should be the road flank of that wood which I had first explored from the heights above. I made a mighty serious business of my repairs and a glittering shop of my repair kit, spanners, pump, and the like, which I spread out orderly upon a rug. It was a trap to catch all childhood, for on such a day, I argued, the children would not be far off. When I paused in my work I listened, but the wood was so full of the noises of summer (though the birds had mated) that I could not at first distinguish these from the tread of small cautious feet stealing across the dead leaves. I rang my bell in an alluring manner, but the feet fled, and I repented, for to a child a sudden noise is very real terror. I must have been at work half an hour when I heard in the wood the voice of the blind woman crying: 'Children, oh, Children! Where are you?' and the stillness made slow to close on the perfection of that cry. She came towards me, half feeling her way between the tree boles, and though a child, it seemed, clung to her skirt, it swerved into the leafage like a rabbit as she drew nearer.

'Is that you?' she said, 'from the other side of the county?'

'Yes, it's me from the other side of the county.'

'Then why didn't you come through the upper woods? They were there just now.'

'They were here a few minutes ago. I expect they knew my car had broken down, and came to see the fun.'

'Nothing serious, I hope? How do cars break down?'

'In fifty different ways. Only mine has chosen the fifty-first.'

She laughed merrily at the tiny joke, cooed with delicious laughter, and pushed her hat back.

'Let me hear,' she said.

'Wait a moment,' I cried, 'and I'll get you a cushion.'

She set her foot on the rug all covered with spare parts, and stooped above it eagerly. 'What delightful things!' The hands through which she saw glanced in the chequered sunlight. 'A box here—another box! Why, you've arranged them like playing shop!'

'I must confess now that I put it out to attract them. I don't need half those things really.'

'How nice of you! I heard your bell in the upper wood. You say they were here before that?'

'I'm sure of it. Why are they so shy? That little fellow in blue who was with you just now ought to have got over his fright. He's been watching me like a Red Indian.'

'It must have been your bell,' she said. 'I heard one of them go past me in trouble when I was coming down. They're shy—so shy even with me.' She turned her face over her shoulder and cried again: 'Children, oh, children! Look and see!'

'They must have gone off together on their own affairs,' I suggested, for there was a murmur behind us of lowered voices broken by the sudden squeaking giggles of childhood. I returned to my tinkerings and she leaned forward, her chin on her hand, listening interestedly.

'How many are they?' I said at last. The work was finished, but I saw no reason to go.

Her forehead puckered a little in thought. 'I don't quite know,' she said simply. 'Sometimes more—sometimes less. They come and stay with me because I love them, you see.'

'That must be very jolly,' I said, replacing a drawer, and as I spoke I heard the inanity of my answer.

'You—you aren't laughing at me?' she cried. 'I—I haven't any of my own. I never married. People laugh at me sometimes about them because—because——'

'Because they're savages,' I returned. 'It's nothing to fret for. That sort laugh at everything that isn't in their own fat lives.'

'I don't know. How should I? I only don't like being laughed at about *them*. It hurts; and when one can't see. . . . I don't want to seem silly,' her chin quivered like a child's as she spoke, 'but we blindies have only one skin, I think. Everything outside hits straight at our souls. It's different with you. You've such good defences in your eyes—looking out—before anyone can really pain you in your soul. People forget that with us.'

I was silent, reviewing that inexhaustible matter—the more than inherited (since it is also carefully taught) brutality of the Christian peoples, beside which the mere heathendom of the West Coast nigger is clean and restrained. It led me a long distance into myself.

'Don't do that!' she said of a sudden, putting her hands before her eyes.

'What?'

She made a gesture with her hand.

'That! It's—it's all purple and black. Don't! That colour hurts.'

'But how in the world do you know about colours?' I exclaimed, for here was a revelation indeed.

'Colours as colours?' she asked.

'No. *Those* Colours which you saw just now.'

'You know as well as I do,' she laughed, 'else you wouldn't have asked that question. They aren't in the world at all. They're in *you* —when you went so angry.'

'D'you mean a dull purplish patch, like port wine mixed with ink?' I said.

'I've never seen ink or port wine, but the colours aren't mixed. They are separate—all separate.'

'Do you mean black streaks and jags across the purple?'

She nodded. 'Yes—if they are like this,' and zig-zagged her finger again, 'but it's more red than purple—that bad colour.'

'And what are the colours at the top of the—whatever you see?'

Slowly she leaned forward and traced on the rug the figure of the Egg itself.

'I see them so,' she said, pointing with a grass stem, 'white, green, yellow, red, purple, and when people are angry or bad, black across the red—as you were just now.'

'Who told you anything about it—in the beginning?' I demanded.

'About the Colours? No one. I used to ask what Colours were when I was little—in table-covers and curtains and carpets, you see —because some colours hurt me and some made me happy. People told me; and when I got older that was how I saw people.' Again she traced the outline of the Egg which it is given to very few of us to see.

'All by yourself?' I repeated.

'All by myself. There wasn't anyone else. I only found out afterwards that other people did not see the Colours.'

She leaned against the tree-bole plaiting and unplaiting chance-plucked grass stems. The children in the wood had drawn nearer. I could see them with the tail of my eye frolicking like squirrels.

'Now I am sure you will never laugh at me,' she went on after a long silence. 'Nor at *them*.'

'Goodness! No!' I cried, jolted out of my train of thought. 'A man who laughs at a child—unless the child is laughing too—is a heathen!'

'I didn't mean that, of course. You'd never laugh *at* children, but I thought—I used to think—that perhaps you might laugh about *them*. So now I beg your pardon. . . . What are you going to laugh at?'

I had made no sound, but she knew.

'At the notion of your begging my pardon. If you had done your duty as a pillar of the State and a landed proprietress you ought to have summoned me for trespass when I barked through your woods the other day. It was disgraceful of me—inexcusable.'

She looked at me, her head against the tree-trunk—long and steadfastly—this woman who could see the naked soul.

'How curious,' she half whispered. 'How very curious.'

'Why, what have I done?'

'You don't understand . . . and yet you understood about the Colours. Don't you understand?'

She spoke with a passion that nothing had justified, and I faced her bewilderedly as she rose. The children had gathered themselves in a roundel behind a bramble bush. One sleek head bent over something smaller, and the set of the little shoulders told me that fingers were on lips. They, too, had some child's tremendous secret. I alone was hopelessly astray there in the broad sunlight.

'No,' I said, and shook my head as though the dead eyes could note. 'Whatever it is, I don't understand yet. Perhaps I shall later— if you'll let me come again.'

'You will come again,' she answered. 'You will surely come again and walk in the wood.'

'Perhaps the children will know me well enough by that time to let me play with them—as a favour. You know what children are like.'

'It isn't a matter of favour but of right,' she replied, and while I wondered what she meant, a dishevelled woman plunged round the bend of the road, loose-haired, purple, almost lowing with agony as she ran. It was my rude, fat friend of the sweetmeat shop. The blind woman heard and stepped forward. 'What is it, Mrs Madehurst?' she asked.

The woman flung her apron over her head and literally grovelled in the dust, crying that her grandchild was sick to death, that the local doctor was away fishing, that Jenny the mother was at her wits' end, and so worth, with repetitions and bellowings.

'Where's the next nearest doctor?' I asked between paroxysms.

'Madden will tell you. Go round to the house and take him with you. I'll attend to this. Be quick!' She half supported the fat woman into the shade. In two minutes I was blowing all the horns of Jericho under the front of the House Beautiful, and Madden, in the pantry, rose to the crisis like a butler and a man.

A quarter of an hour at illegal speeds caught us a doctor five miles away. Within the half-hour we had decanted him, much interested in motors, at the door of the sweetmeat shop, and drew up the road to await the verdict.

'Useful things cars,' said Madden, all man and no butler. 'If I'd had one when mine took sick she wouldn't have died.'

'How was it?' I asked.

'Croup. Mrs Madden was away. No one knew what to do. I drove eight miles in a tax-cart for the doctor. She was choked when we came back. This car 'd ha' saved her. She'd have been close on ten now.'

'I'm sorry,' I said. 'I thought you were rather fond of children from what you told me going to the cross-roads the other day.'

'Have you seen 'em again, sir—this mornin'?'

'Yes, but they're well broke to cars. I couldn't get any of them within twenty yards of it.'

He looked at me carefully as a scout considers a stranger—not as a menial should lift his eyes to his divinely appointed superior.

'I wonder why,' he said just above the breath that he drew.

We waited on. A light wind from the sea wandered up and down the long lines of the woods, and the wayside grasses, whitened already with summer dust, rose and bowed in sallow waves.

A woman, wiping the suds off her arms, came out of the cottage next the sweetmeat shop.

'I've be'n listenin' in de back-yard,' she said cheerily. 'He says Arthur's unaccountable bad. Did ye hear him shruck just now? Unaccountable bad. I reckon t'will come Jenny's turn to walk in de wood next week along, Mr Madden.'

'Excuse me, sir, but your lap-robe is slipping,' said Madden deferentially. The woman started, dropped a curtsey, and hurried away.

'What does she mean by "walking in the wood"?' I asked.

'It must be some saying they use hereabouts. I'm from Norfolk myself,' said Madden. 'They're an independent lot in this county. She took you for a chauffeur, sir.'

I saw the Doctor come out of the cottage followed by a draggle-tailed wench who clung to his arm as though he could make treaty for her with Death. 'Dat sort,' she wailed—'dey're just as much to us dat has 'em as if dey was lawful born. Just as much—just as much! An' God, He'd be just as pleased if you saved 'un, Doctor. Don't take it from me. Miss Florence will tell ye de very same. Don't leave 'im, Doctor!'

'I know, I know,' said the man; 'but he'll be quiet for a while now. We'll get the nurse and the medicine as fast as we can.' He signalled me to come forward with the car, and I strove not to be privy to what followed; but I saw the girl's face, blotched and frozen with grief, and I felt the hand without a ring clutching at my knees when we moved away.

The Doctor was a man of some humour, for I remember he claimed my car under the Oath of AEsculapius, and used it and me without mercy. First we convoyed Mrs Madehurst and the blind woman to wait by the sick-bed till the nurse should come. Next we invaded a neat county town for prescriptions (the Doctor said the trouble was cerebro-spinal meningitis), and when the County Institute, banked and flanked with scared market cattle, reported itself out of nurses for the moment we literally flung ourselves loose upon the county. We conferred with the owners of great houses—magnates at the ends of overarching avenues whose big-boned womenfolk strode away from their tea-tables to listen to the imperious Doctor. At last a white-haired lady sitting under a cedar of Lebanon and surrounded by a court of magnificent Borzois—all hostile to motors—gave the Doctor, who received them as from a princess, written orders which we bore many miles at top speed, through a park, to a French nunnery, where we took over in exchange a pallid-faced and trembling Sister. She knelt at the bottom of the tonneau telling her beads without pause till, by short cuts of the Doctor's invention, we had her to the sweetmeat shop once more. It was a long afternoon crowded with mad episodes that rose and dissolved like the dust of our wheels; cross-sections of remote and incomprehensible lives through which we raced at right angles; and I went home in the dusk, wearied out, to dream of the clashing horns of cattle; round-eyed nuns walking in a garden of graves; pleasant tea-parties beneath shady trees; the carbolic-scented, grey-painted corridors of the County Institute; the steps of shy children in the wood, and the hands that clung to my knees as the motor began to move.

I had intended to return in a day or two, but it pleased Fate to hold me from that side of the county, on many pretexts, till the elder and the wild rose had fruited. There came at last a brilliant day, swept clear from the south-west, that brought the hills within hand's reach —a day of unstable airs and high filmy clouds. Through no merit of my own I was free, and set the car for the third time on that known road. As I reached the crest of the Downs I felt the soft air change, saw it glaze under the sun; and, looking down at the sea, in that instant beheld the blue of the Channel turn through polished silver and dulled steel to dingy pewter. A laden collier hugging the coast steered outward for deeper water, and, across copper-coloured haze, I saw sails rise one by one on the anchored fishing-fleet. In a deep dene behind me an eddy of sudden wind drummed through sheltered oaks, and spun aloft the first dry sample of autumn leaves. When I reached the beach road the sea-fog fumed over the brickfields, and the tide was telling all the groynes of the gale beyond Ushant. In less than an hour summer England vanished in chill grey. We were again the shut island of the North, all the ships of the world bellowing at our perilous gates; and between their outcries ran the piping of bewildered gulls. My cap dripped moisture, the folds of the rug held it in pools or sluiced it away in runnels, and the salt-rime stuck to my lips.

Inland the smell of autumn loaded the thickened fog among the trees, and the drip became a continuous shower. Yet the late flowers

—mallow of the wayside, scabious of the field, and dahlia of the garden—showed gay in the mist, and beyond the sea's breath there was little sign of decay in the leaf. Yet in the villages the house doors were all open, and bare-legged, bare-headed children sat at ease on the damp doorsteps to shout 'pip-pip' at the stranger.

I made bold to call at the sweetmeat shop, where Mrs Madehurst met me with a fat woman's hospitable tears. Jenny's child, she said, had died two days after the nun had come. It was, she felt, best out of the way, even though insurance offices, for reasons which she did not pretend to follow, would not willingly insure such stray lives. 'Not but what Jenny didn't tend to Arthur as though he'd come all proper at de end of de first year—like Jenny herself.' Thanks to Miss Florence, the child had been buried with a pomp which, in Mrs Madehurst's opinion, more than covered the small irregularity of its birth. She described the coffin, within and without, the glass hearse, and the evergreen lining of the grave.

'But how's the mother?' I asked.

'Jenny? Oh, she'll get over it. I've felt dat way with one or two o' my own. She'll get over. She's walkin' in de wood now.'

'In this weather?'

Mrs Madehurst looked at me with narrowed eyes across the counter.

'I dunno but it opens de 'eart like. Yes, it opens de 'eart. Dat's where losin' and bearin' comes so alike in de long run, we do say.'

Now the wisdom of the old wives is greater than that of all the Fathers, and this last oracle sent me thinking so extendedly as I went up the road, that I nearly ran over a woman and a child at the wooded corner by the lodge gates of the House Beautiful.

'Awful weather!' I cried, as I slowed dead for the turn.

'Not so bad,' she answered placidly out of the fog. 'Mine's used to 'un. You'll find yours indoors, I reckon.'

Indoors, Madden received me with professional courtesy, and kind inquiries for the health of the motor, which he would put under cover.

I waited in a still, nut-brown hall, pleasant with late flowers and warmed with a delicious wood fire—a place of good influence and great peace. (Men and women may sometimes, after great effort, achieve a creditable lie; but the house, which is their temple, cannot say anything save the truth of those who have lived in it.) A child's cart and a doll lay on the black-and-white floor, where a rug had been kicked back. I felt that the children had only just hurried away —to hide themselves, most like—in the many turns of the great adzed staircase that climbed statelily out of the hall, or to crouch at gaze behind the lions and roses of the carven gallery above. Then I heard her voice above me, singing as the blind sing—from the soul:

'In the pleasant orchard-closes.'

And all my early summer came back at the call.

'In the pleasant orchard-closes,
　God bless all our gains, say we—
But May God bless all our losses,
　Better suits with our degree.'

She dropped the marring fifth line, and repeated—

'Better suits with our degree!'

I saw her lean over the gallery, her linked hands white as pearl against the oak.

'Is that you—from the other side of the county?' she called.

'Yes, me—from the other side of the county,' I answered, laughing.

'What a long time before you had to come here again.' She ran down the stairs, one hand lightly touching the broad rail. 'It's two months and four days. Summer's gone!'

'I meant to come before, but Fate prevented.'

'I knew it. Please do something to that fire. They won't let me play with it, but I can feel it's behaving badly. Hit it!'

I looked on either side of the deep fireplace, and found but a half-charred hedge-stake with which I punched a black log into flame.

'It never goes out, day or night,' she said, as though explaining. 'In case any one comes in with cold toes, you see.'

'It's even lovelier inside than it was out,' I murmured. The red light poured itself along the age-polished dusky panels till the Tudor roses and lions of the gallery took colour and motion. An old eagle-topped convex mirror gathered the picture into its mysterious heart, distorting afresh the distorted shadows, and curving the gallery lines into the curves of a ship. The day was shutting down in half a gale as the fog turned to stringy scud. Through the uncurtained mullions of the broad window I could see the valiant horsemen of the lawn rear and recover against the wind that taunted them with legions of dead leaves.

'Yes, it must be beautiful,' she said. 'Would you like to go over it?

There's still light enough upstairs.'

I followed her up the unflinching, wagon-wide staircase to the gallery whence opened the thin fluted Elizabethan doors.

'Feel how they put the latch low down for the sake of the children.' She swung a light door inward.

'By the way, where are they?' I asked. 'I haven't even heard them today.'

She did not answer at once. Then, 'I can only hear them,' she replied softly. 'This is one of their rooms—everything ready, you see.'

She pointed into a heavily-timbered room. There were little low gate tables and children's chairs. A dolls' house, its hooked front half open, faced a great dappled rocking-horse, from whose padded saddle it was but a child's scramble to the broad window-seat overlooking the lawn. A toy gun lay in a corner beside a gilt wooden cannon.

'Surely they've only just gone,' I whispered. In the failing light a door creaked cautiously. I heard the rustle of a frock and the patter of feet—quick feet through a room beyond.

'I heard that,' she cried triumphantly. 'Did you? Children, oh, children! Where are you?'

The voice filled the walls that held it lovingly to the last perfect note, but there came no answering shout such as I had heard in the garden. We hurried on from room to oak-floored room; up a step here, down three steps there; among a maze of passages; always mocked by our quarry. One might as well have tried to work an unstopped warren with a single ferret. There were bolt-holes innumerable—recesses in walls, embrasures of deep-slitted windows now darkened, whence they could start up behind us: and abandoned fireplaces, six feet deep in the masonry, as well as the tangle of communicating doors. Above all, they had the twilight for their helper in our game. I had caught one or two joyous chuckles of evasion, and once or twice had seen the silhouette of a child's frock against some darkening window at the end of a passage; but we returned empty-handed to the gallery, just as a middle-aged woman was setting a lamp in its niche.

'No, I haven't seen her either this evening, Miss Florence,' I heard her say, 'but that Turpin he says he wants to see you about his shed.'

'Oh, Mr Turpin must want to see me very badly. Tell him to come to the hall, Mrs Madden.'

I looked down into the hall whose only light was the dulled fire, and deep in the shadow I saw them at last. They must have slipped

117

down while we were in the passages, and now thought themselves perfectly hidden behind an old gilt leather screen. By child's law, my fruitless chase was as good as an introduction, but since I had taken so much trouble I resolved to force them to come forward later by the simple trick, which children detest, of pretending not to notice them. They lay close, in a little huddle, no more than shadows except when a quick flame betrayed an outline.

'And now we'll have some tea,' she said. 'I believe I ought to have offered it you at first, but one doesn't arrive at manners somehow when one lives alone and is considered—h'm—peculiar.' Then with very pretty scorn, 'Would you like a lamp to see to eat by?'

'The firelight's much pleasanter, I think.' We descended into that delicious gloom and Madden brought tea.

I took my chair in the direction of the screen ready to surprise or be surprised as the game should go, and at her permission, since a hearth is always sacred, bent forward to play with the fire.

'Where do you get these beautiful short faggots from?' I asked idly. 'Why, they are tallies!'

'Of course,' she said. 'As I can't read or write I'm driven back on the early English tally for my accounts. Give me one and I'll tell you what it meant.'

I passed her an unburned hazel-tally, about a foot long, and she ran her thumb down the nicks.

'This is the milk-record for the home farm for the month of April last year, in gallons,' said she. 'I don't know what I should have done without tallies. An old forester of mine taught me the system. It's out of date now for every one else; but my tenants respect it. One of them's coming now to see me. Oh, it doesn't matter. He has no business here out of office hours. He's a greedy, ignorant man—very greedy, or—he wouldn't come here after dark.'

'Have you much land then?'

'Only a couple of hundred acres in hand, thank goodness. The other six hundred are nearly all let to folk who knew my folk before me, but this Turpin is quite a new man—and a highway robber.'

'But are you sure I shan't be——?'

'Certainly not. You have the right. He hasn't any children.'

'Ah, the children!' I said, and slid my low chair back till it nearly touched the screen that hid them. 'I wonder whether they'll come out for me.'

There was a murmur of voices—Madden's and a deeper note—at the low, dark side door, and a ginger-headed, canvas-gaitered giant of the unmistakable tenant-farmer type stumbled or was pushed in.

'Come to the fire, Mr Turpin,' she said.

'If—if you please, Miss, I'll—I'll be quite as well by the door.' He clung to the latch as he spoke like a frightened child. Of a sudden I realized that he was in the grip of some almost over-powering fear.

'Well?'

'About that new shed for the young stock—that was all. These first autumn storms settin' in . . . but I'll come again, Miss.' His teeth did not chatter much more than the door-latch.

'I think not,' she answered levelly. 'The new shed—m'm. What did my agent write you on the 15th?'

'I—fancied p'raps that if I came to see you—ma'—man to man like, Miss. But——'

His eyes rolled into every corner of the room wide with horror. He half opened the door through which he had entered, but I noticed it shut again—from without and firmly.

'He wrote what I told him,' she went on. 'You are overstocked already. Dunnett's Farm never carried more than fifty bullocks—even in Mr Wright's time. And *he* used cake. You've sixty-seven and you don't cake. You've broken the lease in that respect. You're dragging the heart out of the farm.'

'I'm—I'm getting some minerals—superphosphates—next week. I've as good as ordered a truck-load already. I'll go down to the station tomorrow about 'em. Then I can come and see you man to man, like, Miss, in the daylight. . . . That gentleman's not going away, is he?' He almost shrieked.

I had only slid the chair a little farther back, reaching behind me to tap on the leather of the screen, but he jumped like a rat.

'No. Please attend to me, Mr Turpin.' She turned in her chair and faced him with his back to the door. It was an old and sordid little piece of scheming that she forced from him—his plea for the new cow-shed at his landlady's expense, that he might with the covered manure pay his next year's rent out of the valuation after, as she made clear, he had bled the enriched pastures to the bone. I could not but admire the intensity of his greed, when I saw him outfacing for its sake whatever terror it was that ran wet on his forehead.

I ceased to tap the leather—was, indeed, calculating the cost of the shed—when I felt my relaxed hand taken and turned softly between the soft hands of a child. So at last I had triumphed. In a moment I would turn and acquaint myself with those quick-footed wanderers. . . .

The little brushing kiss fell in the centre of my palm—as a gift on which the fingers were, once, expected, to close: as the all-faithful, half-reproachful signal of a waiting child not used to neglect even when grown-ups were busiest—a fragrant of the muted code devised very long ago.

Then I knew. And it was as though I had known from the first day when I looked across the lawn at the high window.

I heard the door shut. The woman turned to me in silence, and I felt that she knew.

What time passed after this I cannot say. I was roused by the fall of a log, and mechanically rose to put it back. Then I returned to my place in the chair very close to the screen.

'Now you understand,' she whispered, across the packed shadows.

'Yes, I understand—now. Thank you.'

'I—I only hear them.' She bowed her head in her hands. 'I have no right, you know—no other right. I have neither borne nor lost—neither borne nor lost!'

'Be very glad then,' said I, for my soul was torn open within me.

'Forgive me!'

She was still, and I went back to my sorrow and my joy.

'It was because I loved them so,' she said at last, brokenly. '*That* was why it was, even from the first—even before I knew that they—they were all I should ever have. And I loved them so!'

She stretched out her arms to the shadows and the shadows within the shadow.

'They came because I loved them—because I needed them. I—I must have made them come. Was that wrong, think you?'

'No—no.'

'I—I grant you that the toys and—and all that sort of thing were nonsense, but—but I used to so hate empty rooms myself when I was little.' She pointed to the gallery. 'And the passages all empty. . . . And how could I ever bear the garden door shut? Suppose——'

'Don't! For pity's sake, don't!' I cried. The twilight had brought a cold rain with gusty squalls that plucked at the leaded windows.

'And the same thing with keeping the fire in all night. *I* don't think it so foolish—do you?'

—I looked at the broad brick hearth, saw, through tears, I believe, that there was no unpassable iron on or near it, and bowed my head.

'I did all that and lots of other things—just to make believe. Then they came. I heard them, but I didn't know that they were not mine by right till Mrs Madden told me——'

'The butler's wife? What?'

'One of them—I heard—she saw. And knew Hers! *Not* for me. I didn't know at first. Perhaps I was jealous. Afterwards, I began

to understand that it was only because I loved them, not because——
. . . Oh, you *must* bear or lose,' she said piteously. 'There is no other
way—and yet they love me. They must! Don't they?'

There was no sound in the room except the lapping voices of the
fire, but we two listened intently, and she at least took comfort from
what she heard. She recovered herself and half rose. I sat still in my
chair by the screen.

'Don't think me a wretch to whine about myself like this, but—but
I'm all in the dark, you know, and *you* can see.'

In truth I could see, and my vision confirmed me in my resolve,
though that was like the very parting of spirit and flesh. Yet a little
longer I would stay since it was the last time.

'You think it is wrong, then?' she cried sharply, though I had said
nothing.

'Not for you. A thousand times no. For you it is right. . . . I am
grateful to you beyond words. For me it would be wrong. For me
only. . . .'

'Why?' she said, but passed her hand before her face as she had
done at our second meeting in the wood. 'Oh, I see,' she went on
simply as a child. 'For you it would be wrong.' Then with a little
indrawn laugh, 'And, d'you remember, I called you lucky—once—
at first. You who must never come here again!'

She left me to sit a little longer by the screen, and I heard the sound
of her feet die out along the gallery above.

Lord Lytton

The Haunted and the Haunters

A friend of mine, who is a man of letters and a philosopher, said to me one day, as if between jest and earnest—'Fancy! since we last met, I have discovered a haunted house in the midst of London.'

'Really haunted?—and by what?—ghosts?'

'Well, I can't answer these questions—all I know is this—six weeks ago I and my wife were in search of a furnished apartment. Passing a quiet street, we saw on the window of one of the houses a bill, "Apartments Furnished". The situation suited us: we entered the house—liked the rooms—engaged them by the week—and left them the third day. No power on earth could have reconciled my wife to stay longer, and I don't wonder at it.'

'What did you see?'

'Excuse me—I have no desire to be ridiculed as a superstitious dreamer—nor, on the other hand, could I ask you to accept on my affirmation what you would hold to be incredible without the evidence of your own senses. Let me only say this, it was not so much what we saw or heard (in which you might fairly suppose that we were the dupes of our own excited fancy, or the victims of imposture in others) that drove us away, as it was an undefinable terror which seized both of us whenever we passed by the door of a certain un-furnished room, in which we neither saw nor heard anything. And the strangest marvel of all was, that for once in my life I agreed with my wife—silly woman though she be—and allowed, after the third night, that it was impossible to stay a fourth in that house. Accord-ingly, on the fourth morning, I summoned the woman who kept the house and attended on us, and told her that the rooms did not quite suit us, and we would not stay out our week. She said, dryly: "I know why; you have stayed longer than any other lodger; few ever stayed a second night; none before you, a third. But I take it they have been very kind to you."

'"They—who?" I asked, affecting a smile.

'"Why, they who haunt the house, whoever they are. I don't mind them; I remember them many years ago, when I lived in this house, not as a servant; but I know they will be the death of me some day. I don't care—I'm old, and must die soon, anyhow; and then I shall be with them, and in this house still." The woman spoke with so dreary a calmness, that really it was a sort of awe that prevented my conversing with her farther. I paid for my week, and too happy were I and my wife to get off so cheaply.'

'You excite my curiosity,' said I; 'nothing I should like better than to sleep in a haunted house. Pray give me the address of the one which you left so ignominiously.'

My friend gave me the address; and when we parted, I walked straight towards the house thus indicated.

It is situated on the north side of Oxford Street, in a dull but respectable thoroughfare. I found the house shut up—no bill at the window, and no response to my knock. As I was turning away, a beer-boy, collecting pewter pots at the neighbouring areas, said to me, 'Do you want anyone in that house, sir?'

'Yes, I heard it was to let.'

'Let!—why, the woman who kept it is dead—has been dead these three weeks, and no one can be found to stay there, though Mr J—— offered ever so much. He offered mother, who chars for him, £1 a week just to open and shut the windows, and she would not.'

'Would not!—and why?'

—'The house is haunted; and the old woman who kept it was found dead in her bed, with her eyes wide open. They say the devil strangled her.'

'Pooh!—you speak of Mr J——. Is he the owner of the house?'

'Yes.'

'Where does he live?'

'In G—— Street, No. —.'

'What is he?—in any business?'

'No, sir—nothing particular; a single gentleman.'

I gave the pot-boy the gratuity earned by his liberal information, and proceeded to Mr J——, in G—— Street, which was close by the street that boasted the haunted house. I was lucky enough to find Mr J—— at home—an elderly man, with intelligent countenance and prepossessing manners.

I communicated my name and my business frankly. I said I heard the house was considered to be haunted—that I had a strong desire to examine a house with so equivocal a reputation—that I should be greatly obliged if he would allow me to hire it, though only for a night. I was willing to pay for that privilege whatever he might be inclined to ask. 'Sir,' said Mr J——, with great courtesy, 'the house is at your service, for as short or as long a time as you please. Rent is out of the question—the obligation will be on my side should you be able to discover the cause of the strange phenomena which at present deprive it of all value. I cannot let it, for I cannot even get a servant to keep it in order or answer the door. Unluckily the house is haunted, if I may use that expression, not only by night, but by day; though at night the disturbances are of a more unpleasant and sometimes of a more alarming character.

'The poor old woman who died in it three weeks ago was a pauper whom I took out of a workhouse, for in her childhood she had been known to some of my family, and had once been in such good circumstances that she had rented that house of my uncle. She was a woman of superior education and strong mind, and was the only person I could ever induce to remain in the house. Indeed, since her death, which was sudden, and the coroner's inquest, which gave it a notoriety in the neighbourhood, I have so despaired of finding any person to take charge of it, much more a tenant, that I would willingly let it rent free for a year to anyone who would pay its rates and taxes.'

'How long is it since the house acquired this sinister character?'

'That I can scarcely tell you, but very many years since. The old woman I spoke of said it was haunted when she rented it between thirty and forty years ago. The fact is that my life has been spent in the East Indies and in the civil service of the Company. I returned to England last year on inheriting the fortune of an uncle, amongst whose possessions was the house in question. I found it shut up and uninhabited. I was told that it was haunted, that no one would inhabit it. I smiled at what seemed to be so idle a story. I spent some money in repainting and roofing it—added to its old-fashioned furniture a few modern articles—advertised it, and obtained a lodger for a year. He was a colonel retired on half-pay. He came in with his family, a son and a daughter, and four or five servants: they all left the house the next day, and although they deponed that they had all seen something different, that something was equally terrible to all. I really could not in conscience sue, or even blame, the colonel for breach of agreement.

'Then I put in the old women I have spoken of, and she was empowered to let the house in apartments. I never had one lodger who stayed more than three days. I do not tell you their stories—to no two lodgers have there been exactly the same phenomena repeated. It is better that you should judge for yourself, than enter the house with an imagination influenced by previous narratives; only be prepared to see and to hear something or other, and take whatever precautions you yourself please.'

'Have you never had a curiosity yourself to pass a night in that house?'

'Yes. I passed not a night, but three hours in broad daylight alone in that house. My curiosity is not satisfied, but it is quenched. I have no desire to renew the experiment. You cannot complain, you see, sir, that I am not sufficiently candid; and unless your interest be exceedingly eager and your nerves unusually strong, I honestly add that I advise you *not* to pass a night in that house.'

'My interest *is* exceedingly keen,' said I, 'and though only a coward will boast of his nerves in situations wholly unfamiliar to him, yet my nerves have been seasoned in such variety of danger that I have the right to rely on them—even in a haunted house.'

Mr J—— said very little more; he took the keys of the house out of his bureau, gave them to me—and thanking him cordially for his frankness, and his urbane concession to my wish, I carried off my prize.

Impatient for the experiment, as soon as I reached home I summoned my confidential servant—a young man of gay spirits, fearless temper, and as free from superstitious prejudice as anyone I could think of.

'F——,' said I, 'you remember in Germany how disappointed we were at not finding a ghost in that old castle, which was said to be haunted by a headless apparition? Well, I have heard of a house in London which, I have reason to hope, is decidedly haunted. I mean to sleep there tonight. From what I hear, there is no doubt that something will allow itself to be seen or to be heard—something, perhaps, excessively horrible. Do you think, if I take you with me, I may rely on your presence of mind, whatever may happen?'

'Oh, sir! pray trust me,' answered F——, grinning with delight.

'Very well—then here are the keys of the house—this is the address. Go now—select for me any bedroom you please; and since the house has not been inhabited for weeks, make up a good fire—air the bed well—see, of course, that there are candles as well as fuel. Take with you my revolver and my dagger—so much for my weapons—arm yourself equally well; and if we are not a match for a dozen ghosts, we shall be but a sorry couple of Englishmen.'

—I was engaged for the rest of the day on business so urgent that I had not leisure to think much on the nocturnal adventure to which

I had plighted my honour. I dined alone, and very late, and while dining, read, as is my habit. The volume I selected was one of Macaulay's Essays. I thought to myself that I would take the book with me; there was so much of healthfulness in the style, and practical life in the subjects, that it would serve as an antidote against the influences of superstitious fancy.

Accordingly, about half-past nine, I put the book into my pocket, and strolled leisurely towards the haunted house. I took with me a favourite dog—an exceedingly sharp, bold, and vigilant bull-terrier —a dog fond of prowling about strange ghostly corners and passages at night in search of rats—a dog of dogs for a ghost.

It was a summer night, but chilly, the sky somewhat gloomy and overcast. Still, there was a moon—faint and sickly, but still a moon —and if the clouds permitted, after midnight it would be brighter.

I reached the house, knocked, and my servant opened with a cheerful smile.

'All right, sir, and very comfortable.'

'Oh!' said I, rather disappointed; 'have you not seen nor heard anything remarkable?'

'Well, sir, I must own I have heard something queer.'

'What?—what?'

'The sound of feet pattering behind me; and once or twice small noises like whispers close at my ear—nothing more.'

'You are not at all frightened?'

'I! not a bit of it, sir'; and the man's bold look reassured me on one point—viz. that, happen what might, he would not desert me.

We were in the hall, the street-door closed, and my attention was now drawn to my dog. He had at first ran in eagerly enough, but had sneaked back to the door, and was scratching and whining to get out. After patting him on the head, and encouraging him gently, the dog seemed to reconcile himself to the situation and followed me and F—— through the house, but keeping close at my heels instead of hurrying inquisitively in advance, which was his usual and normal habit in all strange places. We first visited the subterranean apartments, the kitchen and other offices, and especially the cellars, in which last there were two or three bottles of wine still left in a bin, covered with cobwebs, and evidently, by their appearance, undisturbed for many years. It was clear that the ghosts were not winebibbers.

For the rest we discovered nothing of interest. There was a gloomy little backward, with very high walls. The stones of this yard were very damp—and what with the damp, and what with the dust and smoke-grime on the pavement, our feet left a slight impression where we passed. And now appeared the first strange phenomenon witnessed by myself in this strange abode. I saw, just before me, the print of a foot suddenly form itself, as it were. I stopped, caught hold of my servant, and pointed to it. In advance of that footprint as suddenly dropped another. We both saw it. I advanced quickly to the place; the footprint kept advancing before me, a small footprint—the foot of a child: the impression was too faint thoroughly to distinguish the shape, but it seemed to us both that it was the print of a naked foot. This phenomenon ceased when we arrived at the opposite wall, nor did it repeat itself on returning.

We remounted the stairs, and entered the rooms on the ground floor, a dining parlour, a small back-parlour, and a still smaller third room that had been probably appropriate to a footman—all still as death. We then visited the drawing-rooms, which seemed fresh and new. In the front room I seated myself in an armchair. F—— placed on the table the candlestick with which he had lighted us. I told him to shut the door. As he turned to do so, a chair opposite to me moved from the wall quickly and noiselessly, and dropped itself about a yard from my own chair, immediately fronting it.

'Why, this is better than the turning-tables,' said I, with a half-laugh—and as I laughed, my dog put back his head and howled.

F——, coming back, had not observed the movement of the chair. He employed himself now in stilling the dog. I continued to gaze on the chair, and fancied I saw on it a pale blue misty outline of a human figure, but an outline so indistinct that I could only distrust my own vision. The dog now was quiet. 'Put back that chair opposite to me,' said I to F——; 'put it back to the wall.'

F—— obeyed. 'Was that you, sir?' said he, turning abruptly.

'I—what!'

'Why, something struck me. I felt it sharply on the shoulder—just here.'

'No,' said I. 'But we have jugglers present, and though we may not discover their tricks, we shall catch *them* before they frighten *us*.'

We did not stay long in the drawing-rooms—in fact, they felt so damp and so chilly that I was glad to get to the fire upstairs. We locked the doors of the drawing-rooms—a precaution which, I should observe, we had taken with all the rooms we had searched below. The bedroom my servant had selected for me was the best on the floor—a large one, with two windows fronting the street. The four-posted bed, which took up no inconsiderable space, was opposite to the fire, which burned clear and bright; a door in the wall to the left, between the bed and the window, communicated with the room which my servant appropriated to himself.

This last was a small room with sofa-bed, and had no communication with the landing-place—no other door but that which conducted to the bedroom I was to occupy. On either side of my fireplace was a cupboard, without locks, flushed with the wall, and covered with the same dull-brown paper. We examined these cupboards—only hooks to suspend female dresses—nothing else; we sounded the walls—evidently solid—the outer walls of the building. Having finished the survey of these apartments, warmed myself a few moments, and lighted my cigar, I then, still accompanied by F——, went forth to complete my reconnoitre. In the landing-place there was another door; it was closed firmly. 'Sir,' said my servant in surprise, 'I unlocked this door with all the others when I first came; it cannot have got locked from the inside, for it is a——'

Before he had finished his sentence the door, which neither of us then was touching, opened quietly of itself. We looked at each other a single instant. The same thought seized both—some human agency might be detected here. I rushed in first, my servant followed. A small blank dreary room without furniture—a few empty boxes and hampers in a corner—a small window—the shutters closed—not even a fireplace—no other door but that by which we had entered—no carpet on the floor, and the floor seemed very old, uneven, worm-eaten, mended here and there, as was shown by the whiter patches on the wood; but no living being, and no visible place in which a living being could have hidden. As we stood gazing around, the door by which we had entered closed as quietly as it had before opened: we were imprisoned.

For the first time I felt a creep of undefinable horror. Not so my servant. 'Why, they don't think to trap us, sir; I could break that trumpery door with a kick of my foot.'

'Try first if it will open to your hand,' said I, shaking off the vague apprehension that had seized me, 'while I open the shutters and see what is without.'

I unbarred the shutters—the window looked on the little backyard I have before described; there was no ledge without—nothing but sheer descent. No man getting out of that window would have found any footing till he had fallen on the stones below.

F——, meanwhile, was vainly attempting to open the door. He now turned round to me, and asked my permission to use force. And I should here state, in justice to the servant, that, far from evincing any superstitious terrors, his nerve, composure, and even gaiety amidst circumstances so extraordinary compelled my admiration, and made me congratulate myself on having secured a companion in every way fitted to the occasion. I willingly gave him the permission he required. But though he was a remarkably strong man, his force was as idle as his milder efforts; the door did not even shake to his stoutest kick. Breathless and panting, he desisted. I then tried the door myself, equally in vain.

As I ceased from the effort, again that creep of horror came over me; but this time it was more cold and stubborn. I felt as if some strange and ghastly exhalation were rising up from the chinks of that rugged floor, and filling the atmosphere with a venomous influence hostile to human life. The door now very slowly and quietly opened as of its own accord. We precipitated ourselves into the landing-place. We both saw a large pale light—as large as the human figure, but shapeless and unsubstantial—move before us, and ascend the stairs that led from the landing into the attics. I followed the light, and my servant followed me. It entered, to the right of the landing, a small garret, of which the door stood open. I entered in the same instant. The light then collapsed into a small globule, exceedingly brilliant and vivid; rested a moment on a bed in the corner, quivered, and vanished. We approached the bed and examined it—a half-tester, such as is commonly found in attics devoted to servants. On the drawers that stood near it we perceived an old faded silk kerchief, with the needle still left in a rent half repaired. The kerchief was covered with dust; probably it had belonged to the old woman who had last died in that house, and this might have been her sleeping-room.

I had sufficient curiosity to open the drawers; there were a few odds and ends of female dress, and two letters tied round with a narrow ribbon of faded yellow. I took the liberty to possess myself of the letters. We found nothing else in the room worth noticing—nor did the light reappear; but we distinctly heard, as we turned to go, a pattering footfall on the floor—just before us. We went through the other attics (in all, four), the footfall still preceding us. Nothing to be seen—nothing but the footfall heard. I had the letters in my hand; just as I was descending the stairs I distinctly felt my wrist seized, and a faint, soft effort made to draw the letters from my clasp. I only held them the more tightly, and the effort ceased.

We regained the bedchamber appropriated to myself, and I then remarked that my dog had not followed us when we had left it. He was thrusting himself close to the fire, and trembling. I was impatient to examine the letters; and while I read them, my servant opened a little box in which he had deposited the weapons I had ordered him to bring, took them out, placed them on a table close at my bed-head, and then occupied himself in soothing the dog, who, however, seemed to heed him very little.

The letters were short—they were dated; the dates exactly thirty-five years ago. They were evidently from a lover to his mistress, or a husband to some young wife. Not only the terms of expression, but a distinct reference to a former voyage indicated the writer to have been a seafarer. The spelling and handwriting were those of a man imperfectly educated, but still the language itself was forcible. In the expressions of endearment there was a kind of rough wild love; but here and there were dark unintelligible hints at some secret not of love—some secret that seemed of crime. 'We ought to love each other,' was one of the sentences I remember, 'for how everyone else would execrate us if all was known.' Again: 'Don't let anyone be in the same room with you at night—you talk in your sleep.' And again: 'What's done can't be undone; and I tell you there's nothing against us unless the dead could come to life.' Here there was under-lined in a better handwriting (a female's), 'They do!' At the end of the letter latest in date the same female hand had written these words: 'Lost at sea the 4th of June, the same day as——'

I put down the letters, and began to muse over their contents.

Fearing, however, that the train of thought into which I fell might unsteady my nerves, I fully determined to keep my mind in a fit state to cope with whatever of marvellous the advancing night might bring forth. I roused myself—laid the letters on the table—stirred up the fire, which was still bright and cheering—and opened my volume of Macaulay. I read quietly enough till about half-past eleven. I then threw myself dressed upon the bed, and told my servant he might retire to his own room, but must keep himself awake. I bade him leave open the door between the two rooms. Thus alone, I kept two candles burning on the table by my bed-head. I placed my watch beside the weapons, and calmly resumed my Macaulay.

Opposite to me the fire burned clear; and on the hearth-rug, seemingly asleep, lay the dog. In about twenty minutes I felt an exceedingly cold air pass by my cheek, like a sudden draught. I fancied the door to my right, communicating with the landing-place, must have got open; but no—it was closed. I then turned my glance to my left, and saw the flame of the candles violently swayed as by a wind. At the same moment the watch beside the revolver softly slid from the table—softly, softly—no visible hand—it was gone. I sprang up, seizing the revolver with the one hand, the dagger with the other; I was not willing that my weapons should share the fate of the watch. Thus armed, I looked round the floor—no sign of the watch. Three slow, loud, distinct knocks were now heard at the bed-head; my servant called out, 'Is that you, sir?'

'No; be on your guard.'

The dog now roused himself and sat on his haunches, his ears moving quickly backwards and forwards. He kept his eyes fixed on me with a look so strange that he concentrated all my attention on himself. Slowly he rose up, all his hair bristling, and stood perfectly rigid, and with the same wild stare. I had no time, however, to examine the dog. Presently my servant emerged from his room; and if ever I saw horror in the human face, it was then. I should not have recognized him had we met in the streets, so altered was every lineament. He passed by me quickly, saying in a whisper that seemed scarcely to come from his lips, 'Run—run! it is after me!' He gained the door to the landing, pulled it open, and rushed forth. I followed him into the landing involuntarily, calling him to stop; but, without heeding me, he bounded down the stairs, clinging to the balusters, and taking several steps at a time. I heard, where I stood, the street door open—heard it again clap to. I was left alone in the haunted house.

It was but for a moment that I remained undecided whether or not to follow my servant; pride and curiosity alike forbade so dastardly a flight. I re-entered my room, closing the door after me, and proceeded cautiously into the interior chamber. I encountered nothing to justify my servants terror. I again carefully examined the walls, to see if there were any concealed door. I could find no trace of one—not even a seam in the dull-brown paper with which the room was hung. How, then, had the Thing, whatever it was, which had so scared him, obtained ingress except through my own chamber?

I returned to my room, shut and locked the door that opened upon the interior one, and stood on the hearth, expectant and prepared. I now perceived that the dog had slunk into an angle of the wall, and was pressing himself close against it, as if literally trying to force his way into it. I approached the animal and spoke to it; the poor brute was evidently beside itself with terror. It showed all its teeth, the slaver dropping from its jaws, and would certainly have bitten me if I had touched it. It did not seem to recognize me. Whoever has seen at the Zoological Gardens a rabbit fascinated by a serpent, cowering in a corner, may form some idea of the anguish which the dog exhibited. Finding all efforts to soothe the animal in vain, and fearing that his bite might be as venomous in that state as if in the madness of hydrophobia, I left him alone, placed my weapons on the table beside the fire, seated myself, and recommenced my Macaulay.

Perhaps in order not to appear seeking credit for a courage, or rather a coolness, which the reader may conceive I exaggerate, I may be pardoned if I pause to indulge in one or two egotistical remarks.

As I hold presence of mind, or what is called courage, to be precisely proportioned to familiarity with the circumstance that lead to it, so I should say that I had been long sufficiently familiar with all experiments that appertain to the Marvellous. I had witnessed many very extraordinary phenomena in various parts of the world—phenomena that would be either totally disbelieved if I stated them, or ascribed to supernatural agencies. Now, my theory is that the Supernatural is the Impossible, and that what is called supernatural is only a something in the laws of nature of which we have been hitherto ignorant. Therefore, if a ghost rise before me, I have not the right to say, 'So, then, the supernatural is possible,' but rather, 'So, then, the apparition of a ghost is, contrary to received opinion, within the laws of nature—*i.e.* not supernatural.'

Now, in all that I had hitherto witnessed, and indeed in all the wonders which the amateurs of mystery in our age record as facts, a material living agency is always required. On the Continent you will find still magicians who assert that they can raise spirits. Assume for the moment that they assert truly, still the living material form of the magician is present; and he is the material agency by which from some constitutional peculiarities, certain strange phenomena are represented to your natural senses.

Accept again, as truthful, the tales of Spirit Manifestation in America—musical or other sounds—writings on paper, produced by no discernible hand—articles of furniture moved without apparent human agency—or the actual sight and touch of hands, to which no bodies seem to belong—still there must be found the *medium* or living being, with constitutional peculiarities capable of obtaining these signs. In fine, in all such marvels, supposing even that there is no imposture, there must be a human being like ourselves, by whom, or through whom, the effects presented to human beings are produced. It is so with the now familiar phenomena of mesmerism or electro-biology; the mind of the person operated on is affected through a material living agent. Nor, supposing it true that a mesmerised patient can respond to the will or passes of a mesmeriser a hundred miles distant, is the response less occasioned by a material being; it may be through a material fluid—call it

Electric, call it Odic, call it what you will—which has the power of traversing space and passing obstacles, that the material effect is communicated from one to the other.

Hence all that I had hitherto witnessed, or expected to witness, in this strange house, I believed to be occasioned through some agency or medium as mortal as myself; and this idea necessarily prevented the awe with which those who regard as supernatural things that are not within the ordinary operations of nature, might have been impressed by the adventures of that memorable night.

As, then, it was my conjecture that all that was presented, or would be presented, to my senses, must originate in some human being gifted by constitution with the power so to present them, and having some motive so to do, I felt an interest in my theory which, in its way, was rather philosophical than superstitious. And I can sincerely say that I was in as tranquil a temper for observation as any practical experimentalist could be in awaiting the effects of some rare though perhaps perilous chemical combination. Of course, the more I kept my mind detached from fancy, the more the temper fitted for observation would be obtained; and I therefore riveted eye and thought on the strong daylight sense in the page of my Macaulay.

I now became aware that something interposed between the page and the light—the page was overshadowed; I looked up, and I saw what I shall find it very difficult, perhaps impossible, to describe.

It was a Darkness shaping itself out of the air in very undefined outline. I cannot say it was of a human form, and yet it had more resemblance to a human form, or rather shadow, than anything else. As it stood, wholly apart and distinct from the air and the light around it, its dimensions seemed gigantic, the summit nearly touching the ceiling. While I gazed, a feeling of intense cold seized me. An iceberg before me could not more have chilled me; nor could the cold of an iceberg have been more purely physical. I feel convinced that it was not the cold caused by fear. As I continued to gaze, I thought—but this I cannot say with precision—that I distinguished two eyes looking down on me from the height. One moment I seemed to distinguish them clearly, the next they seemed gone; but still two rays of a pale-blue light frequently shot through the darkness, as from the height on which I half-believed, half-doubted, that I had encountered the eyes.

I strove to speak—my voice utterly failed me; I could only think to myself, 'Is this fear? it is *not* fear!' I strove to rise—in vain; I felt as if weighed down by an irresistible force. Indeed, my impression was that of an immense and overwhelming Power opposed to my volition; that sense of utter inadequacy to cope with a force beyond men's, which one may feel *physically* in a storm at sea, in a conflagration, or when confronting some terrible wild beast, or rather, perhaps, the shark of the ocean, I felt *morally*. Opposed to my will was another will, as far superior to its strength as storm, fire, and shark are superior in material force to the force of men.

And now, as this impression grew on me, now came, at last, horror—horror to a degree that no words can convey. Still I retained pride, if not courage; and in my own mind I said, 'This is horror, but it is not fear; unless I fear, I cannot be harmed; my reason rejects this thing; it is an illusion—I do not fear.' With a violent effort I succeeded at least in stretching out my hand towards the weapon on the table; as I did so, on the arm and shoulder I received a strange shock, and my arm fell to my side powerless. And now, to add to my horror, the light began slowly to wane from the candles—they were not, as it were, extinguished, but their flame seemed very gradually withdrawn; it was the same with the fire—the light was extracted from the fuel; in a few minutes the room was in utter darkness.

The dread that came over me, to be thus in the dark with that dark Thing, whose power was so intensely felt, brought a reaction of nerve. In fact, terror had reached that climax, that either my senses must have deserted me, or I must have burst through the spell. I did burst through it. I found voice, though the voice was a shriek. I remember that I broke forth with words like these—'I do not fear, my soul does not fear'; and at the same time I found the strength to rise. Still in that profound gloom I rushed to one of the windows—tore aside the curtain—flung open the shutters; my first thought was—LIGHT. And when I saw the moon high, clear, and calm, I felt a joy that almost compensated for the previous terror. There was the moon, there was also the light from the gas-lamps in the deserted slumberous street. I turned to look back into the room; the moon penetrated its shadow very palely and partially—but still there was light. The dark Thing, whatever it might be, was gone—except that I could yet see a dim shadow which seemed the shadow of that shade, against the opposite wall.

My eye now rested on the table, and from under the table (which was without cloth or cover—an old mahogany round table) there rose a hand, visible as far as the wrist. It was a hand, seemingly, as much of flesh and blood as my own, but the hand of an aged person —lean, wrinkled, small too—a woman's hand.

That hand very softly closed on the two letters that lay on the table: hand and letters both vanished. There then came the same three loud measured knocks I had heard at the bed-head before this extraordinary drama had commenced.

As those sounds slowly ceased, I felt the whole room vibrate sensibly; and at the far end there rose, as from the floor, sparks or globules like bubbles of light, many-coloured—green, yellow, fire-red, azure. Up and down, to and fro, hither, thither, as tiny will-o'-the-wisps, the sparks moved, slow or swift, each at its own caprice. A chair (as in the drawing-room below) was now advanced from the wall without apparent agency, and placed at the opposite side of the table. Suddenly, as forth from the chair, there grew a shape—a woman's shape. It was distinct as a shape of life—ghastly as a shape of death. The face was that of youth, with a strange mournful beauty; the throat and shoulders were bare, the rest of the form in a loose robe of cloudy white. It began sleeking its long yellow hair, which fell over its shoulders; its eyes were not turned towards me, but to the door; it seemed listening, watching, waiting. The shadow of the shade in the background grew darker; and again I thought I beheld the eyes gleaming out from the summit of the shadow—eyes fixed upon that shape.

As if from the door, though it did not open, there grew out another shape equally distinct, equally ghastly—a man's shape—a young man's. It was in the dress of the last century, or rather in a likeness of such dress; for both the male shape and the female, though defined, were evidently unsubstantial, impalpable—sim-ulacra—phantasms; and there was something incongruous, grotes-que, yet fearful, in the contrast between the elaborate finery, the courtly precision of that old-fashioned garb, with its ruffles and lace and buckles, and the corpse-like aspect and ghost-like stillness of the flitting wearer. Just as the male shape approached the female, the dark Shadow started from the wall, all three for a moment wrapped in darkness. When the pale light returned, the two phantoms were as if in the grasp of the Shadow that towered between them; and there was a bloodstain on the breast of the female; and the phantom-male was leaning on its phantom-sword, and blood seemed trickling fast from the ruffles, from the lace; and the darkness of the inter-mediate Shadow swallowed them up—they were gone. And again the bubbles of light shot, and sailed, and undulated, growing thicker and thicker and more wildly confused in their movements.

The closet-door to the right of the fireplace now opened, and from the aperture there came the form of a woman, aged. In her hand she held letters—the very letters over which I had seen *the* Hand close; and behind her I heard a footstep. She turned round as if to listen, then she opened the letters and seemed to read; and over her shoulder I saw a livid face, the face of a man long drowned—bloated, bleached—seaweed tangled in its dripping hair; and at her feet lay a form as of a corpse and beside the corpse there cowered a child, a miserable, squalid child, with famine in its cheeks and fear in its eyes. And as I looked in the old woman's face, the wrinkles and lines vanished, and it became a face of youth—hard-eyed, stony, but still youth; and the Shadow darted forth, and darkened over these phantoms as it had darkened over the last.

Nothing now was left but the Shadow, and on that my eyes were intently fixed, till again eyes grew out of the Shadow—malignant, serpent eyes. And the bubbles of light again rose and fell, and in their disordered, irregular, turbulent maze, mingled with the wan moonlight. And now from these globules themselves as from the shell of an egg, monstrous things burst out; the air grew filled with them; larvæ so bloodless and so hideous that I can in no way describe them except to remind the reader of the swarming life which the solar microscope brings before his eyes in a drop of water—things transparent, supple, agile, chasing each other, devouring each other—forms like nought ever beheld by the naked eye. As the shapes were without symmetry, so their movements were without order. In their very vagrancies there was no sport; they came round me and round, thicker and faster and swifter, swarming over my head, crawling over my right arm, which was outstretched in involuntary command against all evil beings.

Sometimes I felt myself touched, but not by them; invisible hands touched me. Once I felt the clutch as of cold soft fingers at my throat. I was still equally conscious that if I gave way to fear I should be in bodily peril; and I concentrated all my faculties in the single focus of resisting, stubborn will. And I turned my sight from the Shadow—above all, from those strange serpent eyes—eyes that had now become distinctly visible. For there, though in nought else around me, I was aware that there was a *will*, and a will of intense, creative, working evil, which might crush down my own.

The pale atmosphere in the room began now to redden as if in the air of some near conflagration. The larvæ grew lurid as things that live in fire. Again the room vibrated; again were heard the three measured knocks; and again all things were swallowed up in the darkness of the dark Shadow, as if out of that darkness all had come, into that darkness all returned.

As the gloom receded, the Shadow was wholly gone. Slowly as it had been withdrawn, the flame grew again into the candles on the table, again into the fuel in the grate. The whole room came once more calmly, healthfully into sight.

The two doors were still closed, the door communicating with the servants' room still locked. In the corner of the wall, into which he had so convulsively niched himself, lay the dog. I called to him—no movement; I approached—the animal was dead; his eyes protruded; his tongue out of his mouth; the froth gathered round his jaws. I took him in my arms; I brought him to the fire; I felt acute grief for the loss of my poor favourite—acute self-reproach; I accused myself of his death; I imagined he had died of fright. But what was my surprise on finding that his neck was broken—actually twisted out of the vertebræ. Had this been done in the dark?—must it not have been by a hand human as mine?—must there not have been a human agency all the while in that room? Good cause to suspect it. I cannot tell. I cannot do more than state the fact fairly; the reader may draw his own inference.

Another surprising circumstance—my watch was restored to the table from which it had been so mysteriously withdrawn; but it had stopped at the very moment it was so withdrawn; nor, despite all the skill of the watchmaker, has it ever gone since—that is, it will go in a strange erratic way for a few hours, and then comes to a dead stop —it is worthless.

Nothing more chanced for the rest of the night. Nor, indeed, had I long to wait before the dawn broke. Not till it was broad daylight did I quit the haunted house. Before I did so, I revisited the little blind room in which my servant and myself had been for a time imprisoned. I had a strong impression—for which I could not account—that from that room had originated the mechanism of the phenomena—if I may use the term—which had been experienced in my chamber. And though I entered it now in the clear day, with the sun peering through the filmy window, I still felt, as I stood on its floor, the creep of the horror which I had first there experienced the night before, and which had been so aggravated by what had passed in my own chamber. I could not, indeed, bear to stay more than half a minute within those walls. I descended the stairs, and again I heard the footfall before me; and when I opened the street door, I thought I could distinguish a very low laugh. I gained my own home, expecting to find my runaway servant there. But he had not presented himself; nor did I hear more of him for three days, when I received a letter from him, dated from Liverpool, to this effect:

'HONOURED SIR,—I humbly entreat your pardon, though I can scarcely hope that you will think I deserve it, unless—which Heaven forbid!—you saw what I did. I feel that it will be years before I can recover myself; and as to being fit for service, it is out of the question. I am therefore going to my brother-in-law at Melbourne. The ship sails tomorrow. Perhaps the long voyage may set me up. I do nothing now but start and tremble, and fancy It is behind me. I humbly beg you, honoured sir, to order my clothes, and whatever wages are due to me, to be sent to my mother's, at Walworth—John knows her address.'

The letter ended with additional apologies, somewhat incoherent, and explanatory details as to effects that had been under the writer's charge.

This flight may perhaps warrant a suspicion that the man wished to go to Australia, and had been somehow or other fraudulently mixed up with the events of the night. I say nothing in refutation of that conjecture; rather, I suggest it as one that would seem to many persons the most probable solution of improbable occurrences. My own theory remained unshaken. I returned in the evening to the house, to bring away in a hack cab the things I had left there, with my poor dog's body. In this task I was not disturbed, nor did any incident worth note befall me, except that still, on ascending, and descending the stairs I heard the same footfall in advance. On leaving the house, I went to Mr J——'s. He was at home. I returned him the keys, told him that my curiosity was sufficiently gratified, and was about to relate quickly what had passed, when he stopped me, and said, though with much politeness, that he had no longer any interest in a mystery which none had ever solved.

I determined at least to tell him of the two letters I had read, as well as of the extraordinary manner in which they had disappeared, and I then inquired if he thought they had been addressed to the woman who had died in the house, and if there were anything in her early history which could possibly confirm the dark suspicions to which the letters gave rise. Mr J—— seemed startled, and, after musing a few moments, answered, 'I know but little of the woman's earlier history, except, as I before told you, that her family were known to mine. But you revive some vague reminiscences to her prejudice. I will make inquiries, and inform you of their result. Still, even if we could admit the popular superstition that a person who had been either the perpetrator or the victim of dark crimes in life could revisit, as a restless spirit, the scene in which those crimes had been committed, I should observe that the house was infested by strange sights and sounds before the old woman died—you smile—what would you say?'

'I would say this, that I am convinced, if we could get to the bottom of these mysteries, we should find a living human agency.'

'What! you believe it is all an imposture? For what object?'

'Not an imposture in the ordinary sense of the word. If suddenly I were to sink into a deep sleep, from which you could not awake me, but in that sleep could answer questions with an accuracy which I could not pretend to when awake—tell you what money you had in your pocket—nay, describe your very thoughts—it is not necessarily an imposture, any more than it is necessarily supernatural. I should be, unconsciously to myself, under a mesmeric influence, conveyed to me from a distance by a human being who had acquired power over me by previous *rapport*.'

'Granting mesmerism, so far carried, to be a fact, you are right. And you would infer from this that a mesmeriser might produce the extraordinary effects you and others have witnessed over inanimate objects—fill the air with sights and sounds?'

'Or impress our senses with the belief in them—we never having been *en rapport* with the person acting on us? No. What is commonly called mesmerism could not do this; but there may be a power akin to mesmerism, and superior to it—the power that in the old days was called Magic. That such a power may extend to all inanimate objects of matter, I do not say; but if so, it would not be against nature, only a rare power in nature which might be given to constitutions with certain peculiarities, and cultivated by practice to an extraordinary degree. That such a power might extend over the dead —that is, over certain thoughts and memories that the dead may still retain—and compel, not that which ought properly to be called the *soul*, and which is far beyond human reach, but rather a phantom of what has been most earth-stained on earth, to make itself apparent to our senses—is a very ancient though obsolete theory, upon which I will hazard no opinion. But I do not conceive the power would be supernatural.

'Let me illustrate what I mean from an experiment which Paracelsus describes as not difficult, and which the author of the *Curiosities of Literature* cites as credible: A flower perishes; you burn it. Whatever were the elements of that flower while it lived are gone, dispersed, you know not whither; you can never discover nor recollect them. But you can, by chemistry, out of the burnt dust of that flower, raise a spectrum of the flower, just as it seemed in life. It may be the same with the human being. The soul has so much escaped you as the essence of elements of the flower. Still you may make a spectrum of it. And this phantom, though in the popular superstition it is held to be the soul of the departed, must not be confounded with the true soul; it is but the eidolon of the dead form.

'Hence, like the best-attested stories of ghosts or spirits, the thing that most strikes us is the absence of what we hold to be soul—that is, of superior emancipated intelligence. They come for little or no object—they seldom speak, if they do come; they utter no ideas above that of an ordinary person on earth. These American spirit-seers have published volumes of communications in prose and verse, which they assert to be given in the names of the most illustrious dead—Shakespeare, Bacon—heaven knows whom. Those communications, taking the best, are certainly not a whit of higher order than would be communications from living persons of fair talent and education; they are wondrously inferior to what Bacon, Shakespeare, and Plato said and wrote when on earth.

'Nor, what is more notable, do they ever contain an idea that was not on the earth before. Wonderful, therefore, as such phenomena may be (granting them to be truthful), I see much that philosophy may question, nothing that it is incumbent on philosophy to deny—viz. nothing supernatural. They are but ideas conveyed somehow or other (we have not yet discovered the means) from one mortal brain to another. Whether, in so doing, tables walk of their own accord, or fiend-like shapes appear in a magic circle, or bodyless hands rise and remove material objects, or a Thing of Darkness, such as presented itself to me, freeze our blood—still am I persuaded that these are but agencies conveyed, as by electric wires, to my own brain from the brain of another. In some constitutions there is a natural chemistry, and those may produce chemic wonders—in others a natural fluid, call it electricity, and these produce electric wonders. But they differ in this from Normal Science—they are alike objectless, purposeless, puerile, frivolous. They lead on to no grand results; and therefore the world does not heed, and true sages have not cultivated them. But sure I am, that of all I saw or heard, a man, human as myself, was the remote originator; and I believe unconsciously to himself as to the exact effects produced, for this reason: no two persons, you say, have ever told you that they experienced exactly the same thing. Well, observe, no two persons ever experience exactly the same dream. If this were an ordinary imposture, the machinery would be arranged for results that would but little vary; if it were a supernatural agency permitted by the Almighty, it would surely be for some definite end.

'These phenomena belong to neither class; my persuasion is, that they originate in some brain now far distant; that that brain had no distinct volition in anything that occurred; that what does occur reflects but its devious, motley, ever-shifting, half-formed thoughts; in short, that it has been but the dreams of such a brain put into action and invested with a semi-substance. That this brain is of immense power, that it can set matter into movement, that it is malignant and destructive, I believe: some material force must have killed my dog; it might, for aught I know, have sufficed to kill myself, had I been as subjugated by terror as the dog—had my intellect or my spirit given me no countervailing resistance in my will.'

'It killed your dog! that is fearful! indeed, it is strange that no animal can be induced to stay in that house; not even a cat. Rats and mice are never found in it.'

'The instincts of the brute creation detect influences deadly to their existence. Man's reason has a sense less subtle, because it has a resisting power more supreme. But enough; do you comprehend my theory?'

'Yes, though imperfectly—and I accept any crotchet (pardon the word), however odd, rather than embrace at once the notion of ghosts and hobgoblins we imbibed in our nurseries. Still, to my unfortunate house the evil is the same. What on earth can I do with the house?'

'I will tell you what I would do. I am convinced from my own internal feelings that the small unfurnished room at right angles to the door of the bedroom which I occupied, forms a starting-point or receptacle for the influences which haunt the house; and I strongly advise you to have the walls opened, the floor removed—nay, the whole room pulled down. I observe that it is detached from the body of the house, built over the small back-yard, and could be removed without injury to the rest of the building.'

'And you think, if I did that——'

'You would cut off the telegraph wires. Try it. I am so persuaded that I am right, that I will pay half the expense if you will allow me to direct the operations.'

'Nay, I am well able to afford the cost; for the rest, allow me to write to you.'

About ten days afterwards I received a letter from Mr J——, telling me that he had visited the house since I had seen him; that he had found the two letters I had described, replaced in the drawer from which I had taken them; that he had read them with misgivings like my own; that he had instituted a cautious inquiry about the woman to whom I rightly conjectured they had been written. It

141

seemed that thirty-six years ago (a year before the date of the letters), she had married against the wish of her relatives, an American of very suspicious character; in fact, he was generally believed to have been a pirate. She herself was the daughter of very respectable tradespeople, and had served in the capacity of a nursery governess before her marriage. She had a brother, a widower, who was considered wealthy, and who had one child of about six years old. A month after the marriage, the body of this brother was found in the Thames, near London Bridge; there seemed some marks of violence about his throat, but they were not deemed sufficient to warrant the inquest in any other verdict than that of 'found drowned'.

The American and his wife took charge of the little boy, the deceased brother having by his will left his sister the guardian of his only child—and in the event of the child's death, the sister inherited. The child died about six months afterwards—it was supposed to have been neglected and ill-treated. The neighbours deposed to have heard it shriek at night. The surgeon who had examined it after death, said that it was emaciated as if from want of nourishment, and the body was covered with livid bruises. It seemed that one winter night the child had sought to escape—crept out into the back-yard—tried to scale the wall—fallen back exhausted, and been found at morning on the stones in a dying state. But though there was some evidence of cruelty, there was none of murder; and the aunt and her husband had sought to palliate cruelty by alleging the exceeding stubbornness and perversity of the child, who was declared to be half-witted. Be that as it may, at the orphan's death the aunt inherited her brother's fortune.

Before the first wedded year was out, the American quitted England abruptly, and never returned to it. He obtained a cruising vessel, which was lost in the Atlantic two years afterwards. The widow was left in affluence; but reverses of various kinds had befallen her: a bank broke—an investment failed—she went into a small business and became insolvent—then she entered into service, sinking lower and lower, from housekeeper down to maid-of-all-work—never long retaining a place, though nothing peculiar against her character was ever alleged. She was considered sober, honest, and peculiarly quiet in her ways; still nothing prospered with her. And so she had dropped into the workhouse, from which Mr J—— had taken her, to be placed in charge of the very house which she had rented as a mistress in the first year of her wedded life.

Mr J—— added that he had passed an hour alone in the unfurnished room which I had urged him to destroy, and that his impressions of dread while there were so great, though he had neither heard nor seen anything, that he was eager to have the walls bared and the floors removed as I had suggested. He had engaged persons for the work, and would commence any day I would name.

The day was accordingly fixed. I repaired to the haunted house— we went into the blind dreary room, took up the skirting, and then the floors. Under the rafters, covered with rubbish, was found a trap-door, quite large enough to admit a man. It was closely nailed down, with clamps and rivets of iron. On removing these we descended into a room below, the existence of which had never been suspected. In this room there had been a window and a flue, but they had been bricked over, evidently for many years. By the help of candles we examined this place; it still retained some mouldering furniture—three chairs, an oak settle, a table—all of the fashion of about eighty years ago. There was a chest of drawers against the wall, in which we found, half-rotted away, old-fashioned articles of a man's dress, such as might have been worn eighty or a hundred years ago by a gentleman of some rank—costly steel buckles and buttons, like those yet worn in court dresses—a handsome court sword—in a waistcoat which had once been rich with gold lace, but which was now blackened and foul with damp, we found five guineas, a few silver coins, and an ivory ticket, probably for some place of entertainment long since passed away. But our main discovery was in a kind of iron safe fixed to the wall, the lock of which it cost us much trouble to get picked.

In this safe were three shelves and two small drawers. Ranged on the shelves were several small bottles of crystal, hermetically stopped. They contained colourless volatile essences, of what nature I shall say no more than that they were not poisons—phosphor and ammonia entered into some of them. There were also some very curious glass tubes, and a small pointed rod of iron, with a large lump of rock-crystal, and another of amber—also a loadstone of great power.

In one of the drawers we found a miniature portrait set in gold, and retaining the freshness of its colours most remarkably, considering the length of time it had probably been there. The portrait was that of a man who might be somewhat advanced in middle life, perhaps forty-seven or forty-eight.

It was a most peculiar face—a most impressive face. If you could fancy some mighty serpent transformed into man, preserving in the human lineaments the old serpent type, you would have a better idea of that countenance than long descriptions can convey: the width

and flatness of frontal—the tapering elegance of contour disguising
the strength of the deadly jaw—the long, large, terrible eye, glittering
and green as the emerald—and withal a certain ruthless calm, as if
from the consciousness of an immense power. The strange thing was
this—the instant I saw the miniature I recognized a startling likeness
to one of the rarest portraits in the world—the portrait of a man of
a rank only below that of royalty, who in his own day had made a
considerable noise. History says little or nothing of him; but search
the correspondence of his contemporaries, and you find reference to
his wild daring, his bold profligacy, his restless spirit, his taste for the
occult sciences. While still in the meridian of life he died and was
buried, so say the chronicles, in a foreign land. He died in time to
escape the grasp of the law, for he was accused of crimes which
would have given him to the headsman.

After his death, the portraits of him, which had been numerous,
for he had been a munificent encourager of art, were bought up and
destroyed—it was supposed by his heirs, who might have been glad
could they have razed his very name from their splendid line. He had
enjoyed a vast wealth; a large portion of this was believed to have
been embezzled by a favourite astrologer or soothsayer—at all events
it had unaccountably vanished at the time of his death. One portrait
alone of him was supposed to have escaped the general destruction;
I had seen it in the house of a collector some months before. It had
made on me a wonderful impression, as it does on all who behold it
—a face never to be forgotten; and there was that face in the
miniature that lay within my hand. True, that in the miniature the
man was a few years older than in the portrait I had seen, or than the
original was even at the time of his death. But a few years!—why,
between the date in which flourished that direful noble and the date
in which the miniature was evidently painted, there was an interval
of more than two centuries. While I was thus gazing, silent and
wondering, Mr J—— said:

'But is it possible? I have known this man.'

'How—where?' I cried.

'In India. He was high in the confidence of the Rajah of ——, and
wellnigh drew him into a revolt which would have lost the Rajah his
dominions. The man was a Frenchman—his name de V——, clever,
bold, lawless. We insisted on his dismissal and banishment: it must
be the same man—no two faces like his—yet this miniature seems
nearly a hundred years old.'

Mechanically I turned round the miniature to examine the back
of it, and on the back was engraved a pentacle; in the middle of the
pentacle a ladder, and the third step of the ladder was formed by the

date 1765. Examining still more minutely, I detected a spring; this, on being pressed, opened the back of the miniature as a lid. Within-side the lid was engraved 'Mariana to thee—Be faithful in life and in death to ——.' Here follows a name that I will not mention, but it was not unfamiliar to me. I had heard it spoken of by old men in my childhood as the name borne by a dazzling charlatan, who had made a great sensation in London for a year or so, and had fled the country on the charge of a double murder within his own house—that of his mistress and his rival. I said nothing of this to Mr J——, to whom reluctantly I resigned the miniature.

We had found no difficulty in opening the first drawer within the iron safe; we found great difficulty in opening the second: it was not locked, but it resisted all efforts till we inserted in the chinks the edge of a chisel. When we had thus drawn it forth, we found a very singular apparatus in the nicest order. Upon a small thin book, or rather tablet, was placed a saucer of crystal; this saucer was filled with a clear liquid—on that liquid floated a kind of compass, with a needle shifting rapidly round, but instead of the usual points of a compass were seven strange characters, not very unlike those used by astrologers to denote the planets. A very peculiar, but not strong nor displeasing odour, came from this drawer, which was lined with a wood that we afterwards discovered to be hazel. Whatever the cause of this odour, it produced a material effect on the nerves. We all felt it, even the two workmen who were in the room—a creeping tingling sensation from the tips of the fingers to the roots of the hair. Impatient to examine the tablet, I removed the saucer. As I did so the needle of the compass went round and round with exceeding swiftness, and I felt a shock that ran through my whole frame, so that I dropped the saucer on the floor. The liquid was spilt—the saucer was broken—the compass rolled to the end of the room—and at that instant the walls shook to and fro, as if a giant had swayed and rocked them.

The two workmen were so frightened that they ran up the ladder by which we had descended from the trapdoor; but seeing that nothing more happened, they were easily induced to return.

Meanwhile I had opened the tablet: it was bound in a plain red leather, with a silver clasp; it contained but one sheet of thick vellum, and on that sheet were inscribed, within a double pentacle, words in old monkish Latin, which are literally to be translated thus:—'On all that it can reach within these walls—sentient or inanimate, living or dead—as moves the needle, so work my will! Accursed be the house, and restless be the dwellers therein.'

We found no more. Mr J—— burnt the tablet and its anathema.

He razed to the foundations the part of the building containing the secret room with the chamber over it. He had then the courage to inhabit the house himself for a month, and a quieter, better-conditioned house could not be found in all London. Subsequently he let it to advantage, and his tenant has made no complaints.

But my story is not yet done. A few days after Mr J—— had removed into the house, I paid him a visit. We were standing by the open window and conversing. A van containing some articles of furniture which he was moving from his former house was at the door. I had just urged on him my theory that all those phenomena regarded as supermundane had emanated from a human brain; adducing the charm, or rather curse, we had found and destroyed in support of my philosophy. Mr J—— was observing in reply, 'That even if mesmerism, or whatever analogous power it might be called, could really thus work in the absence of the operator, and produce effects so extraordinary, still could those effects continue when the operator himself was dead? and if the spell had been wrought, and, indeed, the room walled up, more than seventy years ago, the probability was, that the operator had long since departed this life'; Mr J——, I say, was thus answering, when I caught hold of his arm and pointed to the street below.

A well-dressed man had crossed from the opposite side, and was accosting the carrier in charge of the van. His face, as he stood, was exactly fronting our window. It was the face of the miniature we had discovered; it was the face of the portrait of the noble three centuries ago.

'Good Heavens!' cried Mr J——, 'that is the face of de V——, and scarcely a day older than when I saw it in the Rajah's court in my youth!'

Seized by the same thought, we both hastened downstairs. I was first in the street; but the man had already gone. I caught sight of him, however, not many yards in advance, and in another moment I was by his side.

I had resolved to speak to him, but when I looked into his face I felt as if it were impossible to do so. That eye—the eye of the serpent —fixed and held me spellbound. And withal, about the man's whole person there was a dignity, an air of pride and station and superiority, that would have made anyone, habituated to the usages of the world, hesitate long before venturing upon a liberty or impertinence. And what could I say? what was it I would ask? Thus ashamed of my first impulse, I fell a few paces back, still, however, following the stranger, undecided what else to do. Meanwhile he turned the corner of the street; a plain carriage was in waiting, with a servant out of livery, dressed like a *valet-de-place*, at the carriage door. In another moment he had stepped into the carriage, and it drove off. I returned to the house. Mr J—— was still at the street door. He had asked the carrier what the stranger had said to him.

'Merely asked whom that house now belonged to.'

The same evening I happened to go with a friend to a place in town called the Cosmopolitan Club, a place open to men of all countries, all opinions, all degrees. One orders one's coffee, smokes one's cigar. One is always sure to meet agreeable, sometimes remarkable, persons.

I had not been two minutes in the room before I beheld at a table, conversing with an acquaintance of mine, whom I will designate by the initial G——, the man—the Original of the Miniature. He was now without his hat, and the likeness was yet more startling, only I observed that while he was conversing there was less severity in the countenance; there was even a smile, though a very quiet and very cold one. The dignity of mien I had acknowledged in the street was also more striking; a dignity akin to that which invests some prince of the East—conveying the idea of supreme indifference and habitual, indisputable, indolent, but resistless power.

G—— soon after left the stranger, who then took up a scientific journal, which seemed to absorb his attention.

I drew G—— aside. 'Who and what is that gentleman?'

'That? Oh, a very remarkable man indeed. I met him last year amidst the caves of Petra—the scriptural Edom. He is the best Oriental scholar I know. We joined company, had an adventure with robbers, in which he showed a coolness that saved our lives; afterwards he invited me to spend a day with him in a house he had bought at Damascus—a house buried amongst almond blossoms and roses—the most beautiful thing! He had lived there for some years, quite as an Oriental, in grand style. I half suspect he is a renegade, immensely rich, very odd; by the by, a great mesmeriser. I have seen him with my own eyes produce an effect on inanimate things. If you take a letter from your pocket and throw it to the other end of the room, he will order it to come to his feet, and you will see the letter wriggle itself along the floor till it has obeyed his command. 'Pon my honour, 'tis true: I have seen him affect even the weather, disperse or collect clouds, by means of a glass tube or wand. But he does not like talking of these matters to strangers. He has only just arrived in England; says he has not been here for a great many years; let me introduce him to you.'

'Certainly! He is English, then? What is his name?'

'Oh!—a very homely one—Richards.'

'And what is his birth—his family?'

'How do I know? What does it signify?—no doubt some parvenu, but rich—so infernally rich!'

G—— drew me up to the stranger, and the introduction was effected. The manners of Mr Richards were not those of an adventurous traveller. Travellers are in general constitutionally gifted with high animal spirits: they are talkative, eager, imperious. Mr Richards was calm and subdued in tone, with manners which were made distant by the loftiness of punctilious courtesy—the manners of a former age. I observed that the English he spoke was not exactly of our day. I should even have said that the accent was slightly foreign. But then Mr Richards remarked that he had been little in the habit for many years of speaking in his native tongue. The conversation fell upon the changes in the aspect of London since he had last visited our metropolis. G—— then glanced off to the moral changes—literary, social, political—the great men who were removed from the stage within the last twenty years—the new great men who were coming on. In all this Mr Richards evinced no interest. He had evidently read none of our living authors, and seemed scarcely acquainted by name with our younger statesmen. Once and only once he laughed; it was when G—— asked him whether he had any thoughts of getting into Parliament. And the laugh was inward —sarcastic—sinister—a sneer raised into a laugh. After a few minutes G—— left us to talk to some other acquaintances who had just lounged into the room, and I then said quietly:

'I have seen a miniature of you, Mr Richards, in the house you once inhabited, and perhaps built, if not wholly, at least in part, in —— Street. You passed by that house this morning.'

Not till I had finished did I raise my eyes to his, and then his fixed my gaze so steadfastly that I could not withdraw it—those fascinating serpent eyes. But involuntarily, and if the words that translated my thought were dragged from me, I added in a low whisper, 'I have been a student in the mysteries of life and nature; of those mysteries I have known the occult professors. I have the right to speak to you thus.' And I uttered a certain pass-word.

'Well,' said he, dryly, 'I concede the right—what would you ask?'

'To what extent human will in certain temperaments can extend?'

'To what extent can thought extend? Think, and before you draw breath you are in China!'

'True. But my thought has no power in China.'

148

'Give it expression, and it may have: you may write down a thought which, sooner or later, may alter the whole condition of China. What is a law but a thought? Therefore thought is infinite— therefore thought has power; not in proportion to its value—a bad thought may make a bad law as potent as a good thought can make a good one.'

'Yes; what you say confirms my own theory. Through invisible currents one human brain may transmit its ideas to other human brains with the same rapidity as a thought promulgated by visible means. And as thought is imperishable—as it leaves its stamp behind it in the natural world even when the thinker has passed out of this world—so the thought of the living may have power to rouse up and revive the thoughts of the dead—such as those thoughts *were in life* —though the thought of the living cannot reach the thoughts which the dead *now* may entertain. Is it not so?'

'I decline to answer, if, in my judgment, thought has the limit you would fix to it; but proceed. You have a special question you wish to put.'

'Intense malignity in an intense will, engendered in a peculiar temperament, and aided by natural means within the reach of science, may produce effects like those ascribed of old to evil magic. It might thus haunt the walls of a human habitation with spectral revivals of all guilty thoughts and guilty deeds once conceived and done within those walls; all, in short, with which the evil will claims *rapport* and affinity—imperfect, incoherent, fragmentary snatches at the old dramas acted therein years ago. Thoughts thus crossing each other haphazard, as in the nightmare of a vision, growing up into phantom sights and sounds, and all serving to create horror, not because those sights and sounds are really visitations from a world without, but that they are ghastly monstrous renewals of what have been in this world itself, set into malignant play by a malignant mortal.

'And it is through the material agency of that human brain that these things would acquire even a human power—would strike as with the shock of electricity, and might kill, if the thought of the person assailed did not rise superior to the dignity of the original assailer—might kill the most powerful animal if unnerved by fear, but not injure the feeblest man, if, while his flesh crept, his mind stood out fearless. Thus, when in old stories we read of a magician rent to pieces by the fiends he had evoked—or still more, in Eastern legends, that one magician succeeds by arts in destroying another— there may be so far truth, that a material being has clothed, from its

149

own evil propensities certain elements and fluids, usually quiescent or harmless, with awful shape and terrific force—just as the lightning that had lain hidden and innocent in the cloud becomes by natural law suddenly visible, takes a distinct shape to the eye, and can strike destruction on the object to which it is attracted.'

'You are not without glimpses of a very mighty secret,' said Mr Richards, composedly. 'According to your view, could a mortal obtain the power you speak of, he would necessarily be a malignant and evil being.'

'If the power were exercised as I have said, most malignant and most evil—though I believe in the ancient traditions that he could not injure the good. His will could only injure those with whom it has established an affinity, or over whom it forces unresisted sway. I will now imagine an example that may be within the laws of nature, yet seem wild as the fables of a bewildered monk.

'You will remember that Albertus Magnus, after describing minutely the process by which spirits may be invoked and commanded, adds emphatically that the process will instruct and avail only to the few—that a *man must be born a magician*!—that is, born with a peculiar physical temperament, as a man is born a poet. Rarely are men in whose constitution lurks this occult power of the highest order of intellect—usually in the intellect there is some twist, perversity, or disease. But, on the other hand, they must possess, to an astonishing degree, the faculty to concentrate thought on a single object—the energic faculty that we call *will*. Therefore, though their intellect be not sound, it is exceedingly forcible for the attainment of what it desires. I will imagine such a person, pre-eminently gifted with this constitution and its concomitant forces. I will place him in the loftier grades of society. I will suppose his desires emphatically those of the sensualist—he has, therefore, a strong love of life. He is an absolute egotist—his will is concentrated in himself—he has fierce passions—he knows no enduring, no holy affections, but he can covet eagerly what for the moment he desires—he can hate implacably what opposed itself to his objects—he can commit fearful crimes, yet feel small remorse—he resorts rather to curses upon others, than to penitence for his misdeeds. Circumstances, to which his constitution guides him, lead him to a rare knowledge of the natural secrets which may serve his egotism. He is a close observer where his passions encourage observation, he is a minute calculator, not from love of truth, but where love of self sharpens his faculties—therefore he can be a man of science.

'I suppose such a being, having by experience learned the power of his arts over others, trying what may be the power of will over his own frame, and studying all that in natural philosophy may increase that power. He loves life, he dreads death; he *wills to live on*. He cannot restore himself to youth, he cannot entirely stay the progress of death, he cannot make himself immortal in the flesh and blood; but he may arrest for a time so prolonged as to appear incredible, if I said it—that hardening of the parts which constitutes old age. A year may age him no more than an hour ages another. His intense will, scientifically trained into system, operates, in short, over the wear and tear of his own frame. He lives on. That he may not seem a portent and a miracle, he *dies* from time to time, seemingly, to certain persons. Having schemed the transfer of a wealth that suffices to his wants, he disappears from one corner of the world, and contrives that his obsequies shall be celebrated. He reappears at another corner of the world, where he resides undetected, and does not revisit the scenes of his former career till all who could remember his features are no more. He would be profoundly miserable if he had affections—he has none but for himself. No good man would accept his longevity, and to no men, good or bad, would he or could he communicate its true secret. Such a man might exist; such a man as I have described I see now before me!—Duke of ——, in the court of ——, dividing time between lust and brawl, alchemists and wizards;—again, in the last century, charlatan and criminal, with name less noble, domiciled in the house at which you gazed today, and flying from the law you had outraged, none knew whither; traveller once more revisiting London, with the same earthly passions which filled your heart when races now no more walked through yonder streets; outlaw from the school of all the nobler and diviner mystics; execrable Image of Life in Death and Death in Life, I warn you back from the cities and homes of healthful men; back to the ruins of departed empires; back to the deserts of nature unredeemed!'

There answered me a whisper so musical, so potently musical, that it seemed to enter into my whole being, and subdue me despite myself. Thus it said:

'I have sought one like you for the last hundred years. Now I have found you, we part not till I know what I desire. The vision that sees through the Past, and cleaves through the veil of the Future, is in you at this hour; never before, never to come again. The vision of no puling fantastic girl, of no sick-bed somnambule, but of a strong man, with a vigorous brain. Soar and look forth!'

As he spoke I felt as if I rose out of myself upon eagle wings. All the weight seemed gone from air—roofless the room, roofless the dome of space. I was not in the body—where I knew not—but aloft over time, over earth.

Again I heard the melodious whisper—'You say right. I have mastered great secrets by the power of Will; true, by Will and by Science I can retard the process of years: but death comes not by age alone. Can I frustrate the accidents which bring death upon the young?'

'No; every accident is a providence. Before a providence snaps every human will.'

'Shall I die at last, ages and ages hence, by the slow, though inevitable, growth of time, or by the cause that I call accident?'

'By a cause you call accident.'

'Is not the end still remote?' asked the whisper, with a slight tremor.

'Regarded as my life regards time, it is still remote.'

'And shall I, before then, mix with the world of men as I did ere I learned these secrets, resume eager interest in their strife and their trouble—battle with ambition, and use the power of the sage to win the power that belongs to kings?'

'You will yet play a part on the earth that will fill earth with commotion and amaze. For wondrous designs have you, a wonder yourself, been permitted to live on through the centuries. All the secrets you have stored will then have their uses—all that now makes you a stranger amidst the generations will contribute then to make you their lord. As the trees and the straws are drawn into a whirlpool —as they spin round, are sucked to the deep, and again tossed aloft by the eddies, so shall races and thrones be plucked into the charm of your vortex. Awful Destroyer—but in destroying, made, against your own will, a Constructor!'

'And that date, too, is far off?'

'Far off; when it comes, think your end in this world is at hand!'

'How and what is the end? Look east, west, south, and north.'

'In the north, where you never yet trod towards the point whence your instincts have warned you, there a spectre will seize you. 'Tis Death! I see a ship—it is haunted—'tis chased—it sails on. Baffled navies sail after that ship. It enters the region of ice. It passes a sky red with meteors. Two moons stand on high, over ice-reefs. I see the ship locked between white defiles—they are ice-rocks. I see the dead strew the decks—stark and livid, green mould on their limbs. All are dead but one man—it is you! But years, though so slowly they come, have then scathed you. There is the coming of age on your brow, and the will is relaxed in the cells of the brain. Still that will, though enfeebled, exceeds all that man knew before you, through the will you live on, gnawed with famine; and nature no longer obeys you in that death-spreading region; the sky is a sky of iron, and the air has iron clamps, and the ice-rocks wedge in the ship. Hark how it cracks and groans. Ice will imbed it as amber imbeds a straw. And a man has gone forth, living yet, from the ship and its dead; and he has clambered up the spikes of an iceberg, and the two moons gaze down on his form. That man is yourself; and terror is on you—terror; and terror has swallowed your will. And I see swarming up the steep ice-rock, grey grisly things. The bears of the north have scented their quarry—they come near you and nearer, shambling and rolling their bulk. And in that day every moment shall seem to you longer than the centuries through which you have passed. And heed this—after life, moments continued make the bliss or the hell of eternity.'

'Hush,' said the whisper; 'but the day, you assure me, is far off—very far! I go back to the almond and rose of Damascus!—sleep!'

The room swam before my eyes. I became insensible. When I recovered, I found G—— holding my hand and smiling. He said, 'You who have always declared yourself proof against mesmerism have succumbed at last to my friend Richards.'

'Where is Mr Richards?'

'Gone, when you passed into a trance—saying quietly to me, "Your friend will not wake for an hour".'

I asked, as collectedly as I could, where Mr Richards lodged.

'At the Trafalgar Hotel.'

'Give me your arm,' said I to G——; 'let us call on him; I have something to say.'

When we arrived at the hotel, we were told that Mr Richards had returned twenty minutes before, paid his bill, left directions with his servant (a Greek) to pack his effects and proceed to Malta by the steamer that should leave Southampton the next day. Mr Richards had merely said of his own movements that he had visits to pay in the neighbourhood of London, and it was uncertain whether he should be able to reach Southampton in time for that steamer; if not, he should follow in the next one.

The waiter asked me my name. On my informing him, he gave me a note that Mr Richards had left for me, in case I called.

The note was as follows: 'I wished you to utter what was in your mind. You obeyed. I have therefore established power over you. For three months from this day you can communicate to no living man what has passed between us—you cannot even show this note to the friend by your side. During three months, silence complete as to me and mine. Do you doubt my power to lay on you this command?—try to disobey me. At the end of the third month, the spell is raised. For the rest I spare you. I shall visit your grave a year and a day after it has received you.'

So ends this strange story, which I ask no one to believe. I write it down exactly three months after I received the above note. I could not write it before, nor could I show to G——, in spite of his urgent request, the note which I read under the gas-lamp by his side.

Arthur Machen

Change

'Here,' said old Mr Vincent Rimmer, fumbling in the pigeon-holes of his great and ancient bureau, 'is an oddity which may interest you.'

He drew a sheet of paper out of the dark place where it had been hidden, and handed it to Reynolds, his curious guest. The oddity was an ordinary sheet of notepaper, of a sort which has long been popular; a bluish grey with slight flecks and streaks of a darker blue embedded in its substance. It had yellowed a little with age at the edges. The outer page was blank; Reynolds laid it open, and spread it out on the table beside his chair. He read something like this:

$$
\begin{array}{ccccccc}
a & aa & e & ee & i & e & ee \\
aa & i & i & o & e & ee & o \\
ee & ee & i & aa & o & oo & o \\
a & o & a & a & e & i & ee \\
e & o & i & ee & a & e & i
\end{array}
$$

Reynolds scanned it with stupified perplexity.

'What on earth is it?' he said. 'Does it mean anything? Is it a cypher, or a silly game, or what?'

Mr Rimmer chuckled. 'I thought it might puzzle you,' he remarked. 'Do you happen to notice anything about the writing; anything out of the way at all?'

Reynolds scanned the document more closely.

'Well, I don't know that there is anything out of the way in the script itself. The letters are rather big, perhaps, and they are rather clumsily formed. But it's difficult to judge handwriting by a few letters, repeated again and again. But, apart from the writing, what is it?'

'That's a question that must wait a bit. There are many strange things related to that bit of paper. But one of the strangest things about it is this; that it is intimately connected with the Darren Mystery.'

'What Mystery did you say? The Darren Mystery? I don't think I ever heard of it.'

'Well, it was a little before your time. And, in any case, I don't see how you could have heard of it. There were, certainly, some very curious and unusual circumstances in the case, but I don't think that they were generally known, and if they were known, they were not understood. You won't wonder at that, perhaps, when you consider that the bit of paper before you was one of those circumstances.'

'But what exactly happened?'

'That is largely a matter of conjecture. But, anyhow, here's the outside of the case, for a beginning. Now, to start with, I don't suppose you've ever been to Meirion? Well, you should go. It's a beautiful county, in West Wales, with a fine sea-coast, and some very pleasant places to stay at, and none of them too large or too popular. One of the smallest of these places, Trenant, is just a village. There is a wooded height above it called the Allt; and down below, the church, with a Celtic cross in the churchyard, a dozen or so of cottages, a row of lodging-houses on the slope round the corner, a few more cottages dotted along the road to Meiros, and that's all. Below the village are marshy meadows where the brook that comes from the hills spreads abroad, and then the dunes, and the sea, stretching away to the Dragon's Head in the far east and enclosed to the west by the beginnings of the limestone cliffs. There are fine, broad sands all the way between Trenant and Porth, the market-town, about a mile and a half away, and it's just the place for children.

'Well, just forty-five years ago, Trenant was having a very successful season. In August there must have been eighteen or nineteen visitors in the village. I was staying in Porth at the time, and, when I walked over, it struck me that the Trenant beach was quite crowded—eight or nine children castle-building and learning to swim, and looking for shells, and all the usual diversions. The grown-up people sat in groups on the edge of the dunes and read and gossiped, or took a turn towards Porth, or perhaps tried to catch prawns in the rock-pools at the other end of the sands. Altogether a very pleasant, happy scene in its simple way, and, as it was a beautiful summer, I have no doubt they all enjoyed themselves very much. I walked to Trenant and back three or four times, and I noticed that most of the children were more or less in charge of a very pretty dark girl, quite young, who seemed to advise in laying out the ground-plan of the castle, and to take off her stockings and tuck up her skirts—we thought a lot of Legs in those days—when the bathers required supervision. She also indicated the kinds of shells which deserved the attention of collectors: an extremely serviceable girl.

'It seemed that this girl, Alice Hayes, was really in charge of the children—or of the greater part of them. She was a sort of nursery-governess or lady of all work to Mrs Brown, who had come down from London in the early part of July with Miss Hayes and little Michael, a child of eight, who refused to recover nicely from his attack of measles. Mr Brown had joined them at the end of the month with the two elder children, Jack and Rosamund. Then, there were the Smiths, with their little family, and the Robinsons with their three; and the fathers and mothers, sitting on the beach every morning, got to know each other very easily. Mrs Smith and Mrs Robinson soon appreciated Miss Hayes's merits as a child-herd; they noticed that Mrs Brown sat placid and went on knitting in the sun, quite safe and unperturbed, while they suffered from recurrent alarms. Jack Smith, though barely fourteen, would be seen dashing through the waves, out to sea, as if he had quite made up his mind to swim to the Dragon's Head, about twenty miles away, or Jane Robinson, in bright pink, would appear suddenly right away among the rocks of the point, ready to vanish into the perilous unknown round the corner. Hence, alarums and excursions, tiring expeditions of rescue and remonstrance, through soft sand or over slippery rocks under a hot sun. And then these ladies would discover that certain of their offspring had entirely disappeared or were altogether missing from the landscape; and dreadful and true tales of children who had driven tunnels into the sand and had been overwhelmed therein rushed to the mind. And all the while Mrs Brown sat serene, confident in the overseership of her Miss Hayes. So, as was to be gathered, the other two took counsel together. Mrs Brown was approached, and something called an arrangement was made, by which Miss Hayes undertook the joint mastership of all three packs, greatly to the ease of Mrs Smith and Mrs Robinson.

It was about this time, I suppose, that I got to know this group of holiday-makers. I had met Smith, whom I knew slightly in town, in the street of Porth, just as I was setting out for one of my morning walks. We strolled together to Trenant on the firm sand down by the water's edge, and introductions went round, and so I joined the party, and sat with them, watching the various diversions of the children and the capable superintendence of Miss Hayes.

'Now there's a queer thing about this little place,' said Brown, a genial man, connected, I believe, with Lloyd's. 'Wouldn't you say

157

this was as healthy a spot as any you could find? Well sheltered from the north, southern aspect, never too cold in winter, fresh sea-breeze in summer: what could you have more?'

'Well,' I replied, 'it always agrees with me very well: a little relaxing, perhaps, but I like being relaxed. Isn't it a healthy place, then? What makes you think so?'

'I'll tell you. We have rooms in Govan Terrace, up there on the hill-side. The other night I woke up with a coughing fit. I got out of bed to get a drink of water, and then had a look out of the windows to see what sort of night it was. I didn't like the look of those clouds in the south-west after sunset the night before. As you can see, the upper windows of Govan Terrace command a good many of the village houses. And, do you know, there was a light in almost every house? At two o'clock in the morning. Apparently the village is full of sick people. But who would have thought it?'

We were sitting a little apart from the rest. Smith had brought a London paper from Porth and he and Robinson had their heads together over the City article. The three women were knitting and talking hard, and down by the blue, creaming water Miss Hayes and her crew were playing happily in the sunshine.

'Do you mind,' I said to Brown, 'if I swear you to secrecy? A limited secrecy: I don't want you to speak of this to any of the village people. They wouldn't like it. And have you told your wife or any of the party about what you saw?'

'As a matter of fact, I haven't said a word to anybody. Illness isn't a very cheerful topic for a holiday, is it? But what's up? You don't mean to say there's some sort of epidemic in the place that they're keeping dark? I say! That would be awful. We should have to leave at once. Think of the children.'

'Nothing of the kind. I don't think that there's a single case of illness in the place—unless you count old Thomas Evans, who has been in what he calls a decline for thirty years. You won't say anything? Then I'm going to give you a shock. The people have a light burning in their houses all night to keep out the fairies.'

I must say it was a success. Brown looked frightened. Not of the fairies; most certainly not; rather at the reversion of his established order of things. He occupied his business in the City; he lived in an extremely comfortable house at Addiscombe; he was a keen though sane adherent of the Liberal Party; and in the world between these points there was no room at all either for fairies or for people who believed in fairies. The latter were almost as fabulous to him as the former, and still more objectionable.

'Look here!' he said at last. 'You're pulling my leg. Nobody believes in fairies. They haven't for hundreds of years. Shakespeare didn't believe in fairies. He says so.'

I let him run on. He implored me to tell him whether it was typhoid, or only measles, or even chicken-pox. I said at last:

'You seem very positive on the subject of fairies. Are you sure there are no such things?'

'Of course I am,' said Brown, very crossly.

'How do you know?'

It is a shocking thing to be asked a question like that, to which, be it observed, there is no answer. I left him seething dangerously.

'Remember,' I said, 'not a word of lit windows to anybody; but if you are uneasy as to epidemics, ask the doctor about it.'

He nodded his head glumly. I knew he was drawing all sorts of false conclusions; and for the rest of our stay I would say that he did not seek me out—until the last day of his visit. I had no doubt that he put me down as a believer in fairies and a maniac; but it is, I consider, good for men who live between the City and Liberal Politics and Addiscombe to be made to realize that there is a world elsewhere. And, as it happens, it was quite true that most of the Trenant people believed in the fairies and were horribly afraid of them.

But this was only an interlude. I often strolled over and joined the party. And I took up my freedom with the young members by contributing posts and a tennis net to the beach sports. They had brought down rackets and balls, in the vague idea that they might be able to get a game somehow and somewhere, and my contribution was warmly welcomed. I helped Miss Hayes to fix the net, and she marked out the court, with the help of many suggestions from the elder children, to which she did not pay the slightest attention. I think the constant disputes as to whether the ball was 'in' or 'out' brightened the game, though Wimbledon would not have approved. And sometimes the elder children accompanied their parents to Porth in the evening and watched the famous Japanese Jugglers or Pepper's Ghost at the Assembly Rooms, or listened to the Mysterious Musicians at the De Barry Gardens—and altogether everybody had, you would say, a very jolly time.

It all came to a dreadful end. One morning when I had come out on my usual morning stroll from Porth, and had got to the camping ground of the party at the edge of the dunes, I found somewhat to my surprise that there was nobody there. I was afraid that Brown had been in part justified in his dread of concealed epidemics, and that some of the children had 'caught something' in the village. So I walked up in the direction of Govan Terrace, and found Brown standing at the bottom of his flight of steps, and looking very much upset.

I hailed him.

'I say,' I began, 'I hope you weren't right, after all. None of the children down with measles, or anything of that sort?'

'It's something worse than measles. We none of us know what has happened. The doctor can make nothing of it. Come in, and we can talk it over.'

Just then a procession came down the steps leading from a house a few doors further on. First of all there was the porter from the station, with a pile of luggage on his truck. Then came the two elder Smith children, Jack and Millicent, and finally, Mr and Mrs Smith. Mr Smith was carrying something wrapped in a bundle in his arms.

'Where's Bob?' He was the youngest; a brave, rosy little man of five or six.

'Smith's carrying him,' murmured Brown.

'What's happened? Has he hurt himself on the rocks? I hope it's nothing serious.'

I was going forward to make my enquiries, but Brown put a hand on my arm and checked me. Then I looked at the Smith party more closely, and I saw at once that there was something very much amiss. The two elder children had been crying, though the boy was going his best to put up a brave face against disaster—whatever it was. Mrs Smith had drawn her veil over her face, and stumbled as she walked, and on Smith's face there was a horror as of ill dreams.

'Look,' said Brown in his low voice.

Smith had half-turned, as he set out with his burden to walk down the hill to the station. I don't think he knew we were there; I don't think any of the party had noticed us as we stood on the bottom step, half-hidden by a blossoming shrub. But as he turned uncertainly, like a man in the dark, the wrappings fell away a little from what he carried, and I saw a little wizened, yellow face peering out; malignant, deplorable.

I turned helplessly to Brown, as that most wretched procession went on its way and vanished out of sight.

'What on earth has happened? That's not Bobby. Who is it?'

'Come into the house,' said Brown, and he went before me up the long flight of steps that led to the terrace.

There was a shriek and a noise of thin, shrill, high-pitched laughter as we came into the lodging-house.

'That's Miss Hayes in blaspheming hysterics,' said Brown grimly.

160

'My wife's looking after her. The children are in the room at the back. I daren't let them go out by themselves in this awful place.' He beat with his foot on the floor and glared at me, awe-struck, a solid man shaken.

'Well,' he said at last, 'I'll tell you what we know; and as far as I can make out, that's very little. However. . . . You know Miss Hayes, who helps Mrs Brown with the children, had more or less taken over the charge of the lot; the young Robinsons and the Smiths, too. You've seen how well she looks after them all on the sands in the morning. In the afternoon she's been taking them inland for a change. You know there's beautiful country if you go a little way inland; rather wild and woody; but still very nice; pleasant and shady. Miss Hayes thought that the all-day glare of the sun on the sands might not be very good for the small ones, and my wife agreed with her. So they took their teas with them and picnicked in the woods and enjoyed themselves very much, I believe. They didn't go more than a couple of miles or three at the outside; and the little ones used to take turns in a go-cart. They never seemed too tired.

'Yesterday at lunch they were talking about some caves at a place called the Darren, about two miles away. My children seemed very anxious to see them, and Mrs Probert, our landlady, said they were quite safe, so the Smiths and Robinsons were called in, and they were enthusiastic, too; and the whole party set off with their tea-baskets, and candles and matches, in Miss Hayes's charge. Somehow they made a later start than usual, and from what I can make out they enjoyed themselves so much in the cool dark cave, first of all exploring, and then looking for treasure, and winding up with tea by candlelight, that they didn't notice how the time was going—nobody had a watch—and by the time they'd packed up their traps and come out from underground, it was quite dark. They had a little trouble making out the way at first, but not very much, and came along in high spirits, tumbling over molehills and each other, and finding it all quite an adventure.

'They had got down in the road there, and were sorting themselves out into the three parties, when somebody called out: "Where's Bobby Smith?" Well, he wasn't there. The usual story; everybody thought he was with somebody else. They were all mixed up in the dark, talking and laughing and shrieking at the top of their voices, and taking everything for granted—I suppose it was like that. But poor little Bob was missing. You can guess what a scene there was. Everybody was much too frightened to scold Miss Hayes, who had no doubt been extremely careless, to say the least of it—not like her.

Robinson pulled us together. He told Mrs Smith that the little chap would be perfectly all right: there were no precipices to fall over and no water to fall into, the way they'd been, that it was a warm night, and the child had had a good stuffing tea, and he would be as right as rain when they found him. So we got a man from the farm, with a lantern, and Miss Hayes to show us exactly where they'd been, and Smith and Robinson and I went off to find poor Bobby, feeling a good deal better than at first. I noticed that the farm man seemed a good deal put out when we told him what had happened and where we were going. "Got lost in the Darren," he said, "indeed, that is a pity." That set Smith off at once; and he asked Williams what he meant; what was the matter with the place? Williams said there was nothing the matter with it at all whatever but it was "a tiresome place to be in after dark". That reminded me of what you were saying a couple of weeks ago about the people here. "Some damned superstitious nonsense," I said to myself, and thanked God it was nothing worse. I thought the fellow might be going to tell us of a masked bog or something like that. I gave Smith a hint in a whisper as to where the land lay; and we went on, hoping to come on little Bob any minute. Nearly all the way we were going through open fields without any cover or bracken or anything of that sort, and Williams kept twirling his lantern, and Miss Hayes and the rest of us called out the child's name; there didn't seem much chance of missing him.

'However, we saw nothing of him—till we got to the Darren. It's an odd sort of place, I should think. You're in an ordinary field, with a gentle upward slope, and you come to a gate, and down you go into a deep, narrow valley; a regular nest of valleys as far as I could make out in the dark, one leading into another, and the sides covered with trees. The famous caves were on one of these steep slopes, and, of course, we all went in. They didn't stretch far; nobody could have got lost in them, even if the candles gave out. We searched the place thoroughly, and saw where the children had had their tea: no signs of Bobby. So we went on down the valley between the woods, till we came to where it opens out into a wide space, with one tree growing all alone in the middle. And then we heard a miserable whining noise, like some little creature that's got hurt. And there under the tree was —what you saw poor Smith carrying in his arms this morning.

'It fought like a wild cat when Smith tried to pick it up, and jabbered some unearthly sort of gibberish. Then Miss Hayes came along and seemed to soothe it; and it's been quiet ever since. The man with the lantern was shaking with terror; the sweat was pouring down his face.'

I stared hard at Brown. 'And,' I thought to myself, 'you are very much in the same condition as Williams.' Brown was obviously overcome with dread.

We sat there in silence.

'Why do you say "it"?' I asked. 'Why don't you say "him"?'

'You saw.'

'Do you mean to tell me seriously that you don't believe that child you helped to bring home was Bobby? What does Mrs Smith say?'

'She says the clothes are the same. I suppose it must be Bobby. The doctor from Porth says the child must have had a severe shock. I don't think he knows anything about it.'

He stuttered over his words, and said at last:

'I was thinking of what you said about the lighted windows. I hoped you might be able to help. Can you do anything? We are leaving this afternoon; all of us. Is there nothing to be done?'

'I am afraid not.'

I had nothing else to say. We shook hands and parted without more words.

The next day I walked over to the Darren. There was something fearful about the place, even in the haze of a golden afternoon. As Brown had said, the entrance and the disclosure of it were sudden and abrupt. The fields of the approach held no hint of what was to come. Then, past the gate, the ground fell violently away on every side, grey rocks of an ill shape pierced through it, and the ash trees on the steep slopes overshadowed all. The descent was into silence, without the singing of a bird, into a wizard shade. At the farther end, where the wooded heights retreated somewhat, there was the open space, or circus, of turf; and in the middle of it a very ancient, twisted thorn tree, beneath which the party in the dark had found the little creature that whined and cried out in unknown speech. I turned about, and on my way back I entered the caves, and lit the carriage candle I had brought with me. There was nothing much to see—I never think there is much to see in caves. There was the place where the children and others before them had taken their tea, with a ring of blackened stones within which many fires and twigs had been kindled. In caves or out of caves, townsfolk in the country are always alike in leaving untidy and unseemly litter behind; and here were the usual scraps of greasy paper, daubed with smears of jam and butter, the half-eaten sandwich, and the gnawed crust. Amidst all this nastiness I saw a piece of folded notepaper, and in sheer idleness picked it up and opened it. You have just seen it. When I asked you if you saw anything peculiar about the writing, you said that the letters were rather big and clumsy. The reason of that is that they were written by a child. I don't think you examined the back of the second leaf. Look: "Rosamund"—Rosamund Brown, that is. And beneath; there, in the corner.

Reynolds looked, and read, and gaped aghast.

'That was—her other name; her name in the dark.'

'Name in the dark?'

'In the dark night of the Sabbath. That pretty girl had caught them all. They were in her hands, those wretched children, like the clay images she made. I found one of those things, hidden in a cleft of the rocks, near the place where they had made their fire. I ground it into dust beneath my feet.'

'And I wonder what her name was?'

'They called her, I think, the Bridegroom and the Bride.'

'Did you ever find out who she was, or where she came from?'

'Very little. Only that she had been a mistress at the Home for Christian Orphans in North Tottenham, where there was a hideous scandal some years before.'

'Then she must have been older than she looked, according to your description.'

'Possibly.'

They sat in silence for a few minutes. Then Reynolds said:

'But I haven't asked you about this formula, or whatever you may call it—all these vowels, here. Is it a cypher?'

'No. But it is really a great curiosity, and it raises some extraordinary questions, which are outside this particular case. To begin with—and I am sure I could go much farther back than my beginning, if I had the necessary scholarship—I once read an English rendering of a Greek manuscript of the second or third century—I won't be certain which. It's a long time since I've seen the thing. The translator and editor of it was of the opinion that it was a Mithraic Ritual; but I have gathered that weightier authorities are strongly inclined to discredit this view. At any rate, it was no doubt an initiation rite into some mystery; possibly it had Gnostic connections; I don't know. But our interest lies in this, that one of the stages or portals, or whatever you call them, consisted almost exactly of that formula you have in your hand. I don't say that the vowels and double vowels are in the same order; I don't think the Greek manuscript has any *aes* or *aas*. But it is perfectly clear that the two documents are of the same kind and have the same purpose. And, advancing a little in time from the Greek manuscript, I don't think it is very surprising that the final operation of an incantation in mediæval and later magic consisted of this wailing on vowels arranged in a certain order.

'But here is something that is surprising. A good many years ago I strolled one Sunday morning into a church in Bloomsbury, the headquarters of a highly respectable sect. And in the middle of a very dignified ritual, there rose quite suddenly, without preface or warning, this very sound, a wild wail of vowels. The effect was astounding, anyhow; whether it was terrifying or merely funny, is a matter of taste. You'll have guessed what I heard: they call it "speaking with tongues", and they believe it to be a heavenly language. And I need scarcely say that they meant very well. But the problem is: how did a congregation of solid Scotch Presbyterians hit on that queer, ancient and not over-sanctified method of expressing spiritual emotion? It is a singular puzzle.

'And that woman? That is not by any means so difficult. The good Scotchmen—I can't think how they did it—got hold of something that didn't belong to them: she was in her own tradition. And, as they say down there: *asakai dasa*: the darkness is undying.'

E. Nesbit

John Charrington's Wedding

No one ever thought that May Forster would marry John Charrington; but he thought differently, and things which John Charrington intended had a queer way of coming to pass. He asked her to marry him before he went up to Oxford. She laughed and refused him. He asked her again next time he came home. Again she laughed, tossed her dainty blonde head, and again refused. A third time he asked her; she said it was becoming a confirmed bad habit, and laughed at him more than ever.

John was not the only man who wanted to marry her: she was the belle of our village *coterie*, and we were all in love with her more or less; it was a sort of fashion, like heliotrope ties or Inverness capes. Therefore we were as much annoyed as surprised when John Charrington walked into our little local Club—we held it in a loft over the saddler's, I remember—and invited us all to his wedding.

'Your wedding?'

'You don't mean it?'

'Who's the happy fair? When's it to be?'

John Charrington filled his pipe and lighted it before he replied. Then he said—

'I'm sorry to deprive you fellows of your only joke—but Miss Forster and I are to be married in September.'

'You don't mean it?'

'He's got the mitten again, and it's turned his head.'

'No,' I said, rising, 'I see it's true. Lend me a pistol someone—or a first-class fare to the other end of Nowhere. Charrington has bewitched the only pretty girl in our twenty-mile radius. Was it mesmerism, or a love-potion, Jack?'

'Neither, sir, but a gift you'll never have—perseverance—and the best luck a man ever had in this world.'

There was something in his voice that silenced me, and all chaff of the other fellows failed to draw him further.

The queer thing about it was that when we congratulated Miss

Forster, she blushed and smiled and dimpled, for all the world as though she were in love with him, and had been in love with him all the time. Upon my word, I think she had. Women are strange creatures.

We were all asked to the wedding. In Brixham everyone who was anybody knew everybody else who was anyone. My sisters were, I truly believe, more interested in the *trousseau* than the bride herself, and I was to be best man. The coming marriage was much canvassed at afternoon tea-tables, and at our little Club over the saddler's, and the question was always asked: 'Does she care for him?'

I used to ask that question myself in the early days of their engagement, but after a certain evening in August I never asked it again. I was coming home from the Club through the churchyard. Our church is on a thyme-grown hill, and the turf about it is so thick and soft that one's footsteps are noiseless.

I made no sound as I vaulted the low lichened wall, and threaded my way between the tombstones. It was at the same instant that I heard John Charrington's voice, and saw Her. May was sitting on a low flat gravestone, her face turned towards the full splendour of the western sun. Its expression ended, at once and for ever, any question of love for him; it was transfigured to a beauty I should not have believed possible, even to that beautiful little face.

John lay at her feet, and it was his voice that broke the stillness of the golden August evening.

'My dear, my dear, I believe I should come back from the dead if you wanted me!'

I coughed at once to indicate my presence, and passed on into the shadow fully enlightened.

The wedding was to be early in September. Two days before I had to run up to town on business. The train was late, of course, for we are on the South-Eastern, and as I stood grumbling with my watch in my hand, whom should I see but John Charrington and May Forster. They were walking up and down the unfrequented end of the platform, arm in arm, looking into each other's eyes, careless of the unsympathetic interest of the porters.

Of course I knew better than to hesitate a moment before burying myself in the booking-office, and it was not till the train drew up at the platform, that I obtrusively passed the pair with my Gladstone, and took the corner in a first-class smoking-carriage. I did this with as good an air of not seeing them as I could assume. I pride myself on my discretion, but if John were travelling alone I wanted his company. I had it.

'Hullo, old man,' came his cheery voice as he swung his bag into my carriage; 'here's luck; I was expecting a dull journey!'

'Where are you off to?' I asked, discretion still bidding me turn my eyes away, though I saw, without looking, that hers were red-rimmed.

'To old Branbridge's,' he answered, shutting the door and leaning out for a last word with his sweetheart.

'Oh, I wish you wouldn't go, John,' she was saying in a low, earnest voice. 'I feel certain something will happen.'

'Do you think I should let anything happen to keep me, and the day after tomorrow our wedding-day?'

'Don't go,' she answered, with a pleading intensity which would have sent my Gladstone on to the platform and me after it. But she wasn't speaking to me. John Charrington was made differently; he rarely changed his opinions, never his resolutions.

He only stroked the little ungloved hands that lay on the carriage door.

'I must, May. The old boy's been awfully good to me, and now he's dying I must go and see him, but I shall come home in time for——' the rest of the parting was lost in a whisper and in the rattling lurch of the starting train.

'You're sure to come?' she spoke as the train moved.

'Nothing shall keep me,' he answered; and we steamed out. After he had seen the last of the little figure on the platform he leaned back in his corner and kept silence for a minute.

When he spoke it was to explain to me that his godfather, whose heir he was, lay dying at Peasmarsh Place, some fifty miles away, and had sent for John, and John had felt bound to go.

'I shall be surely back tomorrow,' he said, 'or, if not, the day after, in heaps of time. Thank heaven, one hasn't to get up in the middle of the night to get married nowadays!'

'And suppose Mr Branbridge dies?'

'Alive or dead I mean to be married on Thursday!' John answered, lighting a cigar and unfolding *The Times*.

At Peasmarsh station we said 'good-bye', and he got out, and I saw him ride off; I went on to London, where I stayed the night.

When I got home the next afternoon, a very wet one, by the way, my sister greeted me with:

'Where's Mr Charrington?'

'Goodness knows,' I answered testily. Every man, since Cain, has resented that kind of question.

'I thought you might have heard from him,' she went on, 'as you're to give him away tomorrow.'

'Isn't he back?' I asked, for I had confidently expected to find him at home.

'No, Geoffrey'—my sister Fanny always had a way of jumping to conclusions, especially such conclusions as were least favourable to her fellow-creatures—'he has not returned, and, what is more, you may depend upon it he won't. You mark my words, there'll be no wedding tomorrow.'

My sister Fanny has a power of annoying me which no other human being possesses.

'You mark my words,' I retorted with asperity, 'you had better give up making such a thundering idiot of yourself. There'll be more wedding tomorrow than ever you'll take the first part in.' A prophecy which, by the way, came true.

But though I could snarl confidently to my sister, I did not feel so comfortable when late that night, I, standing on the doorstep of John's house, heard that he had not returned. I went home gloomily through the rain. Next morning brought a brilliant blue sky, gold sun, and all such softness of air and beauty of cloud as go to make up a perfect day. I woke with a vague feeling of having gone to bed anxious, and of being rather averse to facing that anxiety in the light of full wakefulness.

But with my shaving-water came a note from John which relieved my mind and sent me up to the Forster's with a light heart.

May was in the garden. I saw her blue gown through the hollyhocks as the lodge gates swung to behind me. So I did not go up to the house, but turned aside down the turfed path.

'He's written to you too,' she said, without preliminary greeting, when I reached her side.

'Yes, I'm to meet him at the station at three, and come straight on to the church.'

Her face looked pale, but there was a brightness in her eyes, and a tender quiver about the mouth that spoke of renewed happiness.

'Mr Branbridge begged him so to stay another night that he had not the heart to refuse,' she went on. 'He is so kind, but I wish he hadn't stayed.'

I was at the station at half-past two. I felt rather annoyed with John. It seemed a sort of slight to the beautiful girl who loved him, that he should come as it were out of breath, and with the dust of travel upon him, to take her hand, which some of us would have given the best years of our lives to take.

But when the three o'clock train glided in, and glided out again having brought no passengers to our little station, I was more than annoyed. There was no other train for thirty-five minutes; I calculated that, with much hurry, we might just get to the church in time for the ceremony; but, oh, what a fool to miss that first train! What other man could have done it?

That thirty-five minutes seemed a year, as I wandered round the station reading the advertisements and the time-tables, and the company's by-laws, and getting more and more angry with John Charrington. This confidence in his own power of getting everything he wanted the minute he wanted it was leading him too far. I hate waiting. Everyone does, but I believe I hate it more than anyone else. The three thirty-five was late, of course.

I ground my pipe between my teeth and stamped with impatience as I watched the signals. Click. The signal went down. Five minutes later I flung myself into the carriage that I had brought for John.

'Drive to the church!' I said, as someone shut the door. 'Mr Charrington hasn't come by this train.'

Anxiety now replaced anger. What had become of the man? Could he have been taken suddenly ill? I had never known him have a day's illness in his life. And even so he might have telegraphed. Some awful accident must have happened to him. The thought that he had played her false never—no, not for a moment—entered my head. Yes, something terrible had happened to him, and on me lay the task of telling his bride. I almost wished the carriage would upset, and break my head so that someone else might tell her, not I, who—but that's nothing to do with this story.

It was five minutes to four as we drew up at the churchyard gate. A double row of eager onlookers lined the path from lychgate to porch. I sprang from the carriage and passed up between them. Our gardener had a good front place near the door. I stopped.

'Are they waiting still, Byles?' I asked, simply to gain time, for of course I knew they were by the waiting crowd's attentive attitude.

'Waiting, sir? No, no, sir; why, it must be over by now.'

'Over! Then Mr Charrington's come?'

'To the minute, sir; must have missed you somehow, and, I say, sir,' lowering his voice, 'I never see Mr John the least bit so afore, but my opinion is he's been drinking pretty free. His clothes was all dusty and his face like a sheet. I tell you I didn't like the looks of him at all, and the folks inside are saying all sorts of things. You'll see, something's gone very wrong with Mr John, and he's tried liquor. He looked like a ghost, and in he went with his eyes straight before him, with never a look or a word for one of us: him that was always such a gentleman!'

I had never heard Byles make so long a speech. The crowd in the churchyard were talking in whispers and getting ready rice and slippers to throw at the bride and bridegroom. The ringers were ready with their hands on the ropes to ring out the merry peal as the bride and bridegroom should come out.

A murmur from the church announced them; out they came. Byles was right. John Charrington did not look himself. There was dust on his coat, his hair was disarranged. He seemed to have been in some row, for there was a black mark above his eyebrow. He was deathly pale. But his pallor was not greater than that of the bride, who might have been carved in ivory—dress, veil, orange blossoms, face and all.

As they passed out the ringers stooped—there were six of them—and then, on the ears expecting the gay wedding peal, came the slow tolling of the passing bell.

A thrill of horror at so foolish a jest from the ringers passed through us all. But the ringers themselves dropped the ropes and fled like rabbits out into the sunlight. The bride shuddered, and grey shadows came about her mouth, but the bridegroom led her on down the path where the people stood with the handfuls of rice; but the handfuls were never thrown, and the wedding-bells never rang. In vain the ringers were urged to remedy their mistake: they protested with many whispered expletives that they would see themselves further first.

In a hush like the hush in the chamber of death the bridal pair passed into their carriage and its door slammed behind them.

Then the tongues were loosed. A babel of anger, wonder, conjecture from the guests and the spectators.

'If I'd seen his condition, sir,' said old Forster to me as we drove off, 'I would have stretched him on the floor of the church, sir, by Heaven I would, before I'd have let him marry my daughter!'

Then he put his head out of the window.

—'Drive like hell,' he cried to the coachman; 'don't spare the horses.'

He was obeyed. We passed the bride's carriage. I forbore to look at it, and old Forster turned his head away and swore. We reached home before it.

We stood in the hall doorway, in the blazing afternoon sun, and in about half a minute we heard wheels crunching the gravel. When the carriage stopped in front of the steps old Forster and I ran down.

'Great Heaven, the carriage is empty! And yet——'

I had the door open in a minute, and this is what I saw——

No sign of John Charrington; and of May, his wife, only a huddled heap of white satin lying half on the floor of the carriage and half on the seat.

'I drove straight here, sir,' said the coachman, as the bride's father lifted her out; 'and I'll swear no one got out of the carriage.'

We carried her into the house in her bridal dress and drew back her veil. I saw her face. Shall I ever forget it? White, white and drawn with agony and horror, bearing such a look of terror as I have never seen since except in dreams. And her hair, her radiant blonde hair, I tell you it was white like snow.

As we stood, her father and I, half mad with the horror and mystery of it, a boy came up the avenue—a telegraph boy. They brought the orange envelope to me. I tore it open.

> '*Mr Charrington was thrown from the dogcart on his way to the station at half-past one. Killed on the spot!*'

—And he was married to May Forster in our parish church at *half-past three*, in presence of half the parish.

'*I shall be married, dead or alive!*'

What had passed in that carriage on the homeward drive? No one knows—no one will ever know. Oh, May! oh, my dear!

Before a week was over they laid her beside her husband in our little churchyard on the thyme-covered hill—the churchyard where they had kept their love-trysts.　　　　　　　　　　　　　　——

—Thus was accomplished John Charrington's wedding.

Vincent O'Sullivan

When I Was Dead

—'And yet my heart
Will not confess he owes the malady
That doth my life besiege.'
All's Well that Ends Well.

That was the worst of Ravenel Hall. The passages were long and
gloomy, the rooms were musty and dull, even the pictures were
sombre and their subjects dire. On an autumn evening, when the
wind soughed and wailed through the trees in the park, and the dead
leaves whistled and chattered, while the rain clamoured at the
windows, small wonder that folks with gentle nerves went a-straying
in their wits! An acute nervous system is a grievous burthen on the
deck of a yacht under sunlit skies: at Ravenel the chain of nerves was
prone to clash and jangle a funeral march. Nerves must be pampered
in a tea-drinking community; and the ghost that your grandfather,
with a skinful of port, could face and never tremble, sets you, in your
sobriety, sweating and shivering; or, becoming scared (poor ghost!)
of your bulged eyes and dropping jaw, he quenches expectation by
not appearing at all. So I am left to conclude that it was tea which
made my acquaintance afraid to stay at Ravenel. Even Wilvern gave
over; and as he is in the Guards, and a polo player, his nerves ought
to be strong enough. On the night before he went I was explaining
to him my theory, that if you place some drops of human blood near
you, and then concentrate your thoughts, you will after a while see
before you a man or a woman who will stay with you during long
hours of the night, and even meet you at unexpected places during
the day. I was explaining this theory, I repeat, when he interrupted
me with words, senseless enough, which sent me fencing and parry-
ing strangers—on my guard.

'I say, Alistair, my dear chap!' he began, 'you ought to get out of this place and go up to Town and knock about a bit—you really ought, you know.'

'Yes,' I replied, 'and get poisoned at the hotels by bad food and at the clubs by bad talk, I suppose. No, thank you: and let me say that your care for my health enervates me.'

'Well, you can do as you like,' says he, rapping with his feet on the floor. 'I'm hanged if I stay here after tomorrow—I'll be staring mad if I do!'

He was my last visitor. Some weeks after his departure I was sitting in the library with my drops of blood by me. I had got my theory nearly perfect by this time; but there was one difficulty.

The figure which I had ever before me was the figure of an old woman with her hair divided in the middle, and her hair fell to her shoulders, white on one side and black on the other. She was a very complete old woman; but, alas! she was eyeless, and when I tried to construct the eyes she would shrivel and rot in my sight. But tonight I was thinking, thinking, as I had never thought before, and the eyes were just creeping into the head when I heard a terrible crash outside as if some heavy substance had fallen. Of a sudden the door was flung open and two maidservants entered. They glanced at the rug under my chair, and at that they turned a sick white, cried on God, and huddled out.

'How dare you enter the library in this manner?' I demanded sternly. No answer came back from them, so I started in pursuit. I found all the servants in the house gathered in a knot at the end of the passage.

'Mrs Pebble,' I said smartly, to the housekeeper, 'I want those two women discharged tomorrow. It's an outrage! You ought to be more careful.'

But she was not attending to me. Her face was distorted with terror.

'Ah dear, ah dear!' she went. 'We had better all go to the library together,' says she to the others.

'Am I master of my own house, Mrs Pebble?' I inquired, bringing my knuckles down with a bang on the table.

None of them seemed to see me or hear me: I might as well have been shrieking in a desert. I followed them down the passage, and forbade them with strong words to enter the library. But they trooped past me, and stood with a clutter round the hearth-rug. Then three or four of them began dragging and lifting, as if they were lifting a helpless body, and stumbled with their imaginary burthen over to a sofa. Old Soames, the butler, stood near.

'Poor young gentleman!' he said with a sob. 'I've knowed him since he was a baby. And to think of him being dead like this—and so young, too!'

I crossed the room. 'What's all this, Soames?' I cried, shaking him roughly by the shoulders. 'I'm not dead. I'm here—here!' As he did not stir I got a little scared. 'Soames, old friend!' I called, 'don't you know me? Don't you know the little boy you used to play with? Say I'm not dead, Soames, please, Soames!'

He stooped down and kissed the sofa. 'I think one of the men ought to ride over to the village for the doctor, Mr Soames,' says Mrs Pebble; and he shuffled out to give the order.

Now, this doctor was an ignorant dog, whom I had been forced to exclude from the house because he went about proclaiming his belief in a saving God, at the same time that he proclaimed himself a man of science. He, I was resolved, should never cross my threshold, and I followed Mrs Pebble through the house, screaming out prohibition. But I did not catch even a groan from her, not a nod of the head, nor a cast of the eye, to show that she had heard.

I met the doctor at the door of the library. 'Well,' I sneered, throwing my hand in his face, 'have you come to teach me some new prayers?'

He brushed by me as if he had not felt the blow, and knelt down by the sofa.

'Rupture of a vessel on the brain, I think,' he says to Soames and Mrs Pebble after a short moment. 'He has been dead some hours. Poor fellow! You had better telegraph for his sister, and I will send up the undertaker to arrange the body.'

'You liar!' I yelled. 'You whining liar! How have you the insolence to tell my servants that I am dead, when you see me here face to face?'

He was far in the passage, with Soames and Mrs Pebble at his heels, ere I had ended, and not one of the three turned round.

All that night I sat in the library. Strangely enough, I had no wish to sleep nor, during the time that followed, had I any craving to eat. In the morning the men came, and although I ordered them out, they proceeded to minister about something I could not see. So all day I stayed in the library or wandered about the house, and at night the men came again bringing with them a coffin. Then, in my humour, thinking it a shame that so fine a coffin should be empty I lay the night in it and slept a soft dreamless sleep – the softest sleep I have ever slept. And when the men came the next day I rested still, and the undertaker shaved me. A strange valet!

On the evening after that, I was coming downstairs, when I noted some luggage in the hall, and so learned that my sister had arrived. I had not seen this woman since her marriage, and I loathed her more than I loathed any creature in this ill-organized world. She was very beautiful, I think—tall, and dark, and straight as a ram-rod—and she had an unruly passion for scandal and dress. I suppose the reason I disliked her so intensely was, that she had a habit of making one aware of her presence when she was several yards off. At half-past nine o'clock my sister came down to the library in a very charming wrap, and I soon found that she was as insensible to my presence as the others. I trembled with rage to see her kneel down by the coffin —my coffin; but when she bent over to kiss the pillow I threw away control.

A knife which had been used to cut string was lying upon a table: I seized it and drove it into her neck. She fled from the room screaming.

'Come! come!' she cried, her voice quivering with anguish. 'The corpse is bleeding from the nose.'

Then I cursed her.

On the morning of the third day there was a heavy fall of snow. About eleven o'clock I observed that the house was filled with blacks and mutes and folk of the county, who came for the obsequies. I went into the library and sat still, and waited. Soon came the men, and they closed the lid of the coffin and bore it out on their shoulders. And yet I sat, feeling rather sadly that something of mine had been taken away: I could not quite think what. For half-an-hour perhaps —dreaming, dreaming: and then I glided to the hall door. There was no trace left of the funeral; but after a while I sighted a black thread winding slowly across the white plain.

'I'm not dead!' I moaned, and rubbed my face in the pure snow and tossed it on my neck and hair. 'Sweet God, I am not dead.'

Edith Wharton

Afterward

'Oh there *is* one, of course, but you'll never know it.'

The assertion, laughingly flung out six months earlier in a bright June garden, came back to Mary Boyne with a new perception of its significance as she stood, in the December dusk, waiting for the lamps to be brought into the library.

The words had been spoken by their friend, Alida Stair, as they sat at tea on her lawn at Pangbourne, in reference to the very house of which the library in question was the central, the pivotal 'feature'. Mary Boyne and her husband, in quest of a country place in one of the southern or south-western counties, had, on their arrival in England, carried their problem straight to Alida Stair, who had successfully solved it in her own case; but it was not until they had rejected, almost capriciously, several practical and judicious suggestions that she threw out: 'Well, there's Lyng, in Dorsetshire. It belongs to Hugo's cousins, and you can get it for a song.'

The reason she gave for its being obtainable on these terms—its remoteness from a station, its lack of electric light, hot-water pipes, and other vulgar necessities—were exactly those pleading in its favour with two romantic Americans perversely in search of the economic drawbacks which were associated, in their tradition, with unusual architectural felicities.

'I should never believe I was living in an old house unless I was thoroughly uncomfortable,' Ned Boyne, the more extravagant of the two, had jocosely insisted: 'the least hint of "convenience" would make me think it had been bought out of an exhibition, with the pieces numbered, and set up again.' And they had proceeded to enumerate, with humorous precision, their various doubts and demands, refusing to believe that the house their cousin recommended was *really* Tudor till they learned it had no heating system, or that the village church was literally in the grounds till she assured them of the deplorable uncertainty of the water supply.

'It's too uncomfortable to be true!' Edward Boyne had continued to exult as the avowal of each disadvantage was successively wrung from her; but he had cut short his rhapsody to ask, with a relapse to distrust: 'And the ghost? You've been concealing from us the fact that there is no ghost!'

Mary, at the moment, had laughed with him, yet almost with her laugh, being possessed of several sets of independent perceptions, had been struck by a note of flatness in Alida's answering hilarity.

'Oh, Dorsetshire's full of ghosts, you know.'

'Yes, yes; but that won't do. I don't want to have to drive ten miles to see somebody else's ghost. I want one of my own on the premises. *Is* there a ghost at Lyng?'

His rejoinder had made Alida laugh again, and it was then that she had flung back tantalizingly: 'Oh, there *is* one, of course, but you'll never know it.'

'Never know it?' Boyne pulled her up. 'But what in the world constitutes a ghost except for the fact of its being known for one?'

'I can't say. But that's the story.'

'That there's a ghost, but that nobody knows it's a ghost?'

'Well—not till afterwards, at any rate.'

'Till afterwards?'

'Not till long afterwards.'

'But if it's once been identified as an unearthly visitant, why hasn't its *signalement* been handed down in the family? How has it managed to preserve its incognito?'

Alida could only shake her head. 'Don't ask me. But it has.'

'And then suddenly'—Mary spoke up as if from cavernous depths of divination—'suddenly, long afterwards, one says to one's self "*That was it?*"'

She was startled at the sepulchral sound with which her question fell on the banter of the other two, and she saw the shadow of the same surprise flit across Alida's pupils. 'I suppose so. One just has to wait.'

'Oh, hang waiting!' Ned broke in. 'Life's too short for a ghost who can only be enjoyed in retrospect. Can't we do better than that, Mary?'

But it turned out that in the event they were not destined to, for within three months of their conversation with Mrs Stair they were settled at Lyng, and the life they had yearned for, to the point of planning it in advance in all its daily details, had actually begun for them.

—It was to sit, in the thick December dusk, by just such a wide-hooded fireplace, under just such black oak rafters, with the sense that beyond the mullioned panes the downs were darkened to a deeper solitude: it was for the ultimate indulgence of such sensations that Mary Boyne, abruptly exiled from New York by her husband's business, had endured for nearly fourteen years the soul-deadening ugliness of a Middle Western town, and that Boyne had ground on doggedly at his engineering, till, with a suddenness that still made her blink, the prodigious windfall of the Blue Star Mine had put them at a stroke in possession of life and the leisure to taste it. They had never for a moment meant their new state to be one of idleness; but they meant to give themselves only to harmonious activities. She had her vision of painting and gardening (against a background of grey walls), he dreamed of the production of his long-planned book on the 'Economic Basis of Culture'; and with such absorbing work ahead no existence could be too sequestered: they could not get far enough from the world, or plunge deep enough into the past.

Dorsetshire had attracted them from the first by an air of remoteness out of all proportion to its geographical position. But to the Boynes it was one of the ever-recurring wonders of the whole incredibly compressed island—a nest of counties, as they put it—that for the production of its effects so little of a given quality went so far: that so few miles made a distance, and so short a distance a difference.

'It's that,' Ned had once enthusiastically explained, 'that gives such depth to their effects, such relief to their contrasts. They've been able to lay the butter so thick on every delicious mouthful.'

The butter had certainly been laid on thick at Lyng; the old house hidden under a shoulder of the downs had almost all the finer marks of commerce with a protracted past. The mere fact that it was neither large nor exceptional made it, to the Boynes, abound the more completely in its special charm—the charm of having been for centuries a deep dim reservoir of life. The life had probably not been of the most vivid order: for long periods, no doubt, it had fallen as noiselessly into the past as the quiet drizzle of autumn fell, hour after hour, into the fish pond between the yews; but these backwaters of existence sometimes breed, in their sluggish depths, strange acuities of emotion, and Mary Boyne had felt from the first the mysterious air of intenser memories.

The feeling had never been stronger than on this particular afternoon when, waiting in the library for the lamps to come, she rose from her seat, and stood among the shadows of the hearth. Her husband had gone off, after luncheon, for one of his long tramps on the downs. She had noticed of late that he preferred to go alone; and, in the tried security of their personal relations, had been driven to conclude that his book was bothering him, and that he needed the afternoons to turn over in solitude the problems left from the morning's work. Certainly the book was not going as smoothly as she had thought it would, and there were lines of perplexity between his eyes such as had never been there in his engineering days. He had often, then, looked fagged to the verge of illness, but the native demon of 'worry' had never branded his brow. Yet the few pages he had so far read to her—the introduction, and a summary of the opening chapter—showed a firm hold on his subject, and an increasing confidence in his powers.

The fact threw her into deeper perplexity, since, now that he had done with 'business' and its disturbing contingencies, the one other possible source of anxiety was eliminated. Unless it were his health, then? But physically he had gained since they had come to Dorsetshire, grown robuster, ruddier and fresher-eyed. It was only within the last week that she had felt in him the undefinable change which made her restless in his absence, and as tongue-tied in his presence as though it were *she* who had a secret to keep from him!

The thought that there *was* a secret somewhere between them struck her with a sudden rap of wonder, and she looked about her down the long room.

'Can it be the house?' she mused.

The room itself might have been full of secrets. They seemed to be piling themselves up, as evening fell, like the layers and layers of velvet shadow dropping from the low ceiling, the rows of books, the smoke-blurred sculpture of the hearth.

'Why—of course—the house is haunted!' she reflected.

The ghost—Alida's imperceptible ghost—after figuring largely in the banter of their first month or two at Lyng, had been gradually left aside as too ineffectual for imaginative use. Mary had, indeed, as became the tenant of a haunted house, made the customary inquiries among her rural neighbours, but, beyond a vague 'The du say so, Ma'am,' the villagers had nothing to impart. The elusive spectre had apparently never had sufficient identity for a legend to crystallize about it, and after a time the Boynes had set the matter down to their profit-and-loss account, agreeing that Lyng was one of the few houses good enough in itself to dispense with supernatural enhancements.

'And I suppose, poor ineffectual demon, that's why it beats its beautiful wings in vain in the void,' Mary said laughingly concluded.

'Or, rather,' Ned answered in the same strain, 'why, amid so much that's ghostly, it can never affirm its separate existence as *the* ghost!' And thereupon their invisible housemate had finally dropped out of their references, which were numerous enough to make them soon unaware of the loss.

Now, as she stood on the hearth, the subject of their earlier curiosity revived in her with a new sense of its meaning—a sense gradually acquired through daily contact with the scene of the lurking mystery. It was the house itself, of course, that possessed the ghost-seeing faculty, that communed visually but secretly with its own past; if one could only get into close enough communion with the house, one might surprise its secret, and acquire the ghost-sight on one's own account. Perhaps, in his long hours in this very room, where she never trespassed till the afternoon, her husband *had* acquired it already, and was silently carrying about the weight of whatever it had revealed to him. Mary was too well versed in the code of the spectral world not to know that one would not talk about the ghosts one saw: to do so was almost as great a breach of taste as to name a lady in a club. But this explanation did not really satisfy her. 'What, after all, except for the fun of the shudder,' she reflected, 'would he really care for any of their old ghosts?' And thence she was thrown back once more on the fundamental dilemma: the fact that one's greater or less susceptibility to spectral influences had no particular bearing on the case, since, when one *did* see a ghost at Lyng, one did not know it.

'Not till long afterwards,' Alida Stair had said. Well, supposing Ned *had* seen one when they first came, and had known only within the last week what had happened to him? More and more under the spell of the hour, she threw back her thoughts to the early days of their tenancy, but at first only to recall a lively confusion of unpacking, settling, arranging of books, and calling to each other from remote corners of the house as, treasure after treasure, it revealed itself to them. It was in this particular connection that she presently recalled a certain soft afternoon of the previous October, when, passing from the first rapturous flurry of exploration to a detailed inspection of the old house, she had pressed (like a novel heroine) a panel that opened on a flight of corkscrew stairs leading to a flat ledge of the roof—the roof which, from below, seemed to slope away on all sides too abruptly for any but practiced feet to scale.

The view from this hidden coign was enchanting, and she had flown down to snatch Ned from his papers and give him the freedom of her discovery. She remembered still how, standing at her side, he had passed his arm about her while their gaze flew to the long tossed horizon-line of the downs, and then dropped contentedly back to trace the arabesque of yew hedges about the fish-pond, and the shadow of the cedar of the lawn.

'And now the other way,' he had said, turning her about within his arm; and closely pressed to him, she had absorbed, like some long satisfying draught, the picture of the grey-walled court, the squat lions on the gates, and the lime-avenue reaching up to the highroad under the downs.

It was just then, while they gazed and held each other, that she had felt his arm relax, and heard a sharp 'Hullo!' that made her turn to glance at him.

Distinctly, yes, she now recalled that she had seen, as she glanced, a shadow of anxiety, of perplexity, rather, fall across his face; and, following his eyes, had beheld the figure of a man—a man in loose greyish clothes, as it appeared to her—who was sauntering down the lime-avenue to the court with the doubtful gait of a stranger who seeks his way. Her short-sighted eyes had given her but a blurred impression of slightness and greyishness, with something foreign, or at least unlocal, in the cut of the figure or its dress; but her husband had apparently seen more—seen enough to make him push past her with a hasty 'Wait!' and dash down the stairs without pausing to give her a hand.

A slight tendency to dizziness obliged her, after a provisional clutch at the chimney against which they had been leaning, to follow him first more cautiously; and when she had reached the landing she paused again, for a less definite reason, leaning over the banister to strain her eyes through the silence of the brown sun-flecked depths. She lingered there till, somewhere in those depths, she heard the closing of a door; then, mechanically impelled, she went down the shallow flights of steps till she reached the lower hall.

The front door stood open on the sunlight of the court, and hall and court were empty. The library door was open, too, and after listening in vain for any sound of voices within, she crossed the threshold, and found her husband alone, vaguely fingering the papers on his desk.

He looked up, as if surprised at her entrance, but the shadow of anxiety had passed from his face, leaving it even, as she fancied, a little brighter and clearer than usual.

'What was it? Who was it?' she asked.

'Who?' he repeated, with the surprise still all on his side.

'The man we saw coming towards the house.'

He seemed to reflect. 'The man? Why, I thought I saw Peters; I dashed after him to say a word about the stable drains, but he had disappeared before I could get down.'

'Disappeared? But he seemed to be walking so slowly when we saw him.'

Boyne shrugged his shoulders. 'So I thought; but he must have got up steam in the interval. What do you say to our trying a scramble up Meldon Steep before sunset?'

That was all. At the time the occurrence had been less than nothing, had, indeed, been immediately obliterated by the magic of their first vision from Meldon Steep, a height which they had dreamed of climbing ever since they had first seen its bare spine rising above the roof of Lyng. Doubtless it was the mere fact of the other incident's having occurred on the very day of their ascent to Meldon that had kept it stored away in the fold of memory from which it now emerged; for in itself it had no mark of the portentous. At the moment there could have been nothing more natural than that Ned should dash himself from the roof in the pursuit of dilatory trades-men. It was the period when they were always on the watch for one or the other of the specialists employed about the place; always lying in wait for them, and rushing out at them with questions, reproaches or reminders. And certainly in the distance the grey figure had looked like Peters.

Yet now, as she reviewed the scene, she felt her husband's explana-tion of it to have been invalidated by the look of anxiety on his face. Why had the familiar appearance of Peters made him anxious? Why, above all, if it was of such prime necessity to confer with him on the subject of the stable drains, had the failure to find him produced such a look of relief? Mary could not say that any one of these questions had occurred to her at the time, yet, from the promptness with which they now marshalled themselves at her summons, she had a sense that they must all along have been there, waiting their hour.

2

Weary with her thoughts, she moved to the window. The library was now quite dark, and she was surprised to see how much faint light the outer world still held.

As she peered out into it across the court, a figure shaped itself far down the perspective of bare limes: it looked a mere blot of deeper grey in the greyness, and for an instant, as it moved towards her, her heart thumped to the thought 'It's the ghost!'

She had time, in that long instant, to feel suddenly that the man of whom, two months earlier, she had had a distant vision from the roof, was now, at his predestined hour, about to reveal himself as *not* having been Peters; and her spirit sank under the impending fear of the disclosure. But almost with the next tick of the clock the figure, gaining substance and character, showed itself even to her weak sight as her husband's; and she turned to meet him, as he entered, with the confession of her folly.

'It's really too absurd,' she laughed out, 'but I never *can* remember!'

'Remember what?' Boyne questioned as they drew together.

'That when one sees the Lyng ghost one never knows it.'

Her hand was on his sleeve, and he kept it there, but with no response in his gesture or in the lines of his preoccupied face.

'Did you think you'd seen it?' he asked, after an appreciable interval.

'Why, I actually took *you* for it, my dear, in my mad determination to spot it!'

'Me—just now?' His arm dropped away, and he turned from her with a faint echo of her laugh. 'Really, dearest, you'd better give it up, if that's the best you can do.'

'Oh, yes, I give it up. Have *you*?' she asked, turning round on him abruptly.

The parlour-maid had entered with letters and a lamp, and the light struck up into Boyne's face as he bent above the tray she presented.

'Have *you*?' Mary perversely insisted, when the servant had disappeared on her errand of illumination.

'Have I what?' he rejoined absently, the light bringing out the sharp stamp of worry between his brows as he turned over the letters.

'Given up trying to see the ghost.' Her heart beat a little at the experiment she was making.

Her husband, laying his letters aside, moved away into the shadow of the hearth.

'I never tried,' he said, tearing open the wrapper of a newspaper.

'Well, of course,' Mary persisted, 'the exasperating thing is that there's no use trying, since one can't be sure till so long afterwards.'

He was unfolding the paper as if he had hardly heard her; but after a pause, during which the sheets rustled spasmodically between his hands, he looked up to ask, 'Have you any idea *how long*?'

Mary had sunk into a low chair beside the fireplace. From her seat she glanced over, startled, at her husband's profile, which was projected against the circle of lamplight.

'No; none. Have *you*?' she retorted, repeating her former phrase with an added stress of intention.

Boyne crumpled the paper into a bunch, and then, inconsequently, turned back with it towards the lamp.

'Lord, no! I only meant,' he explained, with a faint tinge of impatience, 'is there any legend, any tradition, as to that?'

'Not that I know of,' she answered; but the impulse to add, 'What makes you ask?' was checked by the reappearance of the parlourmaid, with tea and a second lamp.

With the dispersal of shadows, and the repetition of the daily domestic office, Mary Boyne felt herself less oppressed by that sense of something mutely imminent which had darkened her afternoon. For a few moments she gave herself to the details of her task, and when she looked up from it she was struck to the point of bewilderment by the change in her husband's face. He had seated himself near the farther lamp, and was absorbed in the perusal of his letters; but was it something he had found in them, or merely the shifting of her own point of view, that had restored his features to their normal aspect? The longer she looked the more definitely the change affirmed itself. The lines of tension had vanished, and such traces of fatigue as lingered were of the kind easily attributable to steady mental effort. He glanced up, as if drawn by her gaze, and met her eyes with a smile.

'I'm dying for my tea, you know; and here's a letter for you,' he said.

She took the letter he held out in exchange for the cup she proffered him, and, returning to her seat, broke the seal with the languid gesture of the reader whose interests are all enclosed in the circle of one cherished presence.

Her next conscious motion was that of starting to her feet, the letter falling to them as she rose, while she held out to her husband a newspaper clipping.

'Ned! What's this? What does it mean?'

He had risen at the same instant, almost as if hearing her cry before she uttered it; and for a perceptible space of time he and she studied each other, like adversaries watching for an advantage, across the space between her chair and his desk.

'What's what? You fairly made me jump!' Boyne said at length, moving towards her with a sudden half-exasperated laugh. The shadow of apprehension was on his face again, not now a look of fixed foreboding, but a shifting vigilance of lips and eyes that gave her the sense of his feeling himself invisibly surrounded.

Her hand shook so that she could hardly give him the clipping.

'This article—from the *Waukesha Sentinel*—that a man named Elwell has brought suit against you—that there was something wrong about the Blue Star Mine. I can't understand more than half.'

They continued to face each other as she spoke, and to her astonishment she saw that her words had the almost immediate effect of dissipating the strained watchfulness of his look.

'Oh, *that*!' He glanced down the printed slip, and then folded it with the gestures of one who handles something harmless and familiar. 'What's the matter with you this afternoon, Mary? I thought you'd got bad news.'

She stood before him with her undefinable terror subsiding slowly under the reassurance of his tone.

'You knew about this, then—it's all right?'

'Certainly I knew about it; and it's all right.'

'But what *is* it? I don't understand. What does this man accuse you of?'

'Pretty nearly every crime in the calendar.' Boyne had tossed the clipping down, and thrown himself into an arm-chair near the fire. 'Do you want to hear the story? It's not particularly interesting—just a squabble over interests in the Blue Star.'

'But who is this Elwell? I don't know the name.'

'Oh, he's a fellow I put into it—gave him a hand up. I told you all about him at the time.'

'I dare say. I must have forgotten.' Vainly she strained back among her memories. 'But if you helped him, why does he make this return?'

'Probably some shyster lawyer got hold of him and talked him over. It's all rather technical and complicated. I thought that kind of thing bored you.'

His wife felt a sting of compunction. Theoretically, she deprecated the American wife's detachment from her husband's professional interests, but in practice she had always found it difficult to fix her attention on Boyne's report of the transactions in which his varied interests involved him. Besides, she had felt during their years of exile, that, in a community where the amenities of living could be obtained only at the cost of efforts as arduous as her husband's professional labours, such brief leisure as he and she could command should be used as an escape from immediate preoccupations, a flight to the life they always dreamed of living. Once or twice, now that this new life had actually drawn its magic circle about them, she had asked herself if she had done right; but hitherto such conjectures had been no more than the retrospective excursions of an active fancy.

Now, for the first time, it startled her a little to find how little she knew of the material foundation on which her happiness was built.

She glanced at her husband, and was again reassured by the composure of his face; yet she felt the need of more definite grounds for her reassurance.

'But doesn't this suit worry you? Why have you never spoken to me about it?'

He answered both questions at once. 'I didn't speak of it at first because it *did* worry me—annoyed me, rather. But it's all ancient history now. Your correspondent must have got hold of a back number of the *Sentinel*.'

She felt a quick thrill of relief. 'You mean it's over? He's lost his case?'

There was a just perceptible delay in Boyne's reply. 'The suit's been withdrawn—that's all.'

But she persisted, as if to exonerate herself from the inward charge of being too easily put off. 'Withdrawn it because he saw he had no chance?'

'Oh, he had no chance,' Boyne answered.

She was still struggling with a dimly felt perplexity at the back of her thoughts.

'How long ago was it withdrawn?'

He paused, as if with a slight return of his former uncertainty. 'I've just had the news now; but I've been expecting it.'

'Just now—in one of your letters?'

'Yes; in one of my letters.'

She made no answer, and was aware only, after a short interval of waiting, that he had risen, and, strolling across the room, had placed himself on the sofa at her side. She felt him, as he did so, pass an arm about her, she felt his hand seek hers and clasp it, and turning slowly, drawn by the warmth of his cheek, she met his smiling eyes.

'It's all right—it's all right?' she questioned, through the flood of her dissolving doubts; and 'I give you my word it was never righter!' he laughed back at her, holding her close.

3

One of the strangest things she was afterwards to recall out of all the next day's strangeness was the sudden and complete recovery of her sense of security.

It was in the air when she woke in her low-ceiled, dusky room; it went with her downstairs to the breakfast-table, flashed out at her from the fire, and reduplicated itself from the flanks of the urn and the sturdy flutings of the Georgian teapot. It was as if, in some roundabout way, all her diffused fears of the previous day, with their moment of sharp concentration about the newspaper article—as if this dim questioning of the future, and started return upon the past, had between them liquidated the arrears of some haunting moral obligation. If she had indeed been careless of her husband's affairs, it was, her new state seemed to prove, because her faith in him instinctively justified such carelessness; and his right to her faith had now affirmed itself in the very face of menace and suspicion. She had never seen him more untroubled, more naturally and unconsciously himself, than after the cross-examination to which she had subjected him: it was almost as if he had been aware of her doubts, and had wanted the air cleared as much as she did.

It was as clear, thank Heaven! as the bright outer light that surprised her almost with a touch of summer when she issued from the house for her daily round of the gardens. She had left Boyne at his desk, indulging herself, as she passed the library door, by a last peep at his quiet face, where he bent, pipe in mouth, above his papers; and now she had her own morning's task to perform. The task involved, on such charmed winter days, almost as much happy loitering about the different quarters of her demesne as if spring were already at work there. There were such endless possibilities still before her, such opportunities to bring out the latent graces of the old place, without a single irreverent touch of alteration, that the winter was all too short to plan what spring and autumn executed. And her recovered sense of safety gave, on this particular morning, a peculiar zest to her progress through the sweet still place. She went first to the kitchen-garden, where the espaliered pear-trees drew complicated patterns on the walls, and pigeons were fluttering and preening about the silvery-slated roof of their cot. This was something wrong about the piping of the hothouse, and she was expecting an authority from Dorchester, who was to drive out between trains and make a diagnosis of the boiler. But when she dipped into the damp heat of the greenhouses, among the spiced scents and waxy pinks and reds of old-fashioned exotics—even the flora of Lyng was in the note!—she learned that the great man had not arrived, and, the day being too rare to waste in an artificial atmosphere, she came out again and paced along the springy turf of the bowling green to the gardens behind the house. At their farther end rose a grass terrace, looking across the fish pond and yew hedges to the long house-front with its twisted chimney stacks and blue roof angles all drenched in the pale gold moisture of the air.

Seen thus, across the level tracery of the gardens, it sent her, from open windows and hospitably smoking chimneys, the look of some warm human presence, of a mind slowly ripened on a sunny wall of experience. She had never before had such a sense of her intimacy with it, such a conviction that its secrets were all beneficient, kept, as they said to children, 'for one's good', such a trust in its power to gather up her life and Ned's into the harmonious pattern of the long, long story it sat there weaving in the sun.

She heard steps behind her, and turned, expecting to see the gardener, accompanied by the engineer from Dorchester. But only one figure was in sight, that of a youngish slightly built man, who, for reasons she could not on the spot have given, did not remotely resemble her notion of an authority on hothouse boilers. The new-comer, on seeing her, lifted his hat, and paused with the air of a gentleman—perhaps a traveller—who wishes to make it known that his intrusion is involuntary. Lyng occasionally attracted the more cultivated traveller, and Mary half-expected to see the stranger dissemble a camera, or justify his presence by producing it. But he made no gesture of any sort, and after a moment she asked, in a tone responding to the courteous hesitation of his attitude: 'Is there any-one you wish to see?'

'I came to see Mr Boyne,' he answered. His intonation, rather than his accent, was faintly American, and Mary, at the note, looked at him more closely. The brim of his soft felt hat cast a shade on his face, which, thus obscured, wore to her short-sighted gaze a look of seriousness, as of a person arriving 'on business', and civilly but firmly aware of his rights.

Past experience had made her equally sensible to such claims; but she was jealous of her husband's morning hours, and doubtful of his having given anyone the right to intrude on them.

'Have you an appointment with my husband?' she asked.

The visitor hesitated, as if unprepared for the question.

'I think he expects me,' he replied.

It was Mary's turn to hesitate. 'You see this is his time for work: he never sees anyone in the morning.'

He looked at her a moment without answering; then, as if accepting her decision, he began to move away. As he turned, Mary saw him pause and glance up at the peaceful housefront. Something in his air suggested weariness and disappointment, the dejection of the traveller who has come from far off whose hours are limited by the timetable. It occurred to her that if this were the case, her refusal might have made his errand vain, and a sense of compunction caused her to hasten after him.

'May I ask if you have come a long way?'

He gave her the same grave look. 'Yes—I have come a long way.'

'Then, if you'll go to the house, no doubt my husband will see you now. You'll find him in the library.'

She did not know why she had added the last phrase, except from a vague impulse to atone for her previous inhospitality. The visitor seemed about to express his thanks, but her attention was distracted by the approach of the gardener with a companion who bore all the marks of being the expert from Dorchester.

'This way,' she said, waving the stranger to the house; and an instant later she had forgotten him in the absorption of her meeting with the boilermaker.

The encounter led to such far-reaching results that the engineer ended by finding it expedient to ignore his train, and Mary was beguiled into spending the remainder of the morning in absorbed confabulation among the flower-pots. When the coloquy ended, she was surprised to find that it was nearly luncheon-time, and she half-expected, as she hurried back to the house, to see her husband coming out to meet her. But she found no one in the court but an under-gardener raking the gravel, and the hall, when she entered it, was so silent that she guessed Boyne to be still at work.

Not wishing to disturb him, she turned into the drawing-room, and there, at her writing-table, lost herself in renewed calculations of the outlay to which the morning's conference had pledged her. The fact that she could permit herself such follies had not yet lost its novelty; and somehow, in contrast to the vague fears of the previous days, it now seemed an element of her recovered security, of the sense that, as Ned had said, things in general had never been 'righter'.

She was still luxuriating in a lavish play of figures when the parlour-maid, from the threshold, roused her with an inquiry as to the expediency of serving luncheon. It was one of their jokes that Trimmle announced luncheon as if she were divulging a state secret, and Mary, intent upon her papers, merely murmured an absent-minded assent.

She felt Trimmle wavering doubtfully on the threshold, as if in rebuke of such unconsidered assent; then her retreating steps sounded down the passage, and Mary, pushing away her papers, crossed the hall—and went to the library door. It was still closed, and she wavered in her turn, disliking to disturb her husband, yet anxious that he should not exceed his usual measure of work. As she stood there, balancing her impulses, Trimmle returned with the announcement of luncheon, and Mary, thus impelled, opened the library door.

Boyne was not at his desk, and she peered about her, expecting to discover him before the bookshelves, somewhere down the length of the room; but her call brought no response, and gradually it became clear to her that he was not there.

She turned back to the parlour-maid.

'Mr Boyne must be upstairs. Please tell him that luncheon is ready.'

Trimmle appeared to hesitate between the obvious duty of obedience and an equally obvious conviction of the foolishness of the injunction laid on her. The struggle resulted in her saying: 'If you please, Madam, Mr Boyne's not upstairs.'

'Not in his room? Are you sure?'

'I'm sure, Madam.'

Mary consulted the clock. 'Where is he, then?'

'He's gone out,' Trimmle announced, with the superior air of one who has respectfully waited for the question that a well-ordered mind would have put first.

Mary's conjecture had been right, then. Boyne must have gone to the gardens to meet her, and since she had missed him, it was clear that he had taken the shorter way by the south door, instead of going round to the court. She crossed the hall to the french window opening directly on the yew garden, but the parlour-maid, after another moment of inner conflict, decided to bring out: 'Please, Madam, Mr Boyne didn't go that way.'

Mary turned back. 'Where *did* he go? And when?'

'He went out of the front door, up the drive, Madam.' It was a matter of principle with Trimmle never to answer more than one question at a time.

'Up the drive? At this hour?' Mary went to the door herself, and glanced across the court through the tunnel of bare limes. But its perspective was as empty as when she had scanned it on entering.

'Did Mr Boyne leave no message?'

Trimmle seemed to surrender herself to a last struggle with the forces of chaos.

'No, Madam. He just went out with the gentleman.'

'The gentleman? What gentleman?' Mary wheeled about, as if to front this new factor.

'The gentleman who called, Madam,' said Trimmle resignedly.

'When did a gentleman call? Do explain yourself, Trimmle!'

Only the fact that Mary was very hungry, and that she wanted to consult her husband about the greenhouses, would have caused her to lay so unusual an injunction on her attendant; and even now she was detached enough to note in Trimmle's eye the dawning defiance of the respectful subordinate who has been pressed too hard.

'I couldn't exactly say the hour, Madam, because I didn't let the gentleman in,' she replied, with an air of discreetly ignoring the irregularity of her mistress's course.

'You didn't let him in?'

'No, Madam. When the bell rang I was dressing, and Agnes——'

'Go and ask Agnes, then,' said Mary.

Trimmle still wore her look of patient magnanimity. 'Agnes would not know, Madam, for she had unfortunately burnt her hand in trimming the wick of the new lamp from town'—Trimmle, as Mary was aware, had always been opposed to the new lamp—'and so Mrs Dockett sent the kitchen-maid instead.'

Mary looked again at the clock. 'It's after two! Go and ask the kitchen-maid if Mr Boyne left any word.'

She went into luncheon without waiting, and Trimmle presently brought her there the kitchen-maid's statement that the gentleman had called about eleven o'clock, and that Mr Boyne had gone out with him without leaving any message. The kitchen-maid did not even know the caller's name, for he had written it on a slip of paper, which he had folded and handed to her, with the injunction to deliver it at once to Mr Boyne.

Mary finished her luncheon, still wondering, and when it was over, and Trimmle had brought the coffee to the drawing-room, her wonder had deepened to a first tinge of disquietude. It was unlike Boyne to absent himself without explanation at so unwonted an hour, and the difficulty of identifying the visitor whose summons he had apparently obeyed made his disappearance the more unaccountable. Mary Boyne's experience as the wife of a busy engineer, subject to sudden calls and compelled to keep irregular hours, had trained her to the philosophic acceptance of surprises; but since Boyne's withdrawal from business he had adopted a Benedictine regularity of life. As if to make up for the dispersed and agitated years, with their 'stand-up' lunches, and dinners rattled down to the jolting of the dining-cars, he cultivated the last refinements of punctuality and monotony, discouraging his wife's fancy for the unexpected, and declaring that to a delicate taste there were infinite gradations of pleasure in the recurrences of habit.

Still, since no life can completely defend itself from the unforeseen, it was evident that all Boyne's precautions would sooner or later prove unavailable, and Mary concluded that he had cut short a tiresome visit by walking with his caller to the station, or at least accompanying him for part of the way.

This conclusion relieved her from further preoccupation, and she went out herself to take up her conference with the gardener. Thence she walked to the village post office, a mile or so away; and when she turned towards home the early twilight was setting in.

She had taken a footpath across the downs, and as Boyne, meanwhile, had probably returned from the station by the highroad, there was little likelihood of their meeting. She felt sure, however, of his having reached the house before her; so sure that, when she entered it herself, without even pausing to inquire of Trimmle, she made directly for the library. But the library was still empty, and with an unwonted exactness of visual memory she observed that the papers on her husband's desk lay precisely as they had lain when she had gone in to call him to luncheon.

Then of a sudden she was seized by a vague dread of the unknown. She had closed the door behind her on entering, and as she stood alone in the long silent room, her dread seemed to take shape and sound, to be there breathing and lurking among the shadows. Her short-sighted eyes strained through them, half-discerning an actual presence, something aloof, that watched and knew; and in the recoil from that intangible presence she threw herself on the bell-rope and gave it a sharp pull.

The sharp summons brought Trimmle in precipitately with a lamp, and Mary breathed again at this sobering reappearance of the usual.

'You may bring tea if Mr Boyne is in,' she said, to justify her ring.

'Very well, Madam. But Mr Boyne is not in,' said Trimmle, putting down the lamp.

'Not in? You mean he's come back and gone out again?'

'No, Madam. He's never been back.'

The dread stirred again, and Mary knew that now it had her fast.

'Not since he went out with—the gentleman?'

'Not since he went out with the gentleman.'

'But who *was* the gentleman?' Mary insisted, with the shrill note of someone trying to be heard through a confusion of noises.

'That I couldn't say, Madam.' Trimmle, standing there by the lamp, seemed suddenly to grow less round and rosy, as though eclipsed by the same creeping shade of apprehension.

'But the kitchen-maid knows—wasn't it the kitchen-maid who let him in?'

'She doesn't know either, Madam, for he wrote his name on a folded paper.'

Mary, through her agitation, was aware that they were both designating the unknown visitor by a vague pronoun, instead of the conventional formula which, till then, had kept their allusions within the bounds of conformity. And at the same moment her mind caught at the suggestion of the folded paper.

'But he must have a name! Where's the paper?'

She moved to the desk, and began to turn over the documents that littered it. The first that caught her eye was an unfinished letter in her husband's hand, with his pen lying across it, as though dropped there at a sudden summons.

'My dear Parvis'—who was Parvis?—'I have just received your letter announcing Elwell's death, and while I suppose there is now no further risk of trouble, it might be safer——'

She tossed the sheet aside, and continued her search; but no folded paper was discoverable among the letters and pages of manuscript which had been swept together in a heap, as if by a hurried or a startled gesture.

'But the kitchen-maid *saw* him. Send her here,' she commanded, wondering at her dullness in not thinking sooner of so simple a solution.

Trimmle vanished in a flash, as if thankful to be out of the room, and when she reappeared, conducting the agitated underling, Mary had regained her self-possession, and had her questions ready.

The gentleman was a stranger, yes—that she understood. But what had he said? And above all, what had he looked like? The first question was easily enough answered, for the disconcerting reason that he had said so little—had merely asked for Mr Boyne, and, scribbling something on a bit of paper, had requested that it should at once be carried in to him.

'Then you don't know what he wrote? You're not sure it *was* his name?'

The kitchen-maid was not sure, but supposed it was, since he had written it in answer to her inquiry as to whom she should announce.

'And when you carried the paper in to Mr Boyne, what did he say?'

The kitchen-maid did not think that Mr Boyne had said anything, but she could not be sure, for just as she had handed him the paper and he was opening it, she had become aware that the visitor had followed her into the library, and she had slipped out, leaving the gentlemen together.

'But then, if you left them in the library, how do you know that they went out of the house?'

This question plunged the witness into a momentary inarticulateness, from which she was rescued by Trimmle, who, by means of ingenious circumlocutions, elicited the statement that before she could cross the hall to the back passage she had heard the two gentlemen behind her, and had seen them go out of the front door together.

'Then, if you saw the strange gentleman twice, you must be able to tell me what he looked like.'

But with this final challenge to her powers of expression it became clear that the limit of the kitchen-maid's endurance had been reached. The obligation of going to the front door to 'show in' a visitor was in itself so subversive of the fundamental order of things that it had thrown her faculties into hopeless disarray, and she could only stammer out, after various panting efforts: 'His hat, mum, was different-like, as you might say——'

'Different? How different?' Mary flashed out, her own mind, in the same instant, leaping back to an image left on it that morning, and then lost under layers of subsequent impressions.

'His hat had a wide brim, you mean? and his face was pale—a youngish face?' Mary pressed her, with a white-lipped intensity of interrogation. But if the kitchen-made found any adequate answer to this challenge, it was swept away for her listener down the rushing current of her own convictions. The stranger—the stranger in the garden! Why had Mary not thought of him before? She needed no one now to tell her that it was he who had called for her husband and gone away with him. But who was he, and why had Boyne obeyed him?

4

It leaped out at her suddenly, like a grin out of the dark that they had often called England so little—'such a confoundedly hard place to get lost in'.

A confoundedly hard place to get lost in! That had been her husband's phrase. And now, with the whole machinery of official investigation sweeping its flashlights from shore to shore, and across the dividing straits; now, with Boyne's name blazing from the walls of every town and village, his portrait (how that wrung her!) hawked up and down the country like the image of a hunted criminal; now the little compact populous island, so policed, surveyed, and administered, revealed itself as a Sphinx-like guardian of abysmal mysteries, staring back into his wife's anguished eyes as if with the wicked joy of knowing something they would never know!

In the fortnight since Boyne's disappearance there had been no word of him, no trace of his movements. Even the usual misleading reports that raise expectancy in tortured bosoms had been few and fleeting. No one but the kitchen-maid had seen Boyne leave the house, and no one else had seen 'the gentleman' who accompanied him. All inquiries in the neighbourhood failed to elicit the memory of a stranger's presence that day in the neighbourhood of Lyng. And no one had met Edward Boyne, either alone or in company, in any of the neighbouring villages, or on the road across the downs, or at either of the local railway-stations. The sunny English noon had swallowed him as completely as if he had gone out into the Cimmerian night.

Mary, while every official means of investigation was working at its highest pressure, had ransacked her husband's papers for any trace of antecedent complications, of entanglements or obligations unknown to her, that might throw a ray into the darkness. But if any such had existed in the background of Boyne's life, they had vanished like the slip of paper on which the visitor had written his name. There remained no possible thread of guidance except—if it were indeed an exception—the letter which Boyne had apparently been in the act of writing when he received his mysterious summons. That letter, read and reread by his wife, and submitted by her to the police, yielded little enough to feed conjecture.

'I have just heard of Elwell's death, and while I suppose there is now no further risk of trouble, it might be safer——' That was all. The 'risk of trouble' was easily explained by the newspaper clipping which had apprised Mary of the suit brought against her husband by one of his associates in the Blue Star enterprise. The only new information conveyed by the letter was the fact of its showing Boyne, when he wrote it, to be still apprehensive of the results of the suit, though he had told his wife that it had been withdrawn, and though the letter itself proved that the plaintiff was dead. It took several days of cabling to fix the identity of the 'Parvis' to whom the fragment was addressed, but even after these inquiries had shown him to be a Waukesha lawyer, no new facts concerning the Elwell suit were elicited. He appeared to have had no direct concern in it, but to have been conversant with the facts merely as an acquaintance, and possible intermediary; and he declared himself unable to guess with what object Boyne intended to seek his assistance.

This negative information, sole fruit of the first fortnight's search, was not increased by a jot during the slow weeks that followed. Mary knew that the investigations were still being carried on, but she had a vague sense of their gradually slackening, as the actual march of time seemed to slacken. It was as though the days, flying horror-struck from the shrouded image of the one inscrutable day, gained assurance as the distance lengthened, till at last they fell back into their normal gait. And so with the human imaginations at work on the dark event. No doubt it occupied them still, but week by week and hour by hour it grew less absorbing, took up less space, was slowly but inevitably crowded out of the foreground of consciousness by the new problems perpetually bubbling up from the cloudy cauldron of human experience.

Even Mary Boyne's consciousness gradually felt the same lowering of velocity. It still swayed with the incessant oscillations of conjecture; but they were slower, more rhythmical in their beat. There were even moments of weariness when, like the victim of some poison which leaves the brain clear, but holds the body motionless, she saw herself domesticated with the Horror, accepting its perpetual presence as one of the fixed conditions of life.

These moments lengthened into hours and days, till she passed into a phase of stolid acquiescence. She watched the routine of daily life with the incurious eye of a savage on whom the meaningless processes of civilization make but the faintest impression. She had come to regard herself as part of the routine, a spoke of the wheel, revolving with its motion; she felt almost like the furniture of the room in which she sat, an insensate object to be dusted and pushed about with the chairs and tables. And this deepening apathy held her fast at Lyng, in spite of the entreaties of friends and the usual medical recommendation of 'change'. Her friends supposed that her refusal to move was inspired by the belief that her husband would one day return to the spot from which he had vanished, and a beautiful legend grew up about this imaginary state of waiting. But in reality she had no such belief: the depths of anguish enclosing her were no longer lighted by flashes of hope. She was sure that Boyne would never come back, that he had gone out of her sight as completely as if Death itself had waited that day on the threshold. She had even renounced, one by one, the various theories as to his disappearance which had been advanced by the press, the police, and her own agonized imagination. In sheer lassitude her mind turned from these alternatives of horror, and sank back into the blank fact that he was gone.

No, she would never know what had become of him—no one would ever know. But the house *knew*; the library in which she spent her long lonely evenings knew. For it was here that the last scene had been enacted, here that the stranger had come, and spoken the word which had caused Boyne to rise and follow him. The floor she trod had felt his tread; the books on the shelves had seen his face; and there were moments when the intense consciousness of the old dusky walls seemed about to break out into some audible revelation of their secret. But the revelation never came, and she knew it would never come. Lyng was not one of the garrulous old houses that betray the secrets entrusted to them. Its very legend proved that it had always been the mute accomplice, the incorruptible custodian, of the mysteries it had surprised. And Mary Boyne, sitting face to face with its silence, felt the futility of seeking to break it by any human means.

5

'I don't say it *wasn't* straight, and yet I don't say it *was* straight. It was business.'

Mary, at the words, lifted her head with a start, and looked intently at the speaker.

When, half an hour before, a card with 'Mr Parvis' on it had been brought up to her, she had been immediately aware that the name had been a part of her consciousness ever since she had read it at the head of Boyne's unfinished letter. In the library she had found awaiting her a small sallow man with a bald head and gold eye-glasses, and it sent a tremor through her to know that this was the person to whom her husband's last known thought had been directed.

Parvis, civilly, but without vain preamble—in the manner of a man who has his watch in his hand—had set forth the object of his visit. He had 'run over' to England on business, and finding himself in the neighbourhood of Dorchester, had not wished to leave it without paying his respects to Mrs Boyne; and without asking her, if the occasion offered, what she meant to do about Bob Elwell's family.

The words touched the spring of some obscure dread in Mary's bosom. Did her visitor, after all, know what Boyne had meant by his unfinished phrase? She asked for an elucidation of his question, and noticed at once that he seemed surprised at her continued ignorance of the subject. Was it possible that she really knew as little as she said?

'I know nothing—you must tell me,' she faltered out; and her visitor thereupon proceeded to unfold his story. It threw, even to her confused perceptions, and imperfectly initiated vision, a lurid glare on the whole hazy episode of the Blue Star Mine. Her husband had made his money in that brilliant speculation at the cost of 'getting ahead' of someone less alert to seize the chance; and the victim of

198

his ingenuity was young Robert Elwell, who had 'put him on' to the Blue Star scheme.

Parvis, at Mary's first cry, had thrown her a sobering glance through his impartial glasses.

'Bob Elwell wasn't smart enough, that's all; if he had been, he might have turned round and served Boyne the same way. It's the kind of thing that happens every day in business. I guess it's what the scientists call the survival of the fittest—see?' said Mr Parvis, evidently pleased with the aptness of his analogy.

Mary felt a physical shrinking from the next question she tried to frame; it was as though the words on her lips had a taste that nauseated her.

'But then—you accuse my husband of doing something dishonourable?'

Mr Parvis surveyed the question dispassionately. 'Oh, no, I don't. I don't even say it wasn't straight.' He glanced up and down the long lines of books, as if one of them might have supplied him with the definition he sought. 'I don't say it *wasn't* straight, and yet I don't say it *was* straight. It was business.' After all, no definition in his category could be more comprehensive than that.

Mary sat staring at him with a look of terror. He seemed to her like the indifferent emissary of some evil power.

'But Mr Elwell's lawyers apparently did not take your view, since I suppose the suit was withdrawn by their advice.'

'Oh, yes; they knew he hadn't a leg to stand on, technically. It was when they advised him to withdraw the suit that he got desperate. You see, he'd borrowed most of the money he lost in the Blue Star, and he was up a tree. That's why he shot himself when they told him he had no show.'

The horror was sweeping over Mary in great deafening waves.

'He shot himself? He killed himself because of *that*?'

'Well, he didn't kill himself, exactly. He dragged on two months before he died.' Parvis emitted the statement as unemotionally as a gramophone grinding out its 'record'.

'You mean that he tried to kill himself, and failed? And tried again?'

'Oh, he didn't have to *try* again,' said Parvis grimly.

They sat opposite each other in silence, he swinging his eyeglasses thoughtfully about his finger, she, motionless, her arms stretched along her knees in an attitude of rigid tension.

'But if you knew all this,' she began at length, hardly able to force her voice above a whisper, 'how is it that when I wrote you at the time of my husband's disappearance you said you didn't understand the letter?'

Parvis received this without perceptible embarrassment: 'Why, I didn't understand it—strictly speaking. And it wasn't the time to talk about it, if I had. The Elwell business was settled when the suit was withdrawn. Nothing I could have told you would have helped you to find your husband.'

Mary continued to scrutinize him. 'Then why are you telling me now?'

Still Parvis did not hesitate. 'Well, to begin with, I supposed you knew more than you appear to—I mean about the circumstances of Elwell's death. And then people are talking of it now; the whole matter's been raked up again. And I thought if you didn't know you ought to.'

She remained silent, and he continued: 'You see, it's only come out lately what a bad state Elwell's affairs were in. His wife's a proud woman, and she fought on as long as she could, going to work, and taking sewing at home when she got too sick—something with the heart, I believe. But she had his mother to look after, and the children, and she broke down under it, and finally had to ask for help. That called attention to the case, and the papers took it up, and a sub-scription was started. Everybody out there liked Bob Elwell, and most of the prominent names in the place are down on the list, and people began to wonder why——'

Parvis broke off to fumble in an inner pocket. 'Here,' he continued, 'here's an account of the whole thing from the *Sentinel*—a little sensational, of course. But I guess you'd better look it over.'

He held out a newspaper to Mary, who unfolded it slowly, remembering, as she did so, the evening when, in that same room, the perusal of a clipping from the *Sentinel* had first shaken the depths of her security.

As she opened the paper, her eyes, shrinking from the glaring headlines, 'Widow of Boyne's Victim Forced to Appeal for Aid', ran down the column of text to two portraits inserted in it. The first was her husband's, taken from a photograph made the year they had come to England. It was the picture of him that she liked best, the one that stood on the writing-table upstairs in her bedroom. As the eyes in the photograph met hers, she felt it would be impossible to read what was said of him, and closed her lids with the sharpness of the pain.

'I thought if you felt disposed to put your name down——' she heard Parvis continue.

She opened her eyes with an effort, and they fell on the other portrait. It was that of a youngish man, slightly built, with features somewhat blurred by the shadow of a projecting hat-brim. Where had she seen that outline before? She stared at it confusedly, her heart hammering in her ears. Then she gave a cry.

'This is the man—the man who came for my husband!'

She heard Parvis start to his feet, and was dimly aware that she had slipped backwards into the corner of the sofa, and that he was bending above her in alarm. She straightened herself, and reached out for the paper, which she had dropped.

'It's the man! I should know him anywhere!' she persisted in a voice that sounded to her own ears like a scream.

Parvis's answer seemed to come to her from far off, down endless fog-muffled windings.

'Mrs Boyne, you're not very well. Shall I call somebody? Shall I get a glass of water?'

'No, no, no!' She threw herself towards him, her hand frantically clutching the newspaper. 'I tell you, it's the man! I *know* him! He spoke to me in the garden!'

Parvis took the journal from her, directing his glasses to the portrait. 'It can't be, Mrs Boyne. It's Robert Elwell.'

'Robert Elwell?' Her white stare seemed to travel into space. 'Then it was Robert Elwell who came for him.'

'Came for Boyne? The day he went away from here?' Parvis's voice dropped as hers rose. He bent over laying a fraternal hand on her, as if to coax her gently back into her seat. 'Why, Elwell was dead! Don't you remember?'

Mary sat with her eyes fixed on the picture, unconscious of what he was saying.

'Don't you remember Boyne's unfinished letter to me—the one you found on his desk that day? It was written just after he'd heard of Elwell's death.' She noticed an odd shake in Parvis's unemotional voice. 'Surely you remember!' he urged.

Yes, she remembered: that was the profoundest horror of it. Elwell had died the day before her husband's disappearance; and this was Elwell's portrait; and it was the portrait of the man who had spoken to her in the garden. She lifted her head and looked slowly about the library. The library could have borne witness that it was also the portrait of the man who had come in that day to call Boyne from his unfinished letter. Through the misty surgings of her brain she heard the faint boom of half-forgotten words—words spoken by Alida Stair on the lawn at Pangbourne before Boyne and his wife had ever seen the house at Lyng, or had imagined that they might one day live there.

—'This was the man who spoke to me,' she repeated.

She looked again at Parvis. He was trying to conceal his disturbance under what he probably imagined to be an expression of indulgent commiseration; but the edges of his lips were blue. 'He thinks me mad; but I'm not mad,' she reflected; and suddenly, there flashed upon her a way of justifying her strange affirmation.

She sat quiet, controlling the quiver of her lips, and waiting till she could trust her voice; then she said, looking straight at Parvis: 'Will you answer me one question, please? When was it that Robert Elwell tried to kill himself?'

'When—when?' Parvis stammered.

'Yes; the date. Please try to remember.'

She saw that he was growing still more afraid of her. 'I have a reason,' she insisted.

'Yes, yes. Only I can't remember. About two months before, I should say.'

'I want the date,' she repeated.

Parvis picked up the newspaper. 'We might see here,' he said, still humouring her. He ran his eyes down the page. 'Here it is. Last October—the——'

She caught the words from him. 'The 20th, wasn't it?' With a sharp look at her, he verified. 'Yes, the 20th. Then you *did* know?'

'I know now.' Her gaze continued to travel past him. 'Sunday, the 20th—that was the day he came here first.'

Parvis's voice was almost inaudible. 'Came *here* first?'

'Yes.'

'You saw him twice, then?'

'Yes, twice.' She just breathed it at him. 'He came first on the 20th of October. I remember the date because it was the day we went up Meldon Steep for the first time.' She felt a faint gasp of inward laughter at the thought that but for that she might have forgotten.

Parvis continued to scrutinize her, as if trying to intercept her gaze.

'We saw him from the roof,' she went on. 'He came down the lime-avenue towards the house. He was dressed just as he is in that picture. My husband saw him first. He was frightened, and ran down ahead of me; but there was no one there. He had vanished.'

'Elwell had vanished?' Parvis faltered.

'Yes.' Their two whispers seemed to grope for each other. 'I couldn't think what had happened. I see now. He *tried* to come then; but he wasn't dead enough—he couldn't reach us. He had to wait for two months to die; and then he came back again—and Ned went with him.'

She nodded at Parvis with the look of triumph of a child who has worked out a difficult puzzle. But suddenly she lifted her hands with a desperate gesture, pressing them to her temples.

'Oh, my God! I sent him to Ned—I told him where to go! I sent him to this room!' she screamed.

She felt the walls of books rush towards her, like inward falling ruins; and she heard Parvis, a long way off, through the ruins, crying to her, and struggling to get at her. But she was numb to his touch, she did not know what he was saying. Through the tumult she heard but one clear note, the voice of Alida Stair, speaking on the lawn at Pangbourne.

'You won't know till afterwards,' it said. 'You won't know till long, long afterwards.'